The Homecoming
and other stories

Other writings by the author

The Michael/Lucifer Correspondence
For Everything a Season (verse)
There are Animals in my Alphabet (verse)

BJ Bear and the Magical Ladybug
The Monster of Rainbow Outlook
A Dangerous Surprise
The Ghost of Willow Park
The Star of Bethlehem is Missing

The Homecoming
and other stories

James W. Greig

A Dunbarton North Publication
2013

ISBN 978-0-9917351-0-5

First Printing: June 2013

Illustrations by Gordon C. Greig
Editorial & Publication Srvs. by Matthias Mayer

Printed and bound in Canada

Dunbarton North Publications
96 Hillcrest Drive
Toronto, Ontario, Canada
M6G 2E6

CONTENTS

Introduction

The Bicycle

Millie

The Woman in Black

Sans Souci

The Race

Not a Winner

The Outrageous Cannon

The Lead Soldier

The Vacuous Widow

The War Casualty

The Gift

The Letter

The Homecoming

"An honest tale speeds best,
being plainly told"

Shakespeare, Richard III

Introduction

Storytelling is deeply rooted in the psyche of the human family. It has been with us since the beginning of time and will remain, no doubt, until time has run its course. None of our other social inventions, clever as many of them are, has been able to quench our need or desire to tell stories. Ideologies, creeds, polities, borders and such come and go but the storyteller and the story remain. In whatever form this ancient pastime expresses itself, whether by drawing or dance or song or spoken or written word, it is a safe bet that storytelling will continue to instruct and enchant us so long as civilization endures.

The collection of stories in this small volume might never have been written except for one of my students in an English writing class who had the daring to call me out when I was extolling the worth of writing a short story. Everyone has a story to tell, I said, and the world would be a more forgiving place if everyone could share that story with others. What short story have you ever written, my inquisitive student persisted. Sidestepping his question, I asked if anyone else had a question before instructing everyone to put pen to paper and to hand in their short story no later than the next class. The assignment, I reminded them, would be worth half of their final mark for the term. Though not exemplary pedagogy, it put an end to the grilling.

My student's question, however, did hit its mark and it resulted in some soul searching, and, eventually, to my putting pen to paper and writing a number of short stories (many of which have not survived which is probably for the best). Those that have were written over many years and are now presented here to share with others. I make no pretense of trying to emulate the truly great short story writers, past or present. Some of the stories arose out of life's experiences but most are exercises of the imagination. Younger readers (if there be any) may not be able to relate to the era in which the stories are cast but should be able to identify with the everyday experiences, the highs and the lows, of the young people therein. Hopefully, older readers will be able to connect more readily with both the younger and older characters and may enjoy returning to an earlier time when life seemed simpler and more predictable. The stories run the gamut of emotions from euphoria to despair, but I must confess, at the outset, that the latter emotion is probably more apparent than the former. This unequal proportion I blame on my Scottish ancestry whose austere attitude to life is well-known.

The human condition hasn't changed very much since the Garden of Eden, and storytellers and stories continue the narrative of stumbling and redemption, with faith, hope and love always out there to help us on our journey. If sharing these stories results in the readers also putting pen to paper and sharing with others their life's experiences and imaginative powers, then just maybe it will be a more forgiving world to live in.

The Author
Toronto, 2013

The Bicycle

The bicycle arrived unexpectedly that Tuesday after the Labor Day holiday. It came mysteriously like manna from heaven. But unlike manna it was all black, not white. Yet it must have been a gift from God because there just wasn't any other way.

It was leaning against the fence in the backyard as if it belonged there. Morning glory stems were already entwined in its spokes, and their delicate blossoms brushed against its worn frame.

I approached cautiously, afraid a sudden move might make it disappear. But it didn't. I touched the handlebars and they were solid. At that moment I felt happier than I had ever been. For once in my life, something I had wanted more than anything was mine.

For months I had prayed for a bicycle. I wasn't sure what words to use so I just asked outright hoping that I wasn't being too bold. Lord, please, You have so much, could I have a bicycle. Please. I know there's a war going on and You're busy, but if You let me have a bicycle, I'll never ask You for anything again. Honest I won't.

As the weeks passed and the prayer went unanswered I was sure nothing would happen. Nothing much that was good ever happened. In fact, things only got worse.

One Sunday morning after church, without any warning I can remember, father announced he was leaving. I'm off to the Boston shipyards to help my American cousins beat those backstabbers, he said. I watched as he packed a few things in a canvas bag, brushed his hair and then trimmed his mustache. Mother didn't try to persuade him to stay. Instead, she went upstairs and didn't come down until he was gone.

I can't remember what we talked about on the streetcar. Father looked out the window most of the way to the train station. I was thinking about how I could get a bicycle, which I would need even more now, as I would have more responsibilities with father gone. It occurred to me that maybe this was the way the Lord was answering my prayer, and I felt a little guilty about doubting Him. Now that father was working again, he might be able to spare enough money for a bike. Perhaps he could buy a cheaper one in Boston and send it to me. By the time we reached Union Station, I had worked out in my mind the necessity of father going away even if it meant a lot of pain for mother and me.

Because there were a lot of soldiers at the train station we said our good-byes outside. We shook hands and Father said he didn't want any tears. So there was none, not then. In a few minutes he disappeared inside and I ran as quickly as I could to the iron bridge to watch his train as it left the station. After a long while, train No. 4433 rumbled by and I waved and waved until it was out of sight. Father made no promises, not even that he would write, but I shouted after the train anyway. I would like a bicycle, I yelled as loud as I could.

Not long after, my two brothers left, one after the other. We watched them board the troop trains with their comrades and when I saw how happy they were, laughing and playfully jostling one another, I wished I were going with them. They made promises. We'll beat those Jerries all hollow and bring back a trophy or two, just wait and see. Take care of yourself, Mom, they shouted, and we'll write every week. Long after they were gone, we stayed by the tracks wondering if we would ever see them again.

After my younger brother Tom left, my mother said to me, you're the man of the house now. I only have you left. She ran her thin fingers through my blond hair and smiled as bravely as she could, her hand trembling all the while. Even though we had one another we felt we were all alone in the world. That night I kneeled beside my bed and prayed, Please, Lord, you haven't forgotten about the bicycle, have You?

At first, letters came from faraway places I had never heard of before and I had to look them up in the school atlas. Places like Tobruk and Sicily. Then the letters stopped. Instead, we began receiving telegrams. By the end of the year telegrams stopped coming too. There would be no war trophies. Only tears.

Not long after the last telegram came from the army, mother fell ill. She had struggled to keep her job at the munitions factory but with each paycheck grew weaker and weaker. You're a danger to yourself and to the others, her supervisor said many times. Stay home for a while. The war's not going to be over for a long time. In the end, the warnings ceased and her supervisor took her card out of the time clock and tore it up. And turn in your identity card, he ordered. That night she cried at the kitchen table for a long while. Those were the last tears I can remember. After that she grew silent.

All day long she would sit by the parlor window looking out as if waiting for someone who never came. At night she would wander through the house from room to room like a wraith in the moonlight.

Each passing week the savings in the black and brass strongbox dwindled until there was little left. Mother seemed not to care. I drew up a list of necessities and revised the list from time to time. Soon most all of our household money was gone. My weekend job running errands for neighbors paid for the medicines mother needed, and for a treat once in a while to cheer her up. When summer turned into winter the food list was shortened to keep coal in the fuel bin. At night, in the chill of my room, I prayed from under the covers, please Lord, don't forget.

That winter was the coldest winter in memory and if it

hadn't been for the insurance money that came from my older brother's death, we wouldn't have made it through. But we did and when summer came I understood clearly that even God couldn't do everything. If I were going to have a bicycle for the first day of high school, I had better make an effort myself. After all I was thirteen years old, and even though I wasn't big, I was wiry and strong. And I was smart too. Mental arithmetic was my best subject.

A sign Mr. Collins posted in his grocery store at the beginning of the summer holidays firmed up my resolve to help God out.

Wanted. A dependable delivery boy. Bicycle provided.

I didn't hesitate to present myself as I knew I could do the job. Mr. Collins, on the other hand, seemed hesitant. He looked me over and I knew he was thinking—he's small for his age. He said, however, "Your mom's been poorly since your father left and your brothers been killed. They were good lads too." He tapped a pencil on the counter's edge as he thought the matter through. He said, at last, "You can have the job. The bike's out back."

The weeks flew by that summer. Seven dollars a week was more than most delivery boys got so I figured I'd better work hard. I stayed behind after my deliveries to stack shelves and sweep up. Each Saturday as a bonus, though I never asked or expected it, Mr. Collins gave me a package of meat and sometimes two or three eggs and jelly powders to take home. He didn't even ask for ration coupons.

Things were definitely getting better. I kept a special envelope for the bicycle in a strongbox. Each Sunday morning I put two dollars in it for the bike and a dollar for church collection. I figured God was really behind our good fortune so I thought I would support His work too. Worries began to lift. The rent increase was no problem because now that it was summer I didn't have to buy coal. We ate better too. In addition to the meat and eggs Mr. Collins gave us, I was able to buy rolls and butter, when you could get it, and even an orange once.

We planted radishes and tomatoes and green beans in the backyard in our Victory garden, and despite the crows most of the things grew. Hope was rising. Even mother seemed better. She sunned herself on the porch steps with a closed book on her lap, and though she rarely laughed anymore, she did smile when I would say how pretty she looked.

My last day at Collin's grocery store was the day before Labor Day. I knew I would miss the job and more particularly, the bicycle. I had got really attached to it. It had become more like my friend than anything else. I looked at it longingly as I parked it where I had first seen it resting against the shed behind the store. Take care of yourself, Mr. Collins said as I was leaving. I had never thought of him as sentimental so I was surprised when he walked me to the door and shook my hand quite formally. For a moment I thought his eyes were a little clouded but then it had been a busy day and he was probably tired out. The package he gave me was much heavier than usual. He had put in some candies, and a fruit cake which mother used to buy.

Labor Day was glorious. Mother and I picnicked in the nearby park. We lounged on the grass in the shade of some spreading maples whose leaves were just beginning to show signs of autumn. I looked up into the pale blue sky, wondering what high school was going to be like. None of my brothers had made it that far. Money was always too tight. But mother said I was different. Smarter and more eager. I turned on my side and glanced at her. She seemed at peace. Maybe it was the new medicine the doctor had finally hit upon. Even though I had to dip into my savings, it was worth it to see her happy again, even a little. At the end of the afternoon we walked the long way home. It had been a perfect day.

That night I prayed for my brothers. I knew that some people prayed for those who had died so I didn't think it would hurt. Keep them safe now, I said, especially Tommy because he was always the most frightened about everything. I finally fell asleep, tired and happy, still wondering if high school would be as grand as I imagined it would be. I had missed my target of having the bike by the first day of school, but it didn't seem to matter as much now. Anyway, I'd work on weekends and maybe before the first snowfall I'd have enough money saved.

I awoke early the next morning. On the kitchen table was one of the brown paper bags Mr. Collins had always sent home with me. In it were sandwiches, each wrapped separately in waxed paper. And with the sandwiches was a note. Good luck today. Take some radishes from the garden. This was my first high school lunch, and for some reason I cannot now imagine, it made me feel like I was entering an entirely new world. Yes, I'll take some radishes.

That was when I discovered the bicycle. I recognized it right away. Black wooden handle grips, well-worn. Black wooden pedals. Black handlebars, tire rims and sprockets. Not a bit of shiny chrome anywhere. The tires were worn thin and the inner tubes, I knew from experience, were covered in patches. But nothing mattered now. Lord, thank You. I knew You'd do it. And thank you too Mr. Collins.

The two-mile ride to high school was a dream. I waved to my school chums as I passed them waiting for the bus and hoped they'd be more than a little jealous. The wind felt good against my face and in my hair. I couldn't imagine I would ever be this happy again.

High school was grander than I had expected. The endless corridors, the lockers, the huge auditorium, the cafeteria with the fragrance of shepherd's pie, the smell of newly oiled desks and chairs. And the teachers. They were all so young, at least the lady teachers were, not like the teachers at the elementary school. And the mysterious Principal whom I saw only once emerging from his office with a stern look on his face. I was almost overwhelmed by the novelty and the surprises. I savored every minute. At the end of the school day I was exhausted. My fingers fumbled with the lock as I tried to follow the directions of the Vice-Principal not to let anyone find out my combination. I'm growing up, I thought with pride.

Clutching my schoolbag in one hand, I raced across the school's gravel driveway to the bicycle racks. The slot where I was certain I had left the bike was empty. The excitement of the day drained away as I ran up and down in a panic between the rows. It wasn't there. I searched the schoolyard and the fields beyond the school fence. Someone's playing a trick on me I figured, and felt relieved as I went back to the bicycle rack. I was certain that it would be there, but all the bicycles were gone. I stood alone in the empty yard except for some teachers who were gossiping by the driveway. At my feet leaves swirled around and drifted away.

Why did You give me a bicycle if you were just going to take it away, I cried out, clenching my fists in hopeless anger. I trusted You. I trusted You and You've let me down. Why? Why? What did I do wrong? It was then the tears came.

Later that evening, as I watched the shadows dance across the ceiling of my bedroom, I thought about what mother had said when I told her about the bike. Don't blame the Lord. You put a lock on your locker. Why didn't you put a lock on your bike? And I knew she was right. So I prayed, Lord, I'm sorry I was so rude today. I made a mistake and I blamed You. I shouldn't have been mad at You, so I hope You'll forgive me. And thanks for the letter from father. Maybe, when he comes home, he'll bring a bike with him. Anyway, it was really grand having a bike even for a little while, and I've learned a lesson I won't forget. I'll take better care of the things I love and the people I love too. Good night, Lord, and I hope someone is watching over You.

Millie

If a thirteen-year-old can fall in love at first sight, then Charles Greene fell in love with Millie on that drizzly Sunday evening in late September. Later, he learned falling in love was much easier than falling out of love.

Stirrat Lawfiter was just signing off the radio broadcast with his inimitable laugh and signature line—Beware evil doers! Stirrat Lawfiter is always nearby—when the door bell rang. Charles switched the radio off and dashed to the front door. He was certain his mother and father had returned home from the evening church service and he was eager to share with them this latest episode of his favorite crime fighter. It had been a particularly thrilling chapter in his hero's never-ending war against evil doers. Charles was bursting with excitement.

As expected, his parents were standing on the verandah, but they were not alone. Right there in front of him, not three feet away, was the heroine of the radio broadcast whom Stirrat Lawfiter had just rescued from the clutches of a treacherous uncle. There she was, the identical match of the image he had formed in his mind, and before this stranger spoke a single word he knew what her voice must sound like. He stared, even though he knew he was being quite rude, but she was even more beautiful than the angels carved in stone inside St. Jude's Cathedral around the corner, which he never tired of admiring. There was, however, one significant difference between St. Jude's angels and this real live one. The Cathedral angels were colorless. This young woman, on the other hand, had cherry red lips and coal black eyes to match her coal black hair. She also had red patches on her cheek which he thought was rouge.

Charles was transfixed. He felt a kind of excitement he had never experienced before. And when he tried to speak, nothing came out.

After what seemed an eternity, Mrs. Greene gently pushed Charles to one side and escorted the stranger into the house. Mr. Greene gathered up the overcoats and hung them in the hall closet. It was only then that Charles noticed the young woman's coat was both muddy and torn. Her shoes too were badly scuffed as though she had been running over some rough ground. These discoveries fueled his imagination and confirmed what he had already suspected. This was a matter for Stirrat Lawfiter.

His brief introduction in the parlor to the mystery woman only revealed that her name was Millie. Where she had come from and why she was now a guest at the Greene home remained unanswered. An awkward silence descended. Charles's mood vacillated from high excitability to inner confusion. Leaning against the piano, he tried to contain his roller coaster emotions.

Millie came to his rescue. She was sitting on the piano bench and motioned for him to come and sit beside her. He looked at his father, then at his mother. They nodded their approval. Then he proceeded to take the most difficult four steps he had taken since childhood. When he sat down beside her, he hoped he would never have to get up again.

Millie turned the piano lid up and ran her long red-tipped fingers over the keys. Never before in the Greene household had the piano sounded so alive. And the tunes she played! Popular songs like the ones his grade seven teacher had them sing because she didn't like the ones in the assigned music curriculum. When Millie began at first to hum and then sing the lyrics, Charles knew it couldn't last. Father wouldn't stand for it. Not on Sunday, not on any day of the week. The music was sacrilegious. Devil's music. But nothing happened.

Millie's voice was low and throaty. Charles dared not look into her eyes for fear of what she might read in his. Instead, he glanced at his father who was sitting stiffly in his armchair. When Mr. Greene could endure the music no longer, he stood up and sent Charles to bed. Millie said Goodnight and continued playing the piano. This one's for you, she said. Sweet dreams.

Sleep did not come easy. And later, when he heard quiet voices in the hallway, and became aware of movement beyond the wall partition, he realized Millie was no more than an arm's length away. Until he fell asleep he listened for her every sound.

That night his dreams were full of turbulent clouds and crashing waves and he felt as if he were falling, falling, falling and yet never reaching the bottom. Once or twice, he awoke and listened to his pounding heart in the darkness.

The next morning he woke up to a soft rapping on his door and his mother's gentle voice. The rain had stopped, and sunlight streamed through the window. He got up slowly and sat on the edge of the bed. It was then he smelled a fragrance he thought he would never smell in the Greene house. Tobacco smoke. He opened the door. The smell of tobacco was even stronger in the hallway. Had his mother smelled it too? He rushed to open his bedroom window as wide as possible. Then he opened the window at the end of the hallway and in the bathroom. Cool fall air rushed in and soon he imagined he couldn't smell the smoke anymore. Why would she go and do that, he asked himself anxiously. Father would never allow smoking in the house. Singing popular music was one thing, but smoking was unmistakably from the Pit.

The breakfast table had one extra place setting, but Millie was nowhere in sight. Mr. Greene had left for work earlier than usual and Charles felt a huge sense of relief. Maybe Millie's transgression went unnoticed. Mrs. Greene didn't mention anything but seemed a little distracted as she bustled about the kitchen not accomplishing very much for all of her activity. It was also quite clear that she had no intention of explaining the whys and wherefores of their strange guest who had already broken two of the household's strictest taboos . . . three if you counted wearing makeup.

Charles ate his breakfast quickly, gathered up his school books and left the house in a state of confusion. Whenever he broke any of the family's rules of conduct, silence was never the usual response. He dreaded the thought of sitting around the dining room table at dinner time when he was certain the law would be laid down, guest or not.

As he passed the driveway, he glanced toward the bushes where he thought he had seen someone earlier while looking out the bathroom window. There was no sign of anyone and yet he sensed something wasn't quite right.

The school day crawled by slower than usual. Charles was reprimanded more than once for his inattention, which left Mrs. Fraser shaking her head in puzzlement. Charles was her prize student. Whenever the school inspector made a surprise visit, she counted on Charles to save the day. She kept her fingers crossed, but Charles's state didn't change. He didn't join in the games at recess and made it perfectly clear he had something on his mind and didn't want to be disturbed. When the bell rang, Charles shot out of the school, running as hard as he could.

There was only one thing on his mind. Would Millie still be there when he got home. What if she's gone and I never see her again, not ever. The thought made him quite miserable. When he burst through the back door into the kitchen he tried to appear nonchalant but his breathlessness gave him away.

Mrs. Greene was busy getting ready for the most important event of her day. Until Millie arrived, nothing had smelled more fragrant than the aroma of freshly baked bread which always filled the kitchen before dinner. Charles's mother had only one ambition—the contentment of her husband. If Millie disturbed that contentment, not even his mother, the most tolerant and thoughtful individual he knew, would put up with it. That evening father's homecoming meant different things to mother and son.

A cup of hot milk, which he didn't like, and warm scones, which he did, were on the kitchen table. Nearby was a half-emptied cup of tea. It was certainly Millie's because there was the telltale sign of lipstick on the rim. Millie, however, was not around. When Charles asked as casually as he could where she was, Mrs. Greene told him that Millie had spent the day playing piano and singing. She didn't even ask if she could help, Charles's mother said reproachfully. Doing nothing for most of the day isn't natural. Now she's upstairs having a rest. Can you believe it? Mrs. Greene shook her head as she placed a tray of cherry tarts in the oven.

Charles was crestfallen. He had been looking forward to, at the very least, having a glimpse of their unusual guest. He sipped the milk, avoiding making a face, and devoured the scones. It was not until his mother had said there was something under his plate that his mood lightened.

There it was, he beamed with delight. A bona fide bread wrapper. This one, plus the ones upstairs, were enough to get the picture of Stirrat Lawfiter at the corner store. Ten bread wrappers were not easy to come by in a household where store bought bread was scarce. Millie didn't like home baked so Mrs. Greene had gone out and bought a store one for her.

This unanticipated windfall could not have come at a better time. Charles already knew what he was going to do with the glossy picture of his favorite radio character. Thank you Lord, he said, as he cleared off the table and held Millie's cup longer than need be.

Millie finally appeared at dinner time which, in the Greene household, was the last meal of the day. In spite of what his mother had said, it was clear Millie must have spent some time in the garden because she had a wonderful glow about her. Even the bruise on her right cheek, which Charles had mistaken for rouge, was less noticeable. And now, in addition to her bright red lips, she had done something to emphasize her large dark eyes. This made her doubly attractive, but much less like the angels at St. Jude's. And, the less like St. Jude's angels she became, the more beautiful she seemed to be. This thought disturbed him considerably.

Mr. Greene's disturbance was different from his son's. Later, he willingly confessed he wished he hadn't been quite so impulsive when he had invited Millie to stay with them on that fateful Sunday evening. But now his conscience started to bother him that he was harboring uncharitable thoughts toward a guest who was becoming less and less welcome. He had smelled the tobacco smoke. This, added to the music and the makeup, was upsetting his Christian equanimity.

For the first time in his life Charles wished the saying of grace would never end. As was their custom they held hands while a prayer of thanksgiving was being offered. Millie's hand was soft and cool and delicious. Midway through the prayer, more apologetic than thankful, she squeezed Charles's hand and when he looked at her she smiled mischievously. His face reddened.

Mrs. Greene steered the conversation into safe channels, talking about household routines and gossiping about her neighbors and friends. This surprised Charles. Idle gossip, it seemed, was no longer forbidden fruit.

Throughout the meal Mr. Greene continued in his distracted mood. He only nodded from time to time or added a monosyllable or two. Usually he monopolized table conversation with anecdotes from the office or world events or his wide reading. Sometimes his chat was even mildly humorous, but always moralistic. That night, what there was of it, was blandly neutral.

Millie wisely caught the mood. She said very little, only responding to a question or two Mrs. Greene posed when she was running out of things to say. All in all dinnertime was not a success. Everyone felt a sense of relief when dessert was served and over.

Afterwards, to Charles's surprise, Millie offered to clear things away. She was hopeless at it so he pitched in to get things done as quickly as possible. He helped Millie sort out the cutlery according to purpose and size. He showed her how to place them exactly in the drawers of the sideboard. He cautioned her about stacking plates on top of one another and discreetly carried the fine silver pieces himself into the kitchen. He couldn't remember another time he enjoyed cleaning up after dinner. Millie had managed to turn everything into an adventure.

When the dining room was returned to its pristine condition and the candelabra placed in the center of the table, Mrs. Greene and her helpers joined Mr. Greene in the parlor. He was listening to a radio broadcast and frowning. The news about the war was not good. The bombing of London had not stopped and the outlook for an early end to the conflict seemed remote. Millie sat there at first with a forced expression of interest on her radiant face but soon boredom showed through. She got up and looked through the books on either side of the fireplace, but none caught her fancy. Theology and other esoteric subjects like ancient history and classical literature held little interest for her. Charles watched. She seemed to move like a sleek feline. It made him shiver.

As soon as the radio broadcast was finished, Millie curled up on the piano bench and filled the room with song. This time, without waiting for approval, Charles sat down beside her and sang along. Mrs. Greene repaired Millie's torn coat while Mr. Greene read Bunyan's Pilgrim's Progress. Millie and Charles played some duets and from time to time his hand brushed up against hers. The evening's entertainment ended with a rollicking version of Chopsticks which evoked laughter even from Mr. Greene.

In his room, toiling over his homework, Charles could still smell the fragrance of Millie's hair. It so distracted him that he leafed through his geography textbook aimlessly. Finally he closed it without writing a single line. He wondered if Millie liked him and then felt embarrassed at the thought. When he was at last getting down to business, he smelled tobacco again.

This time however it was not coming from the hallway. It was coming through the window behind him. Charles turned out the light and peered out the window. He could make out two forms on the driveway, whether men or women he could not tell. The red tips of their cigarettes moved as they moved their heads.

Charles quickly drew back out of sight and closed the drapes before putting the light back on. He remembered what he had thought he had seen first thing in the morning. Now he was certain someone had been there. But why would strangers be hiding in bushes and standing in the driveway. For the first time in his life he felt real fear.

Downstairs, the music stopped and moments later he heard Millie's light footsteps on the stairs. When he was certain she was no longer in the hallway, he quietly opened his door and raced down the stairs. His tale about seeing strangers on the driveway came out in gasps. Slow down, his father said. He already knew about the unwanted visitors. They've come for Millie, he whispered, as he closed the door to the hallway.

It was then Charles learned about that Sunday evening and about Millie and her past. She had lived a shameful life on the streets, Mr. Greene said gravely, and now she was a member of a gang. Charles could not believe what he was hearing. It wasn't possible. When she tried to leave them, his father continued, they beat her but she had gotten away and ran to the church.

Mr. Greene produced a rumpled note from his cardigan pocket. He read it aloud. If Millie doesn't leave your house right away, you can expect trouble. The note had been placed under the windshield wiper of the car where he had found it before dinner. He folded the note and put it in the drawer of his writing desk. Your sins will find you out every time, he said solemnly, and implied that Millie had done more than her fair share of sinning.

For a long moment there was silence. Mrs. Greene stopped repairing Millie's torn coat and Mr. Greene sat down in his armchair with Pilgrim's Progress unopened on his lap. Charles leaned against the piano, remembering the pleasurable feeling of Millie's hand. "If there are any more threatening notes, we will have no alternative," Mr. Greene said at last. "Millie will have to go." He opened his book but didn't seem to be reading. Charles looked with desperation at his mother.

She spoke quietly. "We can't turn her away. It wouldn't be right. Good must overcome evil." She picked up the coat and continued with her sewing. Mr. Greene seemed relieved.

"Then we will go to the police even if it puts Millie at greater risk," he said.

Charles found it hard to get to sleep. Goodness overcoming evil was not what Stirrat Lawfiter believed in. Not exactly anyway. Sometimes evil had to be countered with a different kind of evil. At least he wasn't a goodie-goodie. He was clever and used cunning to trap evil people. And he even used force to stop them from doing what they were doing. The thought of putting Millie at any risk by calling the police troubled him.

As he finally dropped off into a restless sleep, he was imagining what Stirrat Lawfiter would do. Again he found himself falling, falling, but never hitting bottom. And there were doors too, closed doors and closed windows he couldn't open and when he tried, they just up and disappeared.

School was a disaster the next day. For the first time in his life he got into trouble. He didn't take out his arithmetic book fast enough and the supply teacher, who lacked Mrs. Fraser's patience, rapped his knuckles with a yardstick. No one laughed even though the temptation was great. Though Charles was usually a gentle person, he was big and could be unforgiving when provoked. He looked straight ahead and for the rest of the day paid close attention because he didn't want to be kept in after school.

That afternoon, on his way home, he made a detour, stopping by the Red and White grocery store with the ten bread wrappers and ten cents in his hand. At first, Mr. Whitney pretended he didn't have any more glossy pictures of Stirrat Lawfiter. Maybe next week, he said. Then with a flourish he reached under the counter and produced the object Charles had set his heart on for months. It was even grander than he had imagined, for it was autographed by Stirrat Lawfiter himself, written just the way he thought it might be— big and bold. He was the bravest person in the world.

Charles flew down the street with the picture carefully placed in his school bag. At the driveway two men with fedoras blocked his way. The taller of the two grabbed Charles by the shoulder and brought his face close. Tell Millie to come out now or you might not get home from school next time. Charles stiffened with defiance. It had not been a good day. He wasn't in any mood to be pushed around. He pulled himself away and ran up the sidewalk and didn't turn around until he was on the verandah. When he did, they had already gone.

Mrs. Greene met him at the door. She had been watching through the window and was about to call the police just as Charles broke away from the two men. Where's Millie, he asked. It was the worst possible answer. She had slipped out of the house sometime in the late morning even though she knew about the note. She just laughed, Mrs. Greene said, when Mr. Greene had warned her about staying in. It was as if she knew about the note already.

Millie had not returned by dinnertime, nor was she there for the evening radio broadcast of news about the war. London was still being bombed and things seemed to be getting worse. Mr. Greene looked grim as the announcer said to stay tuned for an important announcement by the Prime Minister of Great Britain. Once Charles had overheard his father say if things didn't improve he'd have to enlist in the army. That worried him because some of the teachers who had enlisted had already been killed. But that night, he was even more worried about Millie.

Nothing was said about her even though Charles noticed that every now and then Mr. Greene glanced at his watch. While they waited for the Prime Minister's announcement, Mr. Greene read about Pilgrim's journey to the Celestial City while Mrs. Greene busied herself with knitting socks for Uncle Harold who was already overseas. Charles excused himself and went to his room. He said he had homework to do but he had something entirely different in mind. Before he closed the drapes, he peered out the window. He didn't see any red cigarette tips. Maybe, just maybe, Millie was going to be safe after all.

Now he set to work to prepare the most important note he would ever write. He sat down at his desk and took out several sheets of paper. He sharpened the best pencil he had and with a ruler made lines which were barely visible. He wanted his writing to be straight. He wanted everything to be just right for Millie. She deserved it. Then he plunged in. But the words he wrote were not the words he hoped to write. Soon his desk was littered with balls of crumpled notepaper. In desperation he got out his dictionary. When you get stuck for words, he remembered Mrs. Fraser saying, use your dictionary. He rifled through the pages but couldn't find what he was looking for. He finally gave up. The dictionary hadn't helped.

The clock in the hallway chimed ten times. Soon he would have to turn off the light and he hadn't even started his homework. Charles began to panic. Please, please, give me the right words, he prayed. The voice at the door said, Lights out Charles. And he prayed again. This time he wrote the words as they came.

> This picture is for you. I hope you like it as much as I do. I hope you like the autograph especially. It should make you feel safe because Stirrat Lawfiter always knows what to do.

He carefully added his signature. Charles Greene. Then he slipped the picture and note under Millie's door and went back to his room.

Wednesday morning was dull and drizzly once again. Charles looked out the window, but saw no one in the driveway. He had heard Millie come in but wasn't sure what time. It was after midnight, of that he was quite sure. Getting dressed as quickly as he could, he hurried downstairs where Mrs. Greene was busy rolling out bread dough. She whispered to him to be quiet. Millie had come home late and was still sleeping.

To Charles's unanswered question Mrs. Greene explained that Father was going to come home early and talk to Millie and explain that if she went out again they would have to call the police, or else she would have to leave. We were so sure Millie would be saved, she said with a sigh.

Charles left the house unhappy and bewildered. The more he thought the situation through the more he became convinced that Stirrat Lawfiter would have handled things differently. He would have acted. He wouldn't have counted on goodness to overcome evil. He would have outwitted the gangsters and even used force if he had to.

For the first time in his life Charles was disappointed in his father. What kind of soldier would he be if he couldn't even protect Millie. His only consolation was that by this time Millie would have seen the note and picture, and he was certain she would like them. It had taken him months to save up the wrappers. It would take him many more to get enough for another picture. And maybe there wouldn't be another chance because sometimes the offer was discontinued. It didn't matter. Not if Millie liked it. She might even feel safer with it.

Whatever Mr. Greene had said to Millie at lunchtime must have had some effect because that evening she seemed very subdued. She had promised not to leave the house again until they could figure out what they could do to stop the men from bothering her. Everything returned to normal. Even the war seemed to be going better. Mr. Greene spent the evening reading and Mrs. Greene knitted contentedly. Charles and Millie sang and played duets and laughed. The only unusual thing that happened was that Millie excused herself and went to bed early. She didn't mention the picture but Charles could tell she was pleased by the way she looked at him.

There were no scones or toast or hot milk or anything on the kitchen table the next morning. In the parlor was a detective and two policemen on the verandah. Detective Powers was questioning Mr. Greene and writing down the answers in a small, black notebook.

Millie was gone and so were many of their valuables—all the pieces of silver and some rare coins and jewellery that Mrs. Greene had inherited from her parents. It was clear the detective was angry, even though he spoke in a controlled voice.

"You should have reported the threats. You shouldn't have taken Millie in in the first place. We know about her and she can be dangerous. Certainly the other gang members are. She's a real viper. Come to the police station and file a report. Today." Then he closed the notebook and prepared to leave.

Charles listened in disbelief. Perhaps Millie wasn't an angel like the ones at St. Jude's but that didn't mean she was really bad. It occurred to him that maybe she had left a note for him so he ran up to the guest room where she had been. The police had already looked through her things and scattered everything about. He looked on the little pine table for a note, but there was none. He searched through the dresser drawers and on the pillow where Millie's head had rested. He couldn't find either the picture or the note. For a moment, he was sure she had taken them with her and felt happy at the thought. As he was about to leave the room, he glanced into the wastepaper basket. There, torn into a dozen pieces was the picture. Beside the pieces was his note, crumpled up like the ones he had rejected the night before.

After school, Charles went up to his room. He had thought about what he must do all day. Now he would do it. He laid the pieces of the picture on his desk and taped them together. Some of the pieces were too damaged to be of any further use but he didn't care. Someday, he was going to frame that picture and even cover it with glass. He knew he was always going to keep it. And he knew, too, that even though he didn't know what was lurking in Millie's heart, he knew what was in his own.

The
Woman in Black

October, 1943

The woman in black returned every day at exactly the same hour. She sat on the same bench beside the promenade and looked out to sea. She spoke to no one and no one spoke to her. It was as though she were not there at all. After an hour, she got up and walked away in the same direction as she had come. I first noticed her by accident. The waiter had given my table to a pair of honeymooners, and not wanting to disturb their nuptial bliss, I agreed to move to a table beside the window. It was then I observed the woman who even from a distance reminded me of Edwina. She was taller than most women and carried herself in a manner which spoke of good breeding, and exceptional strength. Edwina was like that before she succumbed to the illness that took her life. Once when the stranger glanced back at the hotel, something she rarely did, I was astonished at how much she resembled Edwina when we had first met years before in Brighton. What was even more uncanny was that Edwina had been sitting on the same bench and at the same hour. The hour of afternoon tea.

....

October, 1914

Storm clouds threatened rain that bleak October afternoon. The promenade was deserted except for occasional lovers strolling hand in hand oblivious of the raw weather. How I envied them!

I was about to return to the hotel, where Mama was waiting for me, when a hat appeared from nowhere and blew across my path. I chased after it and stopped it, rather clumsily, by stamping my foot on its broad brim. Looking around helplessly, I first saw Edwina standing beside the bench and waving to attract my attention. I felt more than a little embarrassed when I stooped down and picked up the hat. I realized, on closer inspection, I had crushed it quite badly. I now regretted having chased after it at all. Wondering how I was ever going to make amends, I carried the battered trophy back to its unsuspecting owner.

"I . . . I'm sorry . . . Miss?"

"Marsh. Edwina Marsh."

"The hat . . . it's . . . well, it's . . . how should I put it?"

"Try flattened," the young woman interjected, smiling. "But thank you for rescuing it. If you hadn't, the hat would have been lost at sea. Besides, it was foolish my wearing it on such a windy day."

"I am truly sorry. It was clumsy of me, Miss Marsh. I think I need more practice in rescuing hats in distress. I should introduce myself. Michael Dobson."

"Well, Mr. Dobson, I hope if we should meet up in the future it will be under better circumstances." Edwina smiled again and offered her hand.

"You're not English . . . " It was a question and it hung suspended in midair.

"No. I'm American." At first Edwina seemed puzzled. "It's not a disease," she said, smiling.

Rupert Brooke's look alike realized he had smudged his copybook with a question that must have seemed offensive.

"Of course not. I . . . I didn't mean it quite like that but . . ." Whatever he had intended to say was lost in his thinking about it.

"At least you were half right. My father's American but my Mama was born in London. So I'm a hybrid. You're not American," she said teasingly.

Michael smiled. It was a good repartee. Whoever this American woman was he liked her immediately.

"Could I escort you to wherever you're going. I mean . . . would you like to walk along the promenade. No, you probably wouldn't want to. I'd better not hold you up any longer. It was a pleasure meeting you and if we should meet again I too hope it will be under better circumstances." I turned and walked away in the direction of the hotel. I was normally a very self-contained young man but at that moment my composure was knocked off-balance. I had proceeded a few paces when the impossible happened.

"Mr. Dobson, you didn't wait for an answer."

I stopped and looked back. My pulse had quickened and I hoped my face was not as flushed as it felt. Get a hold of yourself, I thought. You're behaving like a schoolboy.

"If you're staying at the hotel, wait for me. I'll walk with you."

And that is how it began.

. . . .

Agatha Dobson placed afternoon tea above Ascot, Wimbledon and St. Moritz. And, if cleanliness was next to godliness, punctuality held an even more commanding position in her hierarchy of social values.

"I'm sorry, Mama, but I was detained." Michael had the look of a schoolboy about to be caned by the headmaster.

Dame Dobson said nothing. She caught the eye of the

waiter instead and with a brief nod summoned him to pour tea.

"There was a young woman and her hat . . . "

"I know all about it. I observed the incident through the window." It was de rigueur to withhold conversation while being waited upon so Michael scanned the lobby beyond the tea room hoping to catch sight of Edwina. To his dismay, she was chatting with a waiter who was looking adoringly at her. It was not good form to be talking to a waiter with such familiarity. American informality, he thought. He didn't like it.

"Michael . . . Michael." Like Jehovah, Dame Dobson rarely invoked her son's name twice.

Michael forced himself to give Mama his undivided attention. It disturbed him that Edwina seemed to welcome the waiter's attention, and, though he felt like a voyeur, it was difficult to look away.

"You probably already know her name is Edwina Marsh." Dame Dobson expertly placed the fragile cup on the saucer while holding her youngest and most troublesome son in her severe gaze. "Her father, Edmund by name, is a New York banker. Apparently filthy rich but with no pedigree. Self-made." This word was always said in a condescending tone followed by a long sigh. By itself, money did not make the man. Agatha Dobson recovered and continued her recital. "But Elizabeth Marsh, his wife, is a Lascelle. Can you imagine the Lascelles still own property in The City. Some say more property than His Highness the Prince of Wales. The Lascelles trace their ancestry back to 1066 and all that. Now I understand the Marshes are visiting London for the purpose of introducing Edwina to eligible bachelors before they all go off to France. They'll take the lucky trophy back to America with them and, well, it's not terribly civilized there, but I suppose one can get used to their adolescent ways."

Dame Dobson frowned. When she did, she looked rather like a Chihuahua with indigestion. "You're not paying attention, Michael." When she picked up her cup, it rattled on the saucer. She quickly surveyed the diners sitting nearby, hoping they hadn't observed this social lapse.

Contrary to what Dame Dobson thought, Michael was completely absorbed by her account of Edwina's family. He savored every scrap of information. Only once did he glance back into the lobby. The waiter was still there but Edwina was gone. Somehow, this small mercy assured him providence had not deserted him.

"Do you know the Marshes?" he said.

"Of course not."

"Then, how . . . "

"Michael, you are impossible. The manager knows everything and he tells me everything."

She was going to reveal more about her source of intelligence when the waiter Edwina had been talking to came to the table and poured tea. He was handsome enough but not a person of quality. He had the hands of a tradesman. Michael was reassured.

Dame Dobson did not pick up on the subject of the manager. Instead, she delivered a message from the War Office. "You will be offered a commission and will serve on Sir Owen's personal staff. That's final. Perhaps this will expunge the disgrace. You are fortunate the war came along. It will be over in a few months and by that time everyone will have forgotten." The Chihuahua had returned. She raised her gloved hand to stave off any argument. The matter was settled.

"When?" Michael knew this was the only question Mama would answer.

"You will report to General Owen at the beginning of November. So, if Edwina is on your mind, you will have to proceed post-haste." For the first time during the afternoon tea, Agatha Dobson smiled. She loved her hopelessly romantic son more than the others, though she would never under any circumstance reveal her true feelings. "Marsh," she said. "A lugubrious name, isn't it? Reminds one of a swamp."

Michael's attention was wandering once more. Now that he had observed the waiter at close quarters he dismissed this unlikely rival from his thoughts. How to proceed with haste with Edwina, however, was very much on his mind. But he needn't have worried. Dame Dobson had already prepared the way.

....

The following day the weather was still raw and the promenade even more deserted. For Michael, however, it was a day he would never forget. Unlike before, he was no longer envious of lovers, such as the ones on the promenade. Though Edwina and he were not strolling hand in hand, he felt he had joined that rarified company of the lucky ones.

"That was a grand affair last evening. How did your mother ever bring together so many luminaries in such a short time?" Edwina's voice bordered on the musical. The wind played with her long blond hair.

"My mother is a formidable lady. She seldom takes no for an answer. I'm no longer surprised by anything she manages to do. Did your mother and father find the evening agreeable?"

"Yes, very much so. My father was so pleased to meet Sir Owen. Is the General a friend of the family?"

"He was my father's classmate at Winchester and later they served together in South Africa. My father was killed in action there and Sir Owen has been like a surrogate father ever since."

"I'm sorry about your father. I didn't know."

"That was a long time ago. Father was in India before that so I didn't really know him. We come from a long line of the King's soldiers."

"I met your brother Leslie last night. He's on Sir Owen's staff, isn't he?"

"Yes he is and I will be soon as well."

"You will? When?"

"I'm not certain but soon."

For a long moment each was lost in thought. Suddenly a small boy darted in front of them pursued by his nanny. The stout woman was trying to maintain her dignity but was not at her best when running.

"He'll be in bad odour with his nanny if he keeps that up," Edwina observed with a chuckle.

"Like me," said Michael. It was time to come clean.

"You . . . in bad odour with your nanny?" Edwina laughed at the thought.

Michael joined in the laughter. "No, with Mama."

"I can't imagine why," Edwina said with surprise.

"I was reading history at Oxford. Until recently, that is. But, well, I rather spoiled things and was sent down. That's why I'm being attached to Sir Owen's staff . . . to atone for my sin."

"I don't understand."

"It was a prank, really. One of the dons caught me fraternizing with a local girl and reported me. It was a dare and it ended rather badly."

"I'm sorry. But it sounds so old fashioned. Is Oxford really like that?"

"Yes, I'm afraid it is. But I knew the rules and I broke them, so instead of being with Auburn I'll be running messages for Sir Owen."

"With Auburn."

"Forgive me. There are three of us. Auburn is the eldest. He's a flyer. That's what I wanted to be more than anything."

"A flyer. If I were a man, I think that's what I'd like to be too. One of the waiters, in fact he waited on your table yesterday, he wants to be a flyer too. He's an American from California."

"It's not America's war," said Michael coldly.

"I'm afraid he disagrees. He has already signed up and will be leaving for France at the end of the week."

"Oh, I see." Michael felt relieved. "I understand your mother has accepted Mama's invitation to spend the weekend at our country place."

"We're looking forward to it. Especially Papa. He's anxious to talk to Sir Owen about the war. Will it be a long one do you think?"

"Everyone says it will be over by Christmas, but I don't think so. Neither do my brothers or Sir Owen. The General believes it will be the bloodiest war Europe has ever seen."

Edwina shuddered a little and Michael would have liked to put his arm around her. "The wind is picking up. Perhaps we should return to the hotel."

....

September, 1941

"Major Dobson."

I looked up from my newspaper. "Yes."

"Your brother called. He'll be late."

"Thank you, Mr. Hopkins. I'll go in for dinner now. Will you bring him to my table when he arrives."

"Of course."

Even with the war, nothing had changed very much—same room, same table, same décor, and same background music. How many years had we come here to celebrate our anniversary? Twenty-three, no, twenty-four. Were they happy years? They were for me. But for Edwina I wish I really knew. At first there was romance as well as love but afterwards respect replaced romance. And love? I wonder.

One thing had changed. The waiter brought the menu and explained that sole with lemon was the only choice. However, he reported more cheerfully, there was an ample supply of scotch.

"Then I'll begin with a tumbler of scotch."

I looked out the window. A pale light illuminated the

bench beside the promenade and the memories flooded in. Edwina was only dead a month and I had already begun to analyze our marriage. Something I was unable to do while she was still alive.

I wonder what the black cloud was that seemed ever present. Even in her last moments Edwina thoughts were really not with me. Try as she might she couldn't hide it. She was gallant to the last, but the distance between us was too great by then. When did I first notice? It was early, certainly before the war ended. Was it when I came back on my first leave? But I dishonor her memory thinking this way. I must stop.

Fortunately, Auburn arrived, apologizing.

I rose to greet him. "No apologies required, old man. You know that. I'm the one who should be apologizing starting without you."

"Harris called me over just as I was about to leave. Something big is about to happen. I can't say much but it will either make or break us." At that moment Auburn waved to a tall stranger and beckoned him over. "Michael, I'd like you to meet Wing Commander Gregson. Clark, this is my brother, Michael."

"My pleasure. Please join us, Clark. I'm afraid the menu is limited to sole but it's really not that bad. Anyway, there's plenty of scotch."

"Clark commands the best fighter wing in the RAF. He could take on the Luftwaffe by himself and sometimes does."

"That is a gross exaggeration even though there is some small measure of truth in it," Clark said with an ironic smile.

At that moment the waiter appeared. "Compliments of the manager . . . a bottle of Madeira." He poured three glasses and left.

"Cheers. Here's to the fly boys."

"And the sloggers," Auburn added. "How are you feeling, Michael? Really."

"First rate. The wound is healing and I'm becoming

restless. I want to get back into action. I need to."

For a moment conversation dropped off. "It's not the same, is it? Without Edwina." Turning to Clark, Auburn explained, "Michael's wife passed away last month."

"I'm sorry. My condolences. I know how you must feel."

To lighten the moment, I raised my glass. "To Edwina," I said and the others joined in the toast.

I noticed, or thought I did, an unusual expression of pain in the Wing Commander's eyes. It was as though he himself had recently experienced a great loss as well. I was of a mind to ask but demurred. I thought my enquiry might be mistaken for mere inquisitiveness.

For the rest of the evening we talked about what was chiefly on our minds. I wanted to know how the air war was going. They wanted to know about the North African campaign. Soon, mellowed by the scotch, even the war seemed less real to us, at least for the moment. Blackout conditions meant the drive back to London would take longer than usual. Auburn glanced at his watch. It was time to go and report to the Air Marshall. He smiled as he got up from the table.

"Goodbye, Michael. I'm glad we were able to share the best Madeira I've tasted since I can't remember when. I could only have wished the circumstances were better. How long will you stay in Brighton? "

"For ten days or so, I think."

"Then off to Cairo or is that a military secret?"

"If it's a secret, it's the worst kept secret of the war so far. Besides, everyone including the PM is convinced that the RAF is going to win the war."

"It was a great pleasure to meet you, Michael," Clark said, extending his hand.

"Mutual. And be careful when you're flying one of those damned Hurricanes, or have you managed to get your hands on a Spit. "

"Spitfires are hard to come by. But if I ever do you'll be the first to know."

"You're not English."

"No, I'm American."

"We've met before, haven't we?"

"No, I don't think so."

Auburn was beginning to show his impatience. "We'd better be going now, Clark."

"Write," I called out. "You know where I can be reached."

"I will but only if you'll respond. You are the worst correspondent I have ever had the misfortune of writing to."

I watched them until they were out of sight. The bottle of Madeira was empty and I had had enough scotch. I left the dining room and walked out into the moonlit night. The bench on which Edwina had sat, so long ago, was unoccupied. I sat there for a long while, listening to the roll of the waves. I thought of her crushed hat and her smile which bewitched me. You're not English, I had said. No, I'm American. It's not a disease. It was then the tears began. The lights along the promenade and at the hotel suddenly went out as the drone of airplanes joined the sound of the waves crashing on the shore.

Two days later a telegram arrived. It said: Wing Commander Gregson killed in action. Thought you should know. Auburn.

....

April, 1915

Dame Dobson put the newspaper aside and with it her reading glasses. "That scoundrel von Richthofen has downed three more of our boys. I hope Auburn gives him a thrashing." Even at sixty Agatha Dobson's English beauty had not faded. But now a tracery of worry lines gathered in the corner of her eyes. The war was going badly. Sir Owen was right and the rest were wrong. It had not been over by Christmas. "I'm glad Michael is far from the front. He's such a dreamer I'm sure he'd do something rash."

Edwina stopped reading and looked across the drawing room to where her mother-in-law was sitting. She had heard nothing from Michael for several days and was beginning to fear the worst. He was, in fact, doing something rash. He was leading reconnaissance missions in No Man's Land. She remembered his last words before he left for France. I don't intend to spend the war being Owen's carrier pigeon.

"Would you like me to read some more, Leslie?" Edwina picked up the shawl from the floor and arranged it around the young man's shoulders. Leslie did not reply but Dame Dobson answered for him. "Please read some more, Edwina. I'm sure he's listening."

Edwina opened the book and found the place she had left off. She was glad Leslie had come home from the hospital. At Headington House she needed a companion to distract her from the restlessness she felt. Even though he was an invalid, shell-shocked Dr. Moseby explained, and could not reciprocate her attention, caring for Leslie took her mind off herself and her own doubts about the impulsive decision she had made. The same decision other young women like her had made and later lamented. You're making a mistake, her mother had warned, before returning to New York. It's the war and you'll regret it. Now a feeling of guilt was added to the dread of doubt. The thought that Michael might not return home did not trouble her the way she felt it should. Sometimes at night when she couldn't sleep, the thought that the war might end what it had begun, brought relief rather than unhappiness.

"Why don't you accompany Leslie to Brighton," Dame Dobson said. "The sea air would do him good. He always liked the sea. Maybe he would even take up painting again. I won't take no for an answer. Mrs. Abbott will make the arrangements."

"I could never forgive myself if anything happened to you when we were gone," said Edwina.

"Nonsense. If you're afraid a Zeppelin is going to land in our front garden, let me put your mind at ease. Headington House has been around for over three hundred years and I am certain it will stand for at least another three. I'll hear no more of it. Run upstairs and start packing. You are going to leave tomorrow."

"Then at least come with us. It would do you good to be away from here."

Dame Dobson shook her head. I have my reasons for staying was all she would say.

....

October, 1943

The hostess was clearly embarrassed. "I'm truly sorry Major Dobson but the waiter has seated someone at your usual table. Honeymooners," she explained. "There's a table by the window."

"Fine. I wouldn't want to disturb their nuptial bliss."

"I'm so glad you feel that way, Major. They're such a nice couple and they only have today."

The table by the window commanded a splendid view of the promenade and the sea. I had sat there many times before with Mama but for a reason she would never divulge Edwina preferred to sit on the other side of the dining room. From time to time I glanced at the young lieutenant and his bride and the years fell away.

It was December 1914 once more.

Sergeant Tomkin followed the newlyweds into the hotel and laid the travelling cases on the floor beside the lift. He remained at attention until the registration formalities were completed then he approached the couple. "If you have no further need of me, I will leave now Lieutenant Dobson," he said smartly.

"Go along now, Tomkin, and make the best of the remains

of the day."

"Thank you, sir. When should I come back in the morning?"

"Morning," said Edwina, puzzled.

"At six." Michael took his bride's arm and escorted her into the dining room.

"But I don't understand, Michael."

"I'll explain everything over tea, darling."

When the hostess directed them to the table by the window, Edwina resisted. "There must be a table with greater privacy," she said.

"Of course, follow me." The hostess led them across the dining room to a table in a small alcove. "Will this be suitable, Mrs. Dobson?"

"Yes, very suitable," Edwina said. When they were seated, Edwina repeated her earlier question. "Why did you ask Sergeant Tomkin to return tomorrow morning? I don't understand."

"Darling, I've been ordered to report to Sir Owen immediately. I'm sorry. We leave from Southampton tomorrow."

"But, Michael . . . I thought," said Edwina as the tears fell. "Only yesterday you said we would have at least a week."

"Everything's changed, my angel. The Germans are about to launch a major offensive. Please don't cry. I promise we'll have a real honeymoon when I get back. Dry your tears and I'll ask Miss Hannah to play some of our favorites."

"No, Michael, don't go. I'm behaving very foolishly. Forgive me. Let's pretend there's no war, at least for tonight. Do you remember when you chased my silly hat?"

"And stepped on it," Michael added.

Even without being asked, Miss Hannah played our Lisztian favorites and the manager sent a bottle of his best champagne. I never felt closer to Edwina than on that memorable night.

"Waiter."

"Yes, Major Dobson."

"Would you please leave a bottle of champagne in the bridal suite with a note: Best wishes and good luck."

"Of course, sir. Right away."

I tried to remember what we had talked about that night so many years ago when we had pretended the war didn't exist, but couldn't. I couldn't even remember what Edwina was wearing or how she looked. All I remember is how the memory of that night stayed with me as I crawled through No Man's Land in the darkest hours of the night. Without it I could not have survived.

Something else, another memory of that night, but one which I suppressed because it caused me disquiet, something Edwina said or had not said, was trying to free itself. But the roar of a low flying plane drew my attention to the outside and that particular memory fled. It was then I noticed the woman dressed in black approaching the bench. Why her sudden appearance startled me I could not say. Perhaps it was because I was thinking of Edwina and the stranger, for a brief moment, melded with her in my thoughts. The woman sat down and looked out to sea. Is she waiting for someone, I wondered. But no one came. And by the time I had finished afternoon tea she was gone. I went out and walked along the promenade in the same direction she had come, but turned back when my leg began to throb. I was astonished by my bizarre behavior. You're chasing a ghost, I scolded myself. For a long while I sat on the same bench, unsettled by the lost memory which would not, or could not, reach the surface.

I retired early that evening, thinking of Edwina and remembering the happy and not so happy times we had spent together. Most of the wartime marriages of our friends had ended badly, most of them divorced and put the war and that part of their lives behind them. But we stayed together. We had pledged for better or for worse and though we never talked about it there was an unspoken understanding that we would stick it out, no matter what. And I was so deliriously happy having Edwina by my side in both the good and bad times that I couldn't even imagine any other condition.

Was I being selfish? Probably. But the Dobson's were a selfish lot. Mama certainly was. Why else would she have insisted Leslie go off to war to maintain the family tradition . . . he was too gentle, too sensitive, not like Auburn and myself. When I finally fell asleep, I dreamed a dream which awakened me in a sweat. I was aboard a troop ship at Southampton and Edwina was standing on the quay. She knew I was standing at the railing waving to her, shouting that I loved her, even so she paid no attention. She seemed preoccupied and was looking elsewhere. As the ship set sail, I shouted louder and louder but Edwina only turned and walked away without looking back. I tried to get off the ship but the other soldiers held me back and laughed. I struggled and struggled until someone held a bayonet to my throat. Then I awoke. For a long while afterwards I wondered if the lost memory was making itself known at last.

. . . .

April, 1915

"Are you quite comfortable, Leslie," Edwina said. "We can go back to the hotel if you're tired."

"Let's go on," he said. "I . . . I . . . I . . . " He did not finish the sentence.

Edwina laid her hand on his shoulder and continued pushing the wheelchair along the promenade. It was a glorious day, sunny bright and cloudless. She breathed in the salty air and felt the soft breeze brush lazily against her face. Headington House seemed light years away and the dull headache she had been experiencing almost continuously for several weeks was now lifting. Not even the frolicsome antics of some young people who nearly collided with the wheelchair could disturb her serenity. It was one of those golden days one hopes will go on forever.

On the afternoon of the day they left for Brighton, Sir Owen sent word that Michael had been on a secret mission but had returned unharmed. Dame Dobson's mood was expansive. For a few hours Headington House lost its gloom. Stay as long as you wish, Dame Dobson had said, and Edwina decided to do just that. Leslie was not alone in needing the healing that nearness to the sea brings.

Often at night when the household was asleep, she would escape to the belvedere in the garden overlooking the Thames and think about the happy times spent at the family summer place on Cape Cod, and her heart ached for home. England, she now knew, could never fill that place. In fact, since her marriage she felt the pull of family and home more strongly than ever. It was as though she was experiencing the intensity of these familial sentiments for the first time. Strange, she thought, how these stirrings had come now when she should be thinking of her new life with Michael and the promise of fulfillment like no other, a family of her own and growing old with a loved one.

"Go back!" screamed Leslie, as he began to shake uncontrollably and bury himself in his shawl. Something had frightened him, but looking around Edwina saw nothing unusual. A passing soldier with his sweetheart offered his help but Leslie hid beneath the shawl and shouted obscenities. The soldier understood and backed off. "I'm sorry, Ma'am" he said. "I've been there too." There were tears in his eyes as he turned and limped away.

For the rest of the afternoon until early evening Edwina held Leslie's frail body in her arms. From time to time she wiped the sweat from his face and hummed familiar melodies. Gradually, the tremors eased and stopped altogether and Leslie slipped into a troubled sleep. When she knew she could go on no longer without help, she welcomed the gentle knock on the door that brought relief.

Mr. Hopkins, the manager of the hotel, had called around

for a nurse but none was available, so he sent one of the housemaids to stay with the invalid. Reluctant, but exhausted, Edwina withdrew from the room.

"The chef has prepared a special dish for you, Ma'am," the housemaid said with a sympathetic smile. But Edwina was beyond dining. Instead, she left the hotel and sat on the bench beside the promenade. A full moon bathed everything in its silver glow. Yet, not even the majesty of the night could erase the afternoon's trauma. Never before had she come face to face with such profound terror. In those few agonizing hours all of the horrors of war were relived in that tortured mind and body. She wept at the thought. How ashamed she now felt. For weeks, preoccupied with her own sense of regret and disappointment, she had become indifferent to the suffering of thousands of young men like Leslie. Michael, Michael, what am I to do?

"Edwina, Mr. Hopkins said I might find you here."

"Clark, how can it be? I thought you were in France."

"I have been. I know you've had a difficult day, Edwina, so if you would rather be alone for a while I'd understand."

"No, no, please stay. Sit here beside me. It has been a terrible time. I don't want to be alone, not tonight."

"You're trembling. Can I get you something?"

"No, Clark, I'll be alright. I probably look awful."

"Impossible. You'll never look awful to me. Here, please take my handkerchief and dry your tears. Then I'll explain everything. Deal?"

"I haven't heard that expression in a long while. Okay, you have a deal." Edwina carefully brushed the tears from her face and folded the handkerchief. She didn't return it.

"Well, first—why am I in England. The soldiers call it a blighty over there."

"A blighty? I don't understand."

"It's a very special kind of wound. Not serious enough to put you in mortal danger but serious enough to get you shipped back to England. And I can tell you it's a damn sight better than shooting yourself in the foot. Right now there's a splinter of shrapnel in my right lung. And that is what every soldier at the front prays for every night. Not necessarily a splinter in the lung, but a blighty."

"Are you in pain?"

"Only if I think about it, and I try not to. Now, why am I at the hotel. The hospital needed my bed so I agreed to give it up and Mr. Hopkins arranged a room for me here."

"For how long?"

"A week, possibly two. I want to get back to France as soon as they'll let me. Things are not going well over there. They need every pilot who is still sound enough to fly."

"Clark, I'm married now."

"I know. Auburn told me."

"Auburn?"

"We're in the same squadron. He told me about you and Michael. From what he tells me Michael is one brave man. I hope you both will be happy."

For a long moment Edwina said nothing. She handed the handkerchief back and turned away. "I'm not happy, Clark, and I won't be. Not now. Clark, why didn't you say goodbye?"

"I wanted to. Very much. But Michael was with you and I just couldn't. I'm truly sorry. I was going to write but hesitated, not sure I should. Then I met Auburn and he told me of your marriage to Michael. Well, I knew then I couldn't write what I wanted to."

"I waited for you on the bench. Just as we had agreed. I waited for over two hours. I would have waited longer but Mr. Hopkins said you had left. Why, Clark, why. Didn't you realize how much I loved you?" The tears which had dried on her cheeks fell once again. "I was so disappointed and angry, yes, angry. That's why I married Michael. I didn't love him then and I don't love him now."

"But how could I have known. We never spoke of love. Not once. All I was was a waiter, no prospects, no accomplishments. How could I have ever hoped that you would love me."

"I will never love anyone else but you, never. When Michael left from Southampton I looked for you, hoping desperately you might be leaving too. I searched the quay, looked into every face, stayed until the ship was gone. And I cried until I could cry no more."

Mr. Hopkins suddenly appeared, his face ashen, barely able to speak. "Mrs. Dobson, you had better come quickly. Something unspeakable has happened."

The unspeakable had happened. Leslie had taken his life with his service revolver. There would be no more talk of love.

....

October, 1943

"Will you be leaving us today, Major Dobson?"

"No, tomorrow evening."

"Is there anything we can do for you?"

"No, not really. Is Mr. Hopkin's health improving?"

"I'm afraid not. He's had a second stroke. His chances of survival are slim."

"I'm very sorry. I understand a new manager is coming next week."

"Yes. Mr. Hopkin's daughter arrived today. She's packing up the few things they had left behind. We're going to miss Mr. Hopkins. He was a good man."

"He was, indeed. Do you think I might have a word with Mr. Hopkin's daughter?"

"I'm sure she would like that, Major Dobson. You know where the manager's suite is."

"Yes, I spent many happy evenings there."

The small suite of rooms which the Hopkins had occupied for over forty years was along a narrow corridor off the lobby. Michael felt a sadness he couldn't explain. It was not only that a fine man who was almost part of the family was dying. It was as if the world he had known and loved was dying too. Why have I been drawn to these rooms, he wondered, as he knocked on the door.

The daughter bore no family resemblance to either of the Hopkins. She was tall and lithe with dark hair and large brown eyes. I was surprised at her youth. She couldn't have been more than twenty-five. Strange, that I had never noticed her before.

"Miss Hopkins, my name is Michael Dobson."

"Yes, I know. Won't you please come in. I'm just finishing up."

"I'm surprised you know my name, Miss Hopkins."

"Please call me Clara, Major Dobson. You were my father's favorite. I have known your name ever since I can remember. Won't you sit down. I'm afraid there's only that old ottoman but it might be more comfortable than standing. You have an injured leg, I believe."

"I think I will sit down. I hope I'm not delaying you." I was glad of the offer to sit because the wound I thought was healing was beginning to throb again.

"I'm almost finished. We were all saddened by the passing of Mrs. Dobson. I admired her more than any other woman I have ever met. She was so vibrant, so charming. I used to watch and try to imitate her."

"I hope this won't offend you, Clara, but I really don't remember seeing you about the hotel."

Clara smiled. "Mr. Hopkins was old-fashioned as you well know. He believed that a child should neither be seen nor heard. The hotel patrons were his first concern so I was kept out of sight. But I remember seeing you and Mrs. Dobson in the little room in the alcove. I was an adopted child late in their life, Major Dobson, but they loved me dearly and I loved them. I'll miss the hotel more than I can express. But life moves on, doesn't it?"

I understood then why Clara had no family resemblance

and why she was so youthful.

"Well, that's just about everything." She looked about the room inspecting closets and cupboards for the last time. From the drawer of an old writing desk which belonged to the hotel she took out some papers and sorted through them. "Father kept everything," she said. Some of the papers she set aside and others she threw into the fireplace. Suddenly she turned and said, "Here are some letters addressed to Mrs. Michael Dobson c/o my father. Is it possible these letters were meant for your wife? "

The small package of five or six letters was tied with a pale, blue ribbon. The writing was faded on the unopened envelopes, yellowed with age. I turned them over in my hand. On the back of one of the envelopes was the name and return address of C. Gregson, Royal Flying Corps. I untied the ribbon and examined each of the letters. As near as I could tell, they were all dated in 1915 and had come by military post. My hand shook as I studied each wafer-thin envelope, wondering what message was hidden inside.

"Do you think they were intended for your wife?" said Clara astonished at the thought.

I nodded. "Yes, I believe so."

"Why didn't my father give them to her then?"

"Why, indeed," I said, knowing all the while. "I must be going, Clara. I'm glad we met at last and if I can do anything to help don't hesitate to call. I'm leaving tomorrow evening but Mrs. Conway knows where I can be reached. Goodnight and thank you for everything."

The letters burned in my hand as I returned to my room and sank into the armchair. I placed the unopened letters beside an unopened bottle of scotch on the table. Why hadn't Mr. Hopkins given the letters to Edwina? Surely there was only one answer. He was protecting someone. I wonder who. What was Clark Gregson to him? Obviously more than an employee. And what did he know of the relationship between Clark and Edwina? Was he protecting Edwina, not realizing he was denying her the happiness she never had with me? Or was he protecting me because of Mama? The answer would go with Mr. Hopkins to his grave.

At first I thought I might open the letters but I realized the truth would not set me free. One thing I knew. The dark cloud that was ever present throughout our marriage would be there no more, to that extent I was free.

After midnight, I went to the bench where we had first met and tore the letters, one by one, into small pieces. Then I scattered the fragments on the waves and watched them as they drifted away into the darkness. I love you, Edwina, forever.

The next day I walked along the promenade as we had done so many times over the years. Memories of Edwina filled my thoughts each step of the way. How fortunate I had been to love someone as much as I had loved her and how unfortunate she had been not to have been able to love someone in the same way. But perhaps I was wrong. Maybe that love was there, all those years, a love as strong and real as my own for her.

At tea time I sat by the window and looked out as I had done so many times before. I knew I would never come back. I would keep the memories of this place where no one would ever find them. For the last time I watched the woman in black take her place on the bench. She kept looking back toward the hotel as if she were looking for someone. I must meet her, I decided impulsively, and was preparing to leave when the waiter came over with a message. Vice-Air Marshall Dobson was calling from London. Headington House had been destroyed by a German bomb. Cheer up, old boy, he said, at least there wasn't anyone home in that drafty old place. By the time we finished our conversation, the woman in black had left and the bench was now occupied by one of the housemaids from the hotel. As I approached, she recognized me and smiled.

"Good day, Major Dobson, it's a fine day, isn't it?" she

said.

"Yes it is. Was there a woman sitting on the bench when you first came? She was wearing black."

"Yes and they left just as I arrived."

"They," I said puzzled. "She wasn't alone?"

"Oh, no, Major Dobson. She was with an RAF officer."

Sans Souci

The Sans Souci Inn rests among the gentle folds of a valley in England's storied Lake District, a stone's throw from the village of Medford. How this unpretentious English inn came by its grandiose French name remains a mystery, even though I have made several attempts to find out. The inn has no obvious Gallic characteristics. Its architecture is faux Tudor. Its ambience is English through and through and its cuisine, unfortunately, would not tempt a Frenchman's palate. No Brioche de foie gras. No Moules en ecrin. No Escargots de Bourgogne. Of all the times Sans Souci has been my summer home I have never once encountered anyone from France or from anywhere else on the Continent.

Unlike Frederick the Great's extravagant summer palace, the Sans Souci has too few amenities to attract professional tourists looking for a truly carefree experience. Its patrons, like myself, are mainly small business reps and coach-class travelers who have learned to put realism ahead of romance. That a college professor from the U.S. Midwest, as I am, is considered a tycoon in this company illustrates at what end of the economic rainbow most of the guests find themselves. Perhaps it's because I pay my account in dollars that I'm mistaken for the son of a Silicon Valley tycoon.

The inn was swarming with guests by the time I arrived at the beginning of June. A last-minute imbroglio with the Dean over my refusal to support his bid for the Wassaloo College presidency had delayed me by a week. The question on my mind as I checked in was would I get the room I had asked for. It has a million dollar view of the lake and this advantage makes up for all its other shortcomings. But I needn't have worried. Mr. Ablonsky, the manager, greeted me with an expansive smile and informed me that my room reservation was secure. From his nuanced felicitations, I gathered that an additional gratuity would not be out of order. Even in England, I have come to realize, baksheesh can work miracles.

It is my habit upon arrival to partake in one of the few luxuries the Sans Souci offers. I ordered room service between long bouts of sleep for the next few days. The combination of a harsh, interminably long winter and the unpleasantness surrounding the appointment of a new president had worn me thin. For the best part of two days I luxuriated in relaxation, reading and gazing out the window at the breath-taking panorama of a crystalline lake surrounded by verdant hills. Soon Indiana, and all thoughts of a way of life I was beginning to abhor, melted away. For me at least, Sans Souci lived up to its name. Free and easy was exactly how I was beginning to feel. A note slipped under the door, however, changed all that.

Luxury, apparently, is not a sustainable resource at the Sans Souci. Mr. Ablonsky wondered whether I would be coming down to dine for the evening meal. Chateaubriand grande fine was the dinner's piece de resistance and so the exact number of guests who would be dining was a matter of some urgency. Reluctantly, I decided to abandon my monastic lifestyle and join the others. A truly French dish at the inn was an event not to be missed. I wondered if a new chef was on board as I could not remember when we were ever tempted with such a delicacy. The thought of having to wear a dinner jacket (one of the few requirements of the inn) was daunting, but nothing gold can stay, as Robert Frost put it (or was it nothing green). Whatever.

I prefer to dine alone. An even moderately good meal can

be spoiled by conversation. If for practical reasons it is not possible, I made it quite clear to the manager there must always be at least two other diners at the table. My reasoning is that they can engage in small talk while I, reading a book for added protection, can enjoy the meal.

I arrived late on purpose, but the strategy misfired. A gaggle of Australian headmasters, who were turning the inn upside down with their adolescent shenanigans, was already installed at the best tables. As I scanned the room for a refuge from these ebullient Down Under pedants my hopes of enjoying the Chateaubriand in splendid isolation began to disappear.

Although the overabundant foliage of potted ferns of unimaginable proportions made it impossible to see every table, one or two of them had at least one unoccupied place, and mercifully, the other diners were travelers sporting red jackets and orange ties. I was confident they would be too busy exchanging insider information on the latest mega merger, or the rise and fall of the pound, to pay much attention to a late arrival with book in hand.

To my surprise and no little disappointment Miss Tomlinson, an English rose with the bluest eyes in the kingdom and golden hair that would make Rapunzel weep, was not on duty as hostess. In her place was Mrs. Ablonsky, she of hairy chin and protruding eyes. As I approached the reception desk, she summoned one of the waiters and uttered a curt instruction. He nodded and I followed, assuming he would take me to one of the unoccupied places I had already identified.

Instead, he led me through the ferny forest to a table for two which was close to the evening's entertainment, a combo playing old Sinatra tunes as selected by the headmasters' tour guide. En route, I asked the waiter if Miss Tomlinson had the night off. No, he said, in his BBC voice, Miss Tomlinson was no longer an employee. One fewer luxury I thought, as I sat down and waited for my escort to remove the plates and cutlery on the opposite side of the table.

But this was not to be. Instead he said, "Red or white," with an unusual economy of words. "Red," I replied as he turned and headed for the kitchen.

As I was congratulating myself that my strategy had worked, after all, the waiter reappeared. He was not alone. A pace or two behind was a tall, lithe goddess who might have stepped out of a fashion magazine. I sighed, but whether because my privacy was about to be invaded or because of this vision of absolute delight, I could not tell. I half rose from my chair until she was seated, then settled down once again. The waiter had apparently discovered language as he was positively unrestrained in his description of Sans Souci's wine list. "Red," she said dismissively and smiled a Mona Lisa smile.

"I suppose I should introduce myself. Jack Clemson."

"It's a pleasure to meet you, Mr. Clemson. I'm Lisa Dubrova." That Mona Lisa smile reappeared as she unfolded her serviette. "Are you an American?" Her accent was vaguely Eastern European.

"Yes. My home's in Wassaloo, Indiana. It's a small college town in the Midwest, but I was born in New York. The Bronx. Do you know it?"

"Wassaloo? No, I don't think so," Lisa responded.

"I meant the Bronx. I thought everybody's heard of the Bronx."

Lisa's coal-black eyes were large and luminous, strangely so, and certainly disconcerting.

The presentation of the soup course interrupted the exhilarating chit-chat. I glanced at my book wistfully.

"And you're from . . . ?"

"Macicza," she responded.

"Macicza?" I replied, puzzled.

"I thought everybody's heard of Macicza. It's my home town in Hungary."

"But I thought Macicza was in . . . I'm sorry. I feel

downright foolish."

"You needn't. Are you here on business, Jack?"

"No. Holidays. And you?"

"I think you Americans might say a business holiday."

"What business are you in?"

"The travel business. I arrange tours to exotic destinations for young people," Lisa explained.

"Well, you've come to the right place. This is one of the most delightful places anywhere. I've come here for ten years and never tire of it."

"I'll make use of your recommendation if that's okay. Okay is a proper American word, isn't it?"

"Yes, okay is an okay word." I was about to provide the etymology of okay, but resisted. "Will you be staying here long? At the Sans Souci, I mean."

"Just for a few days. I had intended to stay longer but the Sans Souci isn't really French, is it. I'm going to Scotland and then to Paris."

Our conversation dropped off. The silence became awkward. The waiter rescued the moment with the evening's promised piece de resistance. It may have been Chateaubriand, but it definitely was not French.

Lisa asked, "Do you teach at the college in . . . ?"

"Wassaloo. Wassaloo Liberal Arts College. Yes I teach there."

"What subject?"

"Nineteenth Century English Literature. And some creative writing thrown in when the head of the department is mad at me."

"And that's why you've come to the Lake District? Wordsworth and all that."

"Yes, I suppose so." The Chateaubriand was overcooked. Miss Dubrova cut off a small portion but left it on the plate. She sipped from the glass of wine instead. Conversation lagged.

"These Australians are rather rowdy, n'est pas?" said Lisa.

"You speak French," I said, instantly feeling foolish for making such a trite observation, but I live in absolute dread that conversation will lapse into an uncomfortable silence if I don't fill the vacuum.

"Mais oui. My mother was French. I also speak German, Russian, Polish, and Hungarian, of course."

"I'm afraid Americans aren't much interested in speaking foreign languages."

"Pity," she said. "They also seem to be ignorant of geography as well. At least geography outside the United States."

The strains of Waltzing Matilda were fading when she excused herself. She said she had a long day ahead of her on the morrow and must retire for the evening. "Goodnight," she said. "I was teasing about the Bronx. A distant cousin of mine lives there. Bon sewer, as you Americans would say."

As she swept through the room, her long, jet black hair shimmering in the candlelight, every head turned in her direction. The headmasters interrupted their raucous conversation and began whispering to one another. Waltzing with Matilda was no longer on their minds. But then, it was not every day the likes of Lisa Dubrova passed by.

She stopped for a brief moment to say something to Mrs. Ablonsky, then disappeared around a potted fern. The hostess glanced in my direction. The glance was decidedly unfriendly. Whatever Miss Dubrova had said to Mrs. Ablonsky did not put me in a favorable light. I picked up my book and buried myself in it.

Later that evening, alone in the darkness, I became unusually restless. I had been reading, my great passion, but couldn't concentrate, so I turned the lights off and stared out the window. Not that I could see anything except my own reflection.

What was it about Miss Dubrova that unsettled me? Turning this question over in my mind, I decided it was definitely not her charm or even her undeniable attractiveness.

It was her air of Old World superiority that nettled me. Doesn't everyone speak a dozen foreign languages? Doesn't everyone know world geography? Doesn't everyone know this or that? If ever I had the opportunity to engage her in small talk again, I told myself, I would show her what New World superiority is. Still, my restlessness persisted and I recognized that it was more than mental jousting with Miss Dubrova that was disturbing me.

A knock at the door ended my gloomy introspection. I turned on the light and opened the door. Why I didn't connect in my mind, right then and there, this woman smiling her enigmatic smile with the proverbial femme fatale, I can only put down to New World naiveté.

"May I come in?" she said provocatively. "We wouldn't want anyone passing to get the wrong impression, would we?"

"Yes, come in. Of course, come in," I replied. What the 'of course' was meant to convey I couldn't imagine, not then and not now. It was a kind of filler while I collected my confused thoughts. Miss Dubrova (at least she was not wearing a wedding ring so I assumed her marital status as single) settled herself in the armchair beside the bed. What she was wearing can best be described as loose and informal. The word, décolletage, comes to mind.

"I'll come right to the point, Mr. Clemson."

Here it comes, I thought. Please don't look at me like that. What is there about those eyes that intrigue me?

"You're a philatelist," Lisa suddenly announced.

"A philatelist. Yes, I guess I am. Not professional, mind you. An amateur, really." I was not sure whether she was asking a question or making an accusation, hence, my equivocation.

"And now you're probably wondering how I know?"

Not exactly. I was wondering why she cared about my hobby at all. "Yes, I suppose I do. How do you know?"

"Mr. Ablonsky told me. Stop me if I'm being too inquisitive or if you have no interest in revealing anything else about yourself." Miss Dubrova's voice increased by several decibels until she was almost shouting.

She wasn't making much sense and I wondered if she had drunk too much wine at dinner on an empty stomach. "The reason I'm interested is," she continued, suddenly lowering her voice, "I have a friend back home who deals in stamps and things and I think you should meet him."

"Is that all? Well, yes, of course. If it can be arranged, I would be delighted to meet your friend." But I wasn't sure how this could be arranged and, at that point, I couldn't think of anything I would like to do less than meet her Hungarian friend who dealt in stamps and things.

Miss Dubrova got up and walked to the door. "Would you like to go for a walk? Later on, I mean. I'm a dreadful sleeper and a walk at midnight always helps. Yes?"

"Why yes I would like to. I wouldn't want you to be accosted by one of those dreadful Australian headmasters, would I." We both laughed though I wondered why I was laughing. Nothing was making any sense at all. A walk at midnight?

"Then it's settled as you Americans would say. I'll meet you in the lobby. Don't forget. Midnight." As she opened the door and turned once again toward me, I was reminded of Lauren Bacall in some movie or other with Humphrey Bogart, their banter at the door eluding me for the moment.

We met at midnight as arranged. She greeted me with a passionate kiss and took my arm with singular possessiveness. From behind the registration desk Mr. Ablonsky broke into a lascivious smile and winked. A few minutes into the walk Miss Dubrova decided she had a headache and would retire after all. When we returned to the inn, not a soul was up and about, not even an inebriated headmaster. No kiss this time. Just a Thank You and see you in the morning. With a mixture of disappointment and relief I went to bed and dreamed about a Hungarian village populated with dwarfs who pasted their heads with postage stamps.

The next morning I slept in, exhausted by the events of the previous evening. I wouldn't have got up at all but the knocking at the door persisted with increasing vehemence.

"Professor Clemson, please open the door. It's urgent." The agitated voice belonged to Mr. Ablonsky.

I opened the door. "Yes," I said.

"There is a constable downstairs. He wants to talk to you."

"Constable?" It took a few moments for my mind to clear. "Constable? A policeman?"

"Yes."

"I'll be right down. Do you know what it's all about?"

"Miss Dubrova's missing."

"Missing?"

"Worse."

"How worse?"

"Murdered."

"When? How?"

"We don't know. Someone called this morning and said she has been murdered. Hurry and come down." The manager shook his head in disbelief and reminded me of something I didn't need reminding of. "You were with her last. You went for a walk with her at midnight. I saw you with her." With that he turned and left the room, still shaking his head.

The constable was waiting at the registration desk. His unsmiling demeanor was more than a little unnerving. As I approached, he took a small, black notebook from his tunic pocket.

"Inspector Turnbull will be along shortly, Professor Clemson. Sorry to disturb you but I'm afraid I have to ask you a few questions about last night. Just to confirm what others have already told me." He flipped the cover of the notebook over and perused his notes. "This enquiry is informal, Professor, and if you are uncomfortable answering any of the questions please let me know. Let me see. Were you dining with a guest by the name of Lisa Dubrova last evening?"

"Well, yes, I was. At least in one sense I was dining with

her, but actually . . . "

Constable Jenkins interrupted. "This is informal, Professor. Just yes or no for now. You can elaborate your answers when Inspector Turnbull arrives."

"Did this same Miss Dubrova visit you in your room around ten o'clock last night?"

"Yes, she did, but I didn't . . . "

Jenkins frowned. "Did you and Miss Dubrova leave the hotel around midnight?"

"Yes."

Jenkins now smiled. I was not a slow learner after all. "One more question, Professor. Did anyone see you and Miss Dubrova return to the inn . . . together, that is?"

I definitely did not like the inference but, as directed, responded in the negative.

"That is all for now, Professor. You will be staying at the inn today." It was not a question. "Here is something you should read." The title of the small religious tract was Barabbas and You. Jenkin's expression did not reveal whether his inclination was more toward crucifixion or redemption.

Breakfast was usually my favourite meal, but not today. I pushed the plate of bangers and mash aside unfinished and went upstairs. Even my room with a view no longer soothed. I lay on the bed constructing imaginary escape scenarios. I was really asleep and would wake up in a few minutes. But the housemaid had already made up the room, so that scenario was a non-starter. Miss Dubrova had returned home to Macicza because her house caught on fire and her children were all alone. But she had no children (or had she). Well, that scenario was too far-fetched. Anyway, the police had probably checked out whether she had returned home. She decided to leave early for Scotland because the croissants were unusually stale at the Sans Souci and she wanted to make an early start on haggis. But no one I have ever known would want to make an early start on haggis. Had she taken her clothes with her? Probably not. One more scenario up in smoke.

Another knock at the door and the same urgent voice as before.

"Professor, Inspector Turnbull is waiting downstairs," said Mr. Ablonsky. "I should warn you he's in a rather foul mood. You'd better not keep him waiting. I've never seen him so disagreeable."

I decided then and there I must be more aggressive. In England a man is innocent until proven guilty. This is a sacred tenet of British justice. And this isn't France, I reminded myself. I will not be intimidated. I have done nothing wrong, absolutely nothing. How I devoutly wished I had read my book that evening. Who is it can read a woman? The bard of Avon always got it right.

Inspector Turnbull was on the phone but rang off when he noticed me. The few snatches of conversation I overheard confirmed Ablonsky's reading of the inspector's mood. Foul, indeed. I got the sinking feeling that the milk of human kindness would be in short supply today. Turnbull was tall, lean and impeccably dressed. I was certain that when he opened his mouth he would sound like the fictional detective Adam Dalgleish, and I was right. "Perhaps we should use the manager's office." He opened the door marked PRIVATE and disappeared inside. I followed like the proverbial lamb to the slaughter. "Please be seated, Professor Clemson. You know why I'm here," he said crisply.

"Yes, I believe so." It was definitely not for a poetry reading.

"You have already met Constable Jenkins."

"Yes." I glanced in his direction.

Jenkins returned my glance with a smirk. He knew when they had someone on the ropes.

"We do not know whether Miss Dubrova has come to harm in spite of the call to the manager this morning. From an inspection of her room, it would appear that she didn't sleep at the inn last night. Her clothes, cosmetics, travelling cases, toiletries and so on are still in her room. The only things missing are the clothes she was seen wearing last night."

"I see." I wasn't sure of what I saw but I felt I had to say something.

"Before we proceed, would you object to Constable Jenkin's examining your room? It's just a formality." The Inspector, I knew, was testing my reaction.

"Not at all," I said more jauntily than I felt. "On the condition that he put everything back." My smile was forced. The chill up my spine was not.

"Good. Let's proceed." The pages of the notebook were once more unfurled. "Let's make sure I have it right. Last evening you dined with Miss Dubrova. According to witnesses, your conversation seemed quite animated as though you were both well-acquainted. Well, that's neither here nor there, is it? Later, Miss Dubrova visited you in your room. Around ten o'clock. Again, according to one of the housemaids, she was dressed, let's see how Jenkins puts it, "scantily". The same housemaid heard Miss Dubrova shout: you don't have to reveal anything more about yourself, or at least something like that. Still later, you met in the lobby at or around midnight. If you had been quarrelling, you both had made up, as Mr. Ablonsky reports Miss Dubrova embraced you passionately. That's about it. Unless, of course, you have something to add. Nothing you say now will prejudice anything you might like to add later." Turnbull closed the notebook. "Well?"

For some unknown reason a calm settled over me. I think it was because in most detective novels I have read the obvious suspect in a criminal investigation is never the culprit. So Inspector Dalgleish of Scotland Yard (or was it Chief Inspector), this bird in the hand is not worth two in the bush.

"Let's get the facts straight. First, I did not dine with Miss Dubrova. She was seated at my table by the waiter. Second, Miss Dubrova came to my room later, uninvited, to advise me she had a friend in her hometown who is a stamp collector as I am. She thought we should meet. She did raise her voice, why I don't know, but we were not quarrelling. She left after fifteen minutes. I too noticed she was dressed scantily.

"Finally, she asked me to go with her on a walk. We met at midnight. She kissed me, why I can't tell. We walked for about fifteen minutes when she said she had a headache. We returned to the inn. The last time I saw Miss Dubrova was at the lift when she said goodnight. Those are the facts."

I was delighted with my bravura performance. So delighted that I began to take in the room which was one of the most interesting in the hotel. I also unearthed a clue about the origin of the inn's name. French authors populated the shelves and a rather good likeness of Voltaire looked out serenely from behind a smaller bust of Napoleon. Speculating that these treasures did not belong to the present manager, I was about to make the logical leap when Jenkins returned. He was carrying a rather large brown bag which he placed on the manager's desk. A whisper in the inspector's ear ended my moment of imperturbability.

"Are you a cross-dresser, Professor Clemson?" he said with a bemused smile.

"A cross-dresser?"

"A transvestite." He obviously knew the answer before he asked but again he seemed to be measuring my reaction.

"Most certainly not. Why do you ask?"

"Constable Jenkins found some lingerie and other things in your room just now. Here in the bag. Would you like to see them?"

"No, I wouldn't. They're not mine."

"I didn't think so. You won't mind then if we take them with us." He handed the bag to Jenkins whose look of feigned disgust could not be disguised. "I think we have taken enough of your time, Professor." He stood up and walked the few steps to the leaded window, striking a reflective pose as if he were assessing the situation. After a moment, he turned.

"We hope to wrap up the investigation very soon, very

soon, in forty-eight hours, certainly no more than that. Perhaps you should turn your passport in. Just a formality, you understand. So far as we know you were the last person with Miss Dubrova and we, of course, have to regard you as a suspect if Miss Dubrova has indeed been harmed. Good-day, Professor."

Under the circumstances, it was hardly a good day. I watched as Inspector Turnbull, flanked by Jenkins and Mr. Ablonsky, left the inn. I remembered something I read once, something Voltaire had written. Fear follows crime and is its punishment. Truer words were never written, even if you're only accused of a crime.

I waited until Mr. Ablonsky returned. He brushed hurriedly by, not stopping to banter as was his custom, and retired to his office. He glanced back at me as he closed the door. I did not like the expression on his face. It said clearly, your goose is cooked. Whatever he had told Inspector Turnbull on the way to the car was probably still on his mind. He certainly wasn't going to be a witness for the defense.

"A telephone call for you, Professor," the house boy said. "At the registration desk."

"Thank you. Did you get the caller's name?"

"No, sir. But he said it was urgent."

As I picked up the telephone, I noticed the door to the manager's office opened a crack. I turned my back and identified myself to the caller.

"You've had an eventful day, Professor." Unless my imagination was playing tricks the voice was not unfamiliar. "I'm here to offer you a way out of your dilemma. Listen carefully. Do you remember the story of Lazarus? How he came back from the dead and everybody was happy. Well, I might just perform the same miracle. I might bring back Lisa from the dead. How would you like that?"

"Who are you?" I said, glancing back as the door closed slowly.

"All in good time, Professor, in good time. Listen to my

proposal. For twenty-five thousand U.S. dollars Lisa will return to the hotel fit as a fiddle, to coin an expression. And you will be off the hook. Simple as that."

"That's extortion."

"Precisely. Think it over soberly, Professor. British prisons are nasty places, especially for murderers. Sell some of your precious stamps. I hear they're worth a small fortune. I'll be in touch. And don't tell the police about this phone call. Turnbull's already decided you're guilty. Telling him about this business arrangement will only convince him he's right. Bye, bye. I'll call again. Have your answer ready."

My hand was shaking as I put down the phone. The caller was right. Whatever I said now would dig the hole I was in even deeper. Twenty-five thousand dollars. Even if I were inclined to pay, I couldn't raise that kind of money in a few days. Who is this stranger? How does he know about my stamp collection? And where have I heard that voice before? I must keep my cool . . . keep my cool . . . keep my cool . . . I repeated until, to my great relief, I experienced the calm I felt before Jenkins delivered the brown bag with, presumably, Lisa's unmentionables inside. Cross-dresser be damned.

I was tempted to find out what Mr. Ablonsky knew about Lisa Dubrova but something warned me off the idea. Instead, I wandered into the lounge where I felt every eye upon me. The Aussie headmasters had been replaced by a busload of caregivers from Manchester. Their careworn faces looked up at me as I passed. How much do they know, I wondered. Mrs. Ablonksy, especially, was given to gossip with her guests, and caregivers would be her cup of tea. If this was to be my fifteen minutes of fame, I could have done without it.

Like another sinner waiting for divine wrath to fall upon him, I decided to hide among the foliage at the far end of the lounge where no caregiver was likely to venture. It wasn't until I had sat down that I realized how wobbly my legs had become. Like a roller coaster ride my feelings of highs and lows were crowding closer and closer together. Steady, man, steady. Think. Of what? Of what you're going to do. It's not a game, stupid, it's your life, or at least twenty or thirty years of it. What would Holmes do? What would Poirot do? Yes, Poirot. The little grey cells. Now I was on to something. Yes, little grey cells. Go backwards and reconstruct everything. Right from the beginning. What was it that puzzled me at the time but I have since forgotten? Something Lisa Dubrova said at dinner. Something I was about to question but didn't because I wasn't exactly certain and she was so infuriatingly self-assured.

I, too, had a small notebook with a mock leather cover. I opened to the first blank page and wrote: Point One: was the table for two a setup? Point Two: if, yes, who engineered it? must quiz waiter. Point Three: what did Lisa say that puzzled me? Point Four: Miss Dubrova's eyes??? Point Five: why did Lisa say Ablonksy told her about my hobby (never told Ablonsky or did I, try to remember) Point Six: someone must have seen us return to the inn? who? Point Seven: how did the caller know about my hobby? from Lisa? I began running out of points when the waiter with the BBC voice approached. He held in his hand a small notepad. Does everyone in England carry a small notepad with them?

"Is there anything you would like?" he asked nervously.

"Yes, as a matter of fact, there is. I would like some answers. Is extortion a crime in England?"

"I believe it is."

"Is conspiracy to commit extortion a crime?"

"Yes, so far as I know."

"Is an accessory to a criminal act punishable under English law?"

"I'm not a law clerk, Professor, but I suppose it is. Why do you ask?"

"Because you are in serious trouble and Inspector Turnbull will soon be investigating your part in a conspiracy to extort a guest at this hotel. Namely me. Now sit down. You have some explaining to do."

"I can't. Employees cannot sit with the guests. It's against the house rules." He glanced back across the lounge. Mr. Ablonsky motioned to him to return to the kitchen. "I must go. I'll come to your room. This evening. But I must go now."

"After dinner then. I'll wait for you. But make sure you keep your promise. Time is running out." I should have added, for me, but ethical conduct is seldom expected of a murder suspect. Mr. Ablonsky smiled weakly as I passed by. "I'll take dinner in my room this evening," I said. "Shall we say at seven."

"Of course, Professor. But if you should change your mind, please let me know. We're expecting a full house tonight."

"Does that include Miss Dubrova by any chance?" I said nonchalantly.

Mr. Ablonsky's eyeglasses dropped to the floor. He was picking them up as I walked away. I had scored a hit.

Mrs. Ablonsky also dropped something. But it was not her eyeglasses. It was the master room key. I startled her as she was leaving my room. How sharper than a serpent's tooth to have a prying manageress!

"You dropped your key," I said with a mocking smile. I picked it up and handed it to her. "Were you looking for something special? Perhaps I can help. The maids must be very busy today to bring you to the second floor."

Mrs. Ablonsky recovered her composure quickly. She was obviously adept in the craft of being caught while snooping about. "Just making sure Constable Jenkins left everything as he found it, Professor Clemson. Some of them from the station leave things in a mess." She pocketed the key and turned to walk away.

"Do the police come often to the inn? I don't ever remember seeing the police here before." It was a stab in the dark, not that I expected a straight answer.

"Constable Jenkins sometimes. On occasion we have an unruly guest," she said, "but we've never had a murder suspect before. Enjoy your evening, if you can." She turned abruptly and waddled off down the corridor.

Touché, I said to myself. If you're as good at prying as you are at verbal fencing, I'd better watch out. A quick look around the room revealed nothing out of the ordinary. I wondered where Jenkins found the ladies' underthings because the dresser drawers seemed undisturbed. I am not fastidious about many things but drawers must be tidy. Baggage from childhood, I suppose. I arrange everything according to a strict formula, and once disturbed, I defy anyone to put things back exactly as they were before.

The things in the wardrobe were also precisely as I had left them. Only the desk drawer beside the window showed perceptible signs of being rifled through. Was it Jenkins or Ablonsky I wondered. And what were they looking for. So far as I could tell nothing was missing nor was there anything in the drawer which in the slightest way implicated me in Miss Dubrova's disappearance.

One thing caught my attention. A penny postage stamp from my album was lying, half-hidden, under the base of the nightstand lamp. I examined it carefully, trying to recall whether I had taken it out the previous evening. It was not a particularly good stamp and certainly of little value.

I picked up the album from the table and flipped the pages. One or two other stamps were missing, impressive no doubt to someone who was not a collector but, like the penny postage stamp, virtually worthless. I sat down at the table and wrote: Point Eight: Who took the stamps and why?

The irrepressible Belgian detective had more luck with his little grey cells than I did with mine. By dinner time I had a few more questions but no illuminating answers. It was clearly a setup, but by who (or should that be by whom). Mrs. Ablonsky directed the waiter to bring Miss Dubrova to my table. On her way out Miss Dubrova seemed to report something to Mrs. Ablonsky. They both have Eastern European names. Mr. Ablonsky was present when we left the inn but was gone fifteen minutes later. He reported something to Inspector Turnbull which gave him guilt pangs. Now he's uncomfortable around me. My offhanded remark about Miss Dubrova showing up for dinner unsettled him and then I caught Mrs. Ablonsky snooping through my things. Some valueless stamps were missing but the room was not searched, at least, not thoroughly. Puzzling. Where did Lisa's things come from? My musings were interrupted by a knock at the door. It was the waiter, with my dinner.

"Come in. I'm surprised Mr. Ablonsky let you out of his sight. Come in."

"So am I, Professor. If I may say so, I think he's being a trifle Machiavellian. Don't hurry back was the last thing he said to me."

"Please sit down. Yes, there. I won't keep you long but I have to ask a few questions."

"I've thought over what you said earlier about being an accessory to extortion and so on. I'm scared, Professor, really scared. Anything I can do to help, you can count on me. I mean anything."

"Good. Do you read Agatha Christie's novels?"

"Yes, some of them. I'm not a fan of detective stories, though."

"But you do know who Poirot is?"

"Yes, I do."

"Well, my friend, you're going to be Captain Hastings to my Poirot.

"Okay."

"Let's get started. First, who asked you to bring Miss Dubrova to my table?"

"Mrs. Ablonsky."

"What was her motivation, do you think?"

"For my convenience. In serving, I mean."

"That's all."

"Yes, I'm quite certain."

That was definitely not the response I was hoping for. I

tried another tack. "What do you know about Miss Dubrova?"

"Not much. She arrived the day before you did. She kept out of sight. In fact, I think the night she came down for dinner was the only time I saw her after her arrival."

"Has she ever been at the Sans Souci before?"

"Yes, for a day or two last autumn according to Mrs. Ablonsky. The Ablonskys were both away and Miss Tomlinson was the acting manager."

"I see. Why did Miss Tomlinson leave?"

"I don't know. I overheard her talking to Mrs. Ablonsky about an engagement. So, perhaps she's going to be married. But I really can't say."

"What about the Ablonskys? How would you rate them in terms of honesty on a scale from 1 to 10?"

"You promise never to tell." He waited for my silent assurance. "Zero," he said. "They are the most devious couple I have ever had the misfortune to work for."

"I thought as much."

"Is it unusual to leave the registration desk unattended after midnight?"

"Yes, very much so. There is always a night attendant on duty. Usually it's Mr. Ablonsky."

"How often does Constable Jenkins come to the inn?"

"Off and on. Mr. Ablonsky calls him when guests get out of hand. Also, he comes for a drink in the lounge once in a while."

"And Inspector Turnbull?"

"Less frequently. He's friendly with one of the maids. I think there's something going on between them. It's just a guess."

"Are there any single male guests right now at the inn? Myself not included."

"I don't think so. The caregivers are mainly couples and those who aren't are single women."

"Good."

"Have I been any help, Professor?"

"Yes, Hastings, you have. But I have a lot of thinking to do. When does your shift begin tomorrow?"

"I have the entire day free."

"Good. Meet me tomorrow morning around nine in the Dying Stag pub. By then I think I'll have some messages for you to run. And thanks. By the way, I don't even know your name."

"It's Clive Hastings."

"Hastings? Really? You can't mean it."

"Really."

"Well, Hastings, we'll drink tomorrow to our partnership in detection."

"What should I tell Mr. Ablonsky if he asks me what we've been talking about?"

"Tell him the truth. Tell him we've been talking about all the possible murder suspects."

"He won't like it."

"Precisely, Hastings. Goodnight."

"Shall I take the tray away?"

"No, I prefer my steak and kidney pie cold. See you in the morning."

"Goodnight, Professor. You didn't tell me anything about the extortion attempt."

"I will. But now I must try to fit the pieces together. By the way, don't mention the extortion bid to the Ablonsky's."

"I won't. See you in the morning."

Only the English can produce a steak and kidney pie that tastes as good cold as it does hot. Before I started in on the business of the night, I washed it down with a carafe of house wine, and polished off the blancmange. Hastings had not provided many new pieces of the puzzle, but I felt certain he was not part of the conspiracy. That, at least, was reassuring. Whatever the Ablonsky's got out of him would not add to their peace of mind either.

I wished I hadn't stopped smoking. A good pipe would have put me in a Sherlock Holmes frame of mind. And I always did think more clearly with a pipe clenched between my teeth. But I knew this was only wishful thinking. You'll have to brush up on your ratiocination. It's definitely not your strong suit, my philosophy professor at NYU once advised me. Now I was beginning to see his point.

Detectives in the U.S., I remembered, are always making charts and diagrams of the suspects in a crime, cleverly using lines and arrows to link one to the other. So, why not? If it helped solve the crime for them in about an hour's time, with a bunch of commercials thrown in for good measure, it might just work for me as well. Then I could spend the rest of the evening philatelising.

Using the linen serviette which was just the right size (I hoped housekeeping would excuse the abuse of their property), I started out with all the zeal and good intentions of an amateur. By midnight, the serviette was a jumble of boxes and lines which looped and crisscrossed and overlapped. On the basis of the arrows every name on the serviette was at the same time convicted and absolved of being part of the conspiracy.

Frustrated, I gave up and glanced at my watch. It was one o'clock. By my reckoning of Inspector Turnbull's forty-eight hour deadline to arrest a suspect, I had approximately a dozen or so hours left of freedom. I folded the serviette and pushed it to back of the desk drawer.

When in England do as the English do, I finally decided. Who is the most famous English detective? Why, the Belgian Poirot, of course. I had come back to where I started. Little grey cells trump charts and diagrams and lines with arrows every time. I lay on the bed and stared at the ceiling, hoping for an epiphany.

For an hour nothing happened, but then it came. Miss Dubrova's eyes. That's it. That's it. Large, luminous, coal-black eyes. Such eyes as may have looked from heaven, but were never raised to it before. I bounded off the bed and snatched up a pencil. In my little notepad I wrote four questions and beneath each question a task for Clive Hastings. Not even the end of a college term brought as much relief as when I looked at that scribbling. I smiled. And so to bed.

Wordsworth was with me as I dozed off. We must be free or die, who speak the tongue that Shakespeare spake . . . the faith and morals . . . hold . . . which Milton . . . held . . .

Mr. Ablonsky was standing at the registration desk as I passed by on my way to the Dying Stag. He looked even more sheepish than usual. "I'm off to the Dying Stag to meet Clive Hastings," I said, loud enough for everyone to hear. "I'll be back in an hour or so." Mrs. Ablonksy, suddenly appearing from the ladies lounge, glowered at me. Apparently, I was no longer a VIP guest in her books. "And I may just wander about like a cloud looking for daffodils." The Ablonsky's exchanged a skeptical glance. "Bon maton, as we Americans say," I added cheerily. "Glorious day, eh wot?" I dared not look back. A guffaw was lurking in my throat.

Hastings was already at the pub. Later, he would tell me that Mr. Ablonsky had fired him, but for the moment he said nothing. His motivation to be of help, however, had taken a quantum leap. We engaged in some light banter and then got down to business. I slipped across the table the paper with the tasks on it. He read them, looked up, read them again, was puzzled, and then grinned. "You think you've solved the mystery," he said with a chuckle. "I'll work as quickly as I can, but it will take some time."

"Time is a thief and I'm a murder suspect. So please give it your best shot. I'll wait for you at the inn. Come right up to my room. And good luck."

"I'll need it, Hercule" he said and laughed. "As I remember, Captain Hastings was a bit of a loser. I hope you don't see me that way."

"Would I trust you with such an important mission if I thought you were a loser? Now get. I think I'll have some refreshment. Sorry you have to leave."

I watched Hastings as he roared off on his Harley. He was

turning out to be a first-rate detection partner. I wondered if a new role in life was opening up for me. Clemson & Hastings, Private Investigators, Bond St., London, WW1. Hmm, not bad. I turned the prospect over in my mind with increasing relish. Wordsworth's brew, if such it was, hit the spot. Nothing goes down better than a pint on a sultry day.

Throughout the rest of the morning, I kept glancing at my watch as the minutes stretched into hours. Twelve noon came and went, and no Hastings. Just as I was beginning to doubt the efficacy of my plans Hastings returned. The broad smile on his handsome face told me everything I needed to know. "You're brilliant," he said, waving the piece of paper with the tasks scribbled on it. "Now you can rub Inspector Turnbull's nose in it."

"I might just do that. But first tell me what you found out and don't spare the details. Not one juicy bit." As he rattled off the facts he had turned up, I related each to the four questions I had posed to myself the night before. The pieces fit. Everything was still circumstantial, but a reasonable man would see the connection. Even someone as superficial as Inspector Turnbull. "Now, Hastings, it's time to invite Turnbull and Jenkins to the party."

The inspector and his constable arrived shortly after my phone call. I was waiting in the lounge, and even though Turnbull glanced in my direction, he did not seem in a hurry to read me my rights. Instead, he chatted up a pretty housemaid, who I guessed to be his bit on the side, as Clive Hastings rather crudely, but aptly, put it.

The more I observed him the less he reminded me of Adam Dalgleish, detective and poet. No fiction writer could portray accurately someone as nondescript as Turnbull. After he had spread his thin resources of amiability around the inn, he approached me with a smug expression on his face.

"If you have something to add to your previous statement, Professor, perhaps we should adjourn to the manager's office again."

"A good idea Inspector, and I hope Jenkins, sorry, Constable Jenkins will join us."

"Certainly, if you wish. Come along Jenkins."

Calling out to Mr. Ablonsky that he didn't want to be disturbed, Inspector Turnbull closed the door and sat down on the edge of the manager's table, not far from where Jenkins had placed the incriminating brown bag just yesterday.

"Well, Professor, we haven't all day. If you have something to tell us, begin. But I must warn you, anything you say now can and will be used against you. Is that clear'?"

"Yes, Inspector Turnbull, very clear. First, you will be delighted to know, I'm sure no harm has come to Miss Dubrova. In fact, she's as fit as a fiddle, to coin an expression."

"She is? How do you know?"

"Are you an aficionado of amateur theatre, Inspector?"

"Why, yes, I suppose I am."

"Then, you should take in a performance of The Little Medford's Players' production of Anna Karenina."

"I should. Why?"

"Because Miss Dubrova is the star of the show. Did you see Julie Andrews in Victor Victoria?"

"No, I did not. Where is all this babble about the theatre leading to?"

"I'm sorry, let me explain. In her role Miss Andrews is a woman masquerading as a man who is cast in the role of a woman. It's a simple as that."

"It is? You're not suggesting Miss Dubrova is a . . . " Inspector Turnbull cast a bewildered glance at Jenkins who was following the discussion with particular interest.

"No. But Miss Dubrova is playing one person when she herself is actually someone else."

"You're confusing me. Miss Dubrova is actually someone else. Who?"

"Leticia Tomlinson."

Constable Jenkins could not suppress a muffled groan.

"Where is this performance?"

"At the Methodist Chapel on the road to Little Medford. Constable Jenkins can take you there. You're a lay preacher at the chapel, aren't you Jenkins? "

"I didn't take you for a religious man, Jenkins," said a dumbfounded Inspector Turnbull. "The Methodist Chapel, you say, Professor." Turning to the constable, he continued, "How is it you didn't know about this? You must have known all along about Miss Dubrova."

Constable Jenkins wisely decided to say nothing.

"There's more, Inspector. Mr. Jenkins (I decided he would soon be out of work) and, I'm guessing, his accomplice Miss Tomlinson, tried to deprive me of a large sum of Yankee dollars. Jenkins, I'm sure, will want to explain this perfidy to you on the way to the station."

"Jenkins," Inspector Turnbull roared, "what in very hell have you been up to? You have some explaining to do and it better be convincing. Do you hear?"

When Inspector Turnbull swung the door open, the Ablonskys stepped back quickly out of the way and retreated to the shelter of the registration desk. At this fracas, a dozen or so of the caregivers wandered out of the lounge and gathered in the lobby. Their otherwise blank faces flickered with a moment of curiosity. Then, like the animals going into the ark, they returned two by two into the lounge to finish their crossword puzzles or snooze away the rest of the day. "I would never have come here if I had known the inn was a nest of reprobates," one of them said to her companion loud enough for the Ablonskys to hear. "I think it's kind of exciting," was her companion's reply. "Go back to your crossword puzzle, you old fool," was all he got for his candour.

"Goodbye, Inspector. I hope you enjoy the performance tonight," I called out, but he didn't look back.

The dying growl of the Harley announced Hasting's timely arrival. He bounded into the lobby with a grin on his face half-a-mile wide. "You whipped them," he shouted. He ignored the Ablonskys altogether and rushed over to where I was standing beside one of the enormous potted ferns. "You did it, Professor, you did it, but how?"

"Come with me, Hastings. I'll hold nothing back."

"Two pints of your best," he called out cheekily to Mr. Ablonsky. I think this was accompanied by a gesture of which the gentry would definitely not approve. My look of surprise at the absence of Hasting's usual deference to his employers was met with a shrug. Now I'm glad they fired me, he said with a smile.

"In that case you can sit and drink with the guests now. Follow me to Clemson's grotto."

When we were comfortably settled and Wordsworth's brew had been delivered by a giggling waitress whose bountiful charms were not lost on a perspiring Hastings, I kept my promise.

"You've studied Horace, haven't you?" Silence was the answer. "Well, Hastings, that ancient Roman poet once said, if I remember correctly, what's well begun is half done.

"Let me back up. Any time you want to interrupt don't hesitate. Now, about Horace and beginning well. You see, Hastings, it began with Miss Dubrova's eyes. Even at dinner something bothered me about them. But it took an epiphany to help me understand."

"Epiphany?"

"I'm using the word loosely, sorry. Let's just say a revelation from cyberspace. They weren't really her eyes at all. They were contact lenses. And they were bothering her so much she must have floated them on some solution or other. Well, I think that's one of the reasons she never stayed long, at dinner, in my room, and when we went for a walk. You see I was stabbed with a white wench's black eye as your fellow Englishman once said. But I am being too wordy."

"That's how it began?" Hasting said.

"Well, sort of. It reminded me of something else which

bothered me. Something Miss Dubrova misspoke. She said her hometown was Macicza . . . "

"And that Macicza was in Hungary. That's why you asked me to look it up."

"Precisely, Hastings. Macicza is in Czechoslovakia. She said Americans are ignorant of geography. But to her sorrow she was wrong."

"Come on, Professor. Macicza is an obscure village. Surely you're not saying you know every small village in Europe."

"I'll say no more. False eyes and false information made me suspicious that Miss Dubrova was not who she said she was."

"I see that. But how did you connect her to Jenkins?"

"A professor of mine at NYU once told me that ratiocination wasn't my strong suit. Well, I've since proved him wrong."

"Ratiocination? I've never once come across that word in any of my correspondence courses from the Open University."

"Pity. It simply means the power of logical reasoning. Jenkins gave me a religious pamphlet after the interview. I didn't think much about it at the time but the would-be extortioner also talked about Lazarus and miracles and because I thought the voice on the phone was familiar I made the leap. Jenkins must be a religious man, and moreover, he probably was the caller. But not an Anglican as few Anglicans are religious. That, by the way, is called a syllogism. If not Anglican, then maybe Methodist. Methodists are pious but totally unscrupulous."

"So you sent me off to enquire at the Methodist Chapel."

"Exactly."

"And that's where I found out that Jenkins was a lay preacher there and I saw the play bill about the Little Medford Players."

"And the photo of Miss Dubrova. Only one other bit of information was needed. If Miss Dubrova was not who she said she was, who was she? I asked myself who knew about

Miss Dubrova. Remember you yourself supplied the information. Not the Ablonskys but the delightful Miss Tomlinson who conveniently left the employ of the Sans Souci just before I arrived. But here's a mystery. I can't remember telling her about my hobby."

"But you did admire her, Professor. Don't you remember how disappointed you were she was no longer the evening hostess?"

"Was it that obvious," I sighed. "Well then, at some point in time I was probably trying to impress her by boasting about my one and only asset. A fool at forty is a fool indeed. Oh well, that's behind me now. But there was one other question."

"Who took the stamps from the album?" Hastings joined in. "Why do you think Jenkins was so foolish? He took them to an antique dealer right here in Medford."

"Because he thought an upright Methodist lay preacher and trustworthy constable was above suspicion."

"Professor Clemson, I can't figure out how they thought they could get away with it."

"Well, Jenkins was an insider. He convinced himself he could control the investigation for forty-eight hours until me, the patsy, paid up. As for Miss Tomlinson, she was so sure of her Thespian craft she believed she could fool everyone."

"She certainly fooled Mrs. Ablonsky and the entire Sans Souci staff."

"Indeed she did. Including yourself I might add."

"And you, too, Professor."

"Well, at least for a few hours."

"I still can't see Constable Jenkins and Leticia as accomplices. They have absolutely nothing in common. Nothing. He's a. . .a straitlaced prude and she's, well, she's. . ."

"Inexpressible," I said. "I think greed was Leticia's motive. An actor of her talent has the West End of London in mind. And the extortion money was her ticket out of Medford.

"But Jenkins, poor soul, was besotted with Miss Tomlinson. And love can make us fiends as well as angels. At least Kingsley thought so. Besides, lay preachers are notoriously vulnerable to the weaknesses of the flesh. Well, now that you're fired, what are you going to do?"

"I'm going to get on my Harley and drive to Milton Keynes," Hastings said with a chuckle.

"Milton Keynes? Why?"

"I'm going to find out whether the Open University has a course on private detection."

"A splendid idea. And if and when you graduate, look me up. I have a distinct feeling we could be the Poirot and Hastings of a new generation."

The Sans Souci still drowses among those gentle folds of a valley in England's Lake District. But I have moved on. In fact, I've moved on both in time and space to a new century and a new locale. Thanks to the National Council for the Endowment of the Arts, I spend my summers now in New Hampshire researching the roots of Frost's poetic genius. And you would be surprised, as I was, that even in the rustic Town of Exeter crime flourishes.

The Race

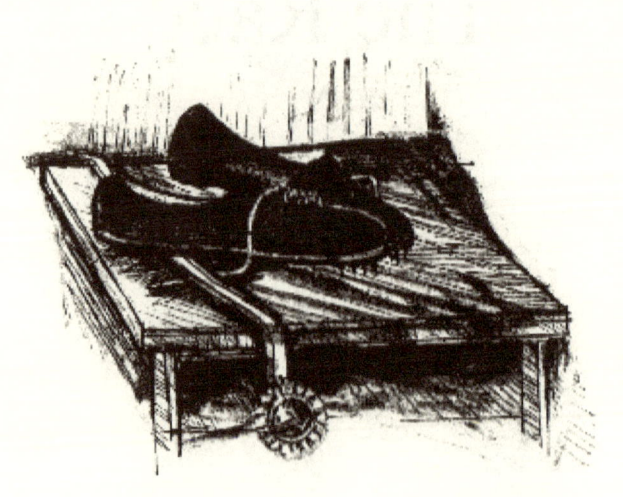

Bobby Atherton had all the keys to success. Money, talent and intelligence. Little wonder he was voted the Highbourne Public School graduate most likely to succeed, though many of us wished he wouldn't. Things came too easy to him.

The Atherton family lived in a grand house on a large corner lot with an expansive lawn and a spacious garden in the back, complete with belvedere, artificial pond, and sumptuous wrought iron fountain. There were always two cars parked in the driveway, sleek and expensive. And before his surgeon father went off to war, they always seemed to have extra ration coupons for gasoline. Bobby was always dressed preppy and had money to spare. There is no question about our envy. He had so much and we had so little. It seemed unfair. And this inequality was the subject of much whinging and complaining.

Almost every Saturday afternoon his inner circle of friends went to the Atherton place to amuse and be amused by the scion of Dr. Albert Atherton. We watched movies, and if weather permitted, went outside to play quoits and tether ball and chase one another through a cedar maze. We were Bobby's bought companions. Not that it stopped us from showing up regularly because we left neither hungry or empty-handed. Mrs. Atherton gave each of us things we couldn't always get during the war, even oranges. Nevertheless, the generosity of the Atherton family did little to soften our resentment which was always lurking there beneath our best manners.

Bobby and I were rivals of a sort. I thought of him as such, but in his eyes I wasn't significant enough to be one. Regardless, I had two things going for me that Bobby lacked.

First, his looks were spoiled by a pasty complexion and irregular features. The girls avoided him and swarmed around me, and that was the main reason for our friendship. Bobby knew by staying close to me he would get some attention, at least. So my good looks were useful and I played them for all they were worth.

The other advantage was even more powerful in my estimation. Dr. Atherton was overseas in the Medical Corps. Before the war, he had been Bobby's main cheerleader. Whenever Bobby took part in an event, Dr. Atherton was sure to be there, encouraging his only son and chatting up the coach, judges and anyone else who seemed important. Unlike Dr. Atherton, my father was still at home and accessible. Even though he didn't attend every school event, I could talk to him about things and get his advice. He was clever in his own way and understood how things worked in the real world.

One event that brought our rivalry to a head each year was the district Sports Day. It was held in June in the stadium of a nearby high school. Highbourne was the smallest public school in the district and therefore not a contender as far as soccer, hockey and baseball were concerned. It had however achieved a reputation in the 100 yard dash. Old Mr. Nelson years before had competed in that event at the Olympics.

He coached Highbourne runners with a skill and passion that produced a steady stream of winners. The school's halls were lined with photos of those who had gone on to greater glory at high school, and even college, track events. The glass display case beside the principal's office was filled with silver-plated championship cups, inscribed with the names of past and present winners. There wasn't a boy at Highbourne who didn't want to be among those worthies and who wouldn't make any sacrifice for the honor.

Bobby took the possibility of achieving celebrity status as a birthright. I coveted it, egged on by my father who had little regard for losers. If you're not first you're nothing at all, was his rule of life.

Bobby Atherton was fast. He once told us God had made him fast for a purpose, that he had a mission in life that would be revealed to him someday. Bobby wasn't boasting. On top of everything else, he was religious and never boasted about anything he had or could do. His accomplishments were legion. He excelled in art, music, sports and was always at the top of his class. His effortless success made us even more envious.

Spring was late in our last year of school. It wasn't until the middle of April that Mr. Nelson asked us to sign up for Sports Day. More than a dozen hopefuls did so and showed up for the first coaching session a week later. I looked them over and knew that by Sports Day only three or four of us would be left.

Bobby was a sure bet. He had already won a gold ribbon in the 100 yard dash the year before, and besides, Mr. Nelson was grooming him for bigger things down the road. I had placed second in that same race, so I had a silver to my credit. Nelson needed me, my father said, to keep Bobby on his toes, so I was pretty sure I would be there at the end too.

Besides me, there were some newcomers to the school, tall and gangly with good legs. They had shown promise in the soccer competition in the autumn and were tough, even if they weren't too smart. They would be there too, at least two of them anyway. As it turned out, I was right sooner than I expected.

At the third training session only four of us remained. The others were told to go home. It was then we discovered why so many were let go so early. Mr. Nelson was retiring from teaching in June and this was his last "kick at the can" he told us. You four are going to help me be remembered as the best damned coach in the county. This was the first time he had ever used profanity, so we knew he meant it. He warned us that the next six weeks would be the toughest we had ever known and, if we weren't up to it, we had better go home with the others. He only had time for winners, just like my father.

At the end of two grueling hours of practice, as we sat exhausted on the steps of the school, Mr. Nelson dropped a bombshell—our running shoes weren't good enough. We all had to have the best running shoes available. Not professional track shoes, because they weren't allowed, but the next best thing. He said it might be a sacrifice, looking directly at me, but in the end it would be worth it. We had one week. He hoped we wouldn't let him down.

No one said anything. We were all too stunned at the thought. I glanced at Bobby but he turned away. It wasn't going to be much of a sacrifice for the Atherton family. Lawrence and George stared at their shoes and shook their heads. At least one of them was close to tears.

Bobby finally broke the silence. He said, almost apologetically, he would like to help. But no one took him up on his offer. We wouldn't take charity, not from him. After a while we broke up and went our separate ways.

After supper, I gingerly broached the subject of new running shoes, first with my mother, who said little, and then with my father. At first he was silent. He kept spreading small amounts of tobacco into cigarette paper, expertly rolling them, and then placing the completed cigarettes on the table, one after the other.

When he finally did speak he started calmly, but his words soon turned hard. He didn't have a soft job like Mr. Nelson and he didn't earn the money teachers made either. His voice rose in anger. He was only a factory worker earning a factory worker's pay. Nelson was an old fool, putting foolish ideas into the heads of stupid boys. There would be no new running shoes. That was final.

I ran up to my room and for a long while I sat in darkness. Turning it over and over in my mind, I thought about Bobby's offer. After all, the Athertons had lots of money and even if I took it as a loan they wouldn't need the money right away. I could pay them back a little at a time. And Bobby needed me, and so did Mr. Nelson if he was going to achieve his dream. But in the end I knew I couldn't take anything from him. I would have to do it on my own.

The days following Coach Nelson's bombshell raced by. I got up early to do my homework because his iron rule was, no homework, no practice. I also paid particularly close attention in class because I didn't want to give him any reason to keep me after school. And when the exhausting practice sessions ended I hurried to the bowling alley to set up pins. By the time I got home around ten it was time to tumble into bed, but not before I got the miniature tea chest from the kitchen cupboard and put the two dollars I had earned in it.

I went to sleep those nights knowing I could do it. I could. And lo and behold, by the weekend I had enough money for the running shoes and a dollar and change to spare. Mother agreed to go with me after Monday's practice to buy the shoes. I was sure Mr. Nelson would give me an extra day.

The others were outfitted in their new shoes that Monday. It made a difference. Mr. Nelson had been right, but then he always was. Bobby finished first twice and tied for first once. I tied for second once and finished last once and third once. But I didn't care because I knew the next time we'd all be even. So I ran hard anyway and Mr. Nelson clapped me on the back and said, with the new shoes I might just come in first this year.

After practice I raced home full of expectation and happiness at the thought of having not only new running shoes but really good ones for a change. Mother was sitting at the kitchen table with the tea-chest near her outstretched hand. I burst through the door and shouted, Mom Let's go, but she didn't stir or even look up. And when she finally did, it was with tears in her eyes. I held her hand gently. What's the matter Mom? She looked at me sadly and opened the lid. The chest was empty.

At first I couldn't believe my eyes. The money was all there when I had left for school. I had counted it twice. Then, from the expression on Mother's face, I knew where it had gone. Father had taken it.

I shook with anger, then with a sense of hopelessness. I knew he was spending the money in the beer parlor, getting drunk, and would come home all teary eyed and sorry for what he had done. I didn't know what was worse, losing the money or seeing him in such a pathetic state.

I ran out of the house and didn't stop until I reached the bowling alley. I would make up the money and buy those running shoes, but this time I'd ask Mr. Nelson to keep the money for me. And even if I were exhausted I would run harder than ever and would keep running until I had the new shoes and then maybe I would come in first like Mr. Nelson said I might.

On Wednesday night I got careless. One of the bowling pins struck my ankle when I didn't get out of the way fast enough. The pain shot through my entire right leg. I thought I was going to be sick. Mr. Carrie, the bowling hall manager, called to me. I shouted back that everything was okay, not to worry, and kept setting up pins. But I could hardly walk.

That night I limped home and crept into bed. I cried then, not out of pain, but out of frustration. I would never beat Bobby now and this would be my last chance. Next year he was going to a private school. Why weren't things fair?

That night I dreamed I came in first and everybody in the stadium stood up and cheered and cheered. Father was there and he was smiling and waving at me, telling everybody that I was his boy, that I was going to be the best runner there ever was, just wait and see, then hoisting me on his shoulders and carrying me home.

On Monday, Mr. Nelson took out his wallet and handed me the money I'd given him. It was just enough for the running shoes. My ankle was still swollen but the bandage I had tied around it helped.

At the practice I ran harder, like I promised myself, and when I got home I soaked my foot in Epsom salts. It helped. We went, mom and me, to the shoe store and I bought the best running shoes in the shop—better than the ones Lawrence and George had, and just as good as Bobby's. Now nothing was going to stop me. Nothing.

The week before Sports Day Mr. Nelson trimmed the school team to three. George was asked to drop out. Not looking back, he ran across the schoolyard. We might have felt sorry for him if we had had the time but Mr. Nelson was pushing us harder than ever. Now I was finishing in second place, and once I even came in first. Mr. Nelson was surprised. Bobby even more so. Putting his arm around my shoulder, he shook his head and grinned. At last he took me as a rival.

Sports Day arrived finally. It was a cheerless day, with rain threatening. The night before Mr. Nelson had given us one of his usual pep talks, but this time it was more sentimental. Don't let me down, he said, and cleared his throat. Knock their socks off for me and for Highbourne.

I thought about this as we got into his car. Bobby sat up front and Lawrence and me in the back. No one said much most of the way to the stadium. My hands felt sweaty and my mouth dry. Even Bobby didn't seem as relaxed as usual.

In the car Mr. Nelson told us about other Sports Days in his long teaching career and how he was going to miss them the most. He confided in us he didn't much like teaching, and now he wished he had only coached. Yes, he'd made a bad choice—but that was life. I should have been a high school, or maybe a college coach. I guess it wasn't meant to be.

I was only half listening. Instead I was wondering if my father would come. He hadn't said anything, but now that he wasn't working he had the time. I made a wish.

The stadium was packed with noisy spectators. Even a few high school students had skipped classes and were trying to look inconspicuous in the crowd of younger kids. The competitors were assembled according to event under the bleachers, waiting their turn. Bobby, Lawrence and I eyed those slated for the 100 yard dash. We looked at one another. The competition wasn't going to be easy.

I was certain that some of the boys from other schools were at least a year older. We didn't know where they had come from. They weren't around the year before when Bobby won the gold and I the silver. The mystery was solved as soon as we heard them speak. They were war refugees from England and Scotland. They were also unknown to Mr. Nelson, or perhaps not. Perhaps he knew about them and they were the reason he worked us so hard. I looked down at my running shoes and made another wish.

Bobby had seemed preoccupied during the past week. Even Mr. Nelson was annoyed with his favorite. I'm sure whatever was bothering Bobby was one of the reasons I beat him even though I didn't like to admit it. But he never said anything and whenever he was asked what was upsetting him he shook his head and wouldn't answer. I was of two minds about it. On the one hand, deep down, I liked Bobby and didn't want him to be like this. But, as my father said, whatever was bothering him might give me an edge in the race.

The gramophone record scratched out the national anthem. Afterwards, an announcement blared over the PA system that all high school students not in class should report to the Vice-Principal's office at once. A clergyman opened Sports Day with a prayer and scripture reading: They that wait upon the Lord shall renew their strength, they shall mount up with wings as eagles, they shall run, and not be weary, and they shall walk, and not faint. He intoned the words solemnly and tried to explain their meaning but his voice was drowned out by the noise from the stands. He gave up finally and made room for the Master of Ceremonies.

Dr. Brock, Chairman of the School Board, briefly spelled out how the events would proceed and ended with a warning against booing competitors. Then he said he wanted to introduce a real war hero, one of their own, a man from their community of whom they were patently proud.

When he announced his name, Dr. Albert Atherton, my mouth fell agape. I glanced at Bobby, but he turned away. So the mystery of his strange manner had been solved. But why the irritation I wondered. Why not happiness?

I got up and walked to the end of the bleachers to get a better view of the dignitaries. There on the platform beside Dr. Brock was Bobby's father. He was stooped a little and his right sleeve was pinned to his uniform. He made some remarks and waved his left hand to the crowd. Few of us understood why the teachers stood up and applauded and cheered after a moment of silence.

When I got back to the others, Mr. Nelson was sitting with Bobby, talking to him softly. I stood close enough to listen. You don't have to run today, the coach said gently. Believe me, I'll understand. But Bobby only shook his head. He was going to run. Mr. Nelson patted his shoulder and walked away. I stooped over and tightened the laces of my running shoes. Bobby and I would run against one another for the last time. I massaged my bruised ankle and took a deep breath. What had the clergyman said? They shall run and not be weary.

When our event was called, the twelve of us got up and took our places. The first, second and third place holders from four schools. There would be a second batch of twelve runners and at the end of the day the top three from the first group would compete with the top three of the second for the championship.

After we had properly positioned ourselves and were waiting for the starter pistol to sound, I prayed. Please let me win and let my father be here to see it. The pistol fired and we were off. I could hear nothing except the pounding of my heart in those brief seconds to the finish line. Then there were cheers and, in spite of Dr. Brock's warning, some boos.

When I looked around, one of the teachers tapped me on the shoulder and led me to the judges' table. Bobby was already there and one of the boys we didn't know. The stranger had come in first, Bobby second, and me third. We both had made it to the second round.

Mr. Nelson looked neither pleased nor displeased. He consoled Lawrence, and briefly put his arms around Bobby and me and drew us closer. I don't recall everything he said but at the end he declared it was up to us to uphold the honor of Highhourne and, with a smile, my reputation too.

Towards late afternoon, we were called out again. This time there were only six of us. As we lined up, I scanned the bleachers hoping to catch a glimpse of my father, hoping he might be there and wave to me. But there wasn't much time.

As I stared at the ground, waiting for the starter's pistol, I suddenly felt alone. I knew that Dr. Atherton was there to cheer Bobby on, as he always did, but I wasn't sure there was anyone for me. I wondered too if this was the way it was always going to be.

I ran. I didn't feel any pain in my ankle. I only had one thought in mind. And, when I crossed the finish line, I kept running. I didn't want to stop. I didn't want to know.

No teacher tapped me on the shoulder this time. There was no judges' table. No ribbon. Bobby was there with the gold once again, and beside him was Dr. Atherton, his left arm around his shoulders.

Not a Winner

After miles of breathtakingly beautiful scenery, on the outskirts of Waynesborough about a mile past Evan's Tree Farm, the view is suddenly interrupted by a pair of over-sized billboards a few hundred yards apart. On the first, a leprechaun perched on a pot of gold invites you to visit Winner's Bakery. On the second, a montage of assorted baked goods boasts—Winner's Bakery is the Nation's Best. Your Patriotic Duty to Stop. Farther on, closer to town, are several buildings, many old, some new, but all flying the Winner's banner.

The newest of these is the Office Building, in front of which, in reserved parking spots, is apparently evidence of the pot of gold: President Ralph Winner's silver Bentley, Vice-President Janet Winner's hunter's green Jaguar, Executive Vice-President Ben Winner's red Viper, and Comptroller Thelma Winner's yellow Porsche. Nearby, a sign points to where visitors can register for a tour. Immediately inside, beside the sign-up desk, on an artist's easel, is a large photograph of a young woman. She is Winner's Employee of the Year. Her name is Daisy Yeats.

Daisy was attractive, despite a low opinion of herself. Whenever she looked into a mirror, which she avoided, she would frown in disappointment. Admittedly, she wasn't a classical beauty. She wasn't a Helen of Troy, whose face according to the poet launched a thousand ships and started a bloody war, nor a Greta Garbo who attracted thousands of suitors according to Hollywood lore. But, with her flowing auburn hair, large and pretty green eyes, tiny well-shaped ears, slightly upturned nose and flawless complexion, she turned heads wherever she went. She was, in that most inelegant of expressions, a real looker. In grade school her friends remember her as pretty, yet shy and uncertain of herself. This shyness persisted into high school. There, unfortunately, it was perceived as being unfriendly and 'stuck-up,' an entirely wrong perception.

What distressed Daisy even more than her looks was her name. None of her friends or classmates or cousins (of whom there were many in the combined Sullivan and Yeats' clans) was called Daisy. In fact, the only other Daisy she knew was a comic strip character—a dumb blonde with long legs and other exaggerated extremities, whose companion was a big oafish fellow called, paradoxically, Li'l Abner, with brawn but even fewer smarts than herself. Had she asked her mother why she had given her only daughter this most un-Irish of names she might have felt somewhat better about herself and this story would never have been written.

But of course she was too diffident and chose to suffer in silence when she might have been relieved to know that not all Daisy's were dumb blondes. There were some who were not always lucky in love, perhaps, and not ending up so well either, but at least they were well-placed in life and regarded by many as rather beautiful.

The truth about the name-giving is that Mrs. Yeats had a serious addiction that many of her friends and certainly most of her extended family thought was more grievous than alcoholism and debauchery. In fact, if Bernard Yeats had known about it he would not have pursued Maureen Sullivan, but instead would have run in the opposite direction. But he didn't run, at least not until they were married and Maureen was about to have their first child. Then he bolted, knowing full-well that by leaving at that sanctified moment he was endangering his mortal soul in the eyes of the church. He told his best friend before he disappeared—it was worth the risk.

Maureen's affliction? *An addiction to reading.* Never was she seen without a book in hand, morning, noon and night. How she kept her vice under wraps during their brief courtship is a mystery.

Just before Daisy was born, Maureen fell in love with an author who had long fallen out of favor. Without a doubt Henry James has a place in American letters, but this new-found devotee placed him on a pedestal rather higher than he deserved.

Maureen was reading with enormous delight James's novella Daisy Miller, the story of a young pretty thing, innocent and vulnerable, whose father is Croesus-rich. This permits his daughter, Daisy, to travel to Europe and mingle with Russian royalty in Geneva and the glitterati of Rome and, unfortunately, be pursued by handsome young fortune hunters. Maureen was enchanted, no doubt, by the thought that her baby, if it were a girl, would perhaps one day be in a similar romantic narrative, hopefully not involving gigolos and certainly not catching a fatal fever among the ruins of the Roman coliseum and dying a week or so later, as did James's heroine. In any event, she called the baby Daisy, for better or for worse.

Every morning Daisy had a decision to make. Should she walk or take the bus to Winner's bakery, where she operated a packaging machine. Lately she mostly walked to save the fare because she wanted to buy a hat she had seen in nearby Milverton. The hat was identical to the one her mother, Maureen, used to wear on Saturday evenings when the two of them would go to the local park, sit close to the bandstand, and listen to a musical ensemble of one sort or another entertain the summer crowd. While Maureen read, Daisy would be transported into a dream world by the music, especially the piano. She imagined having a piano like her friend Emily, only she wouldn't hate practicing. She would practice and practice until she was the best piano player in the world. She never realized her dream but decided she could at least have the hat. It would remind her of happier days before her mother's sudden death, the day after Daisy graduated from high school.

Today she took the bus. It was slow but Daisy didn't mind. It would give her time to finish the book she had started reading the night before. She became distracted, however, as she thought about the hat and how she had come to see it in the first place. If Eddie hadn't invited her to a movie in Milverton, she wouldn't have seen it at all.

Eddie was kind of a mystery, or at least her feelings for him were. He was called Mr. Fixit at the bakery, able to do just about anything. He was good-looking in a rough hewn sort of way, not smooth like some of the boys she had dated in high school. He often gave her a ride home from work (especially when it was raining) which was really helpful because she was determined to save up for the hat.

What Daisy didn't know was that Eddie was helping her out because, of all the girls at the bakery who were crazy about him, he was crazy about her. He wanted her to have the hat and anything else she might set her mind on. Daisy sensed this but was puzzled that when Eddie left her at the door of the boarding house where she lived, he never even once hinted he might like to come in and spend some time with her.

Ben Winner, the owner's son, drove her home a few times as well and always tried to talk her into letting him come in for a drink or whatever, as he put it. But Daisy wasn't interested in alcohol or 'whatever' so she always put him off.

It wasn't long before he stopped offering to drive her home, and at first she wondered why. Then she decided she didn't like or want his attention anyway. Mrs. Longmore, her landlady, confided in her that she had heard some bad things about Ben. "Stay away from him," she warned. "He can't be trusted. Hurts people."

After a while, she closed the book and looked outside, every now and then catching her reflection in the window. It occurred to her that she shared many of the same circumstances as the book's heroine. Alone, without family, except some relatives who didn't keep in touch. Not exactly dirt poor but just getting by week by week. Living in a boarding house with a grim future. Not attractive and no special talents. Her few friends and acquaintances already married, some with children. Two young men interested in her, one more than the other. The one poor, not particularly ambitious, but sincere, thoughtful and probably loyal. The other rich, well-educated, adventurous but probably not trustworthy and certainly self-centered. If only my mother were still around to help me sort things out, Daisy sighed. The bus stopped suddenly and jolted her out of her fanciful reverie.

When Daisy got off, she found Eddie waiting for her. He took her by the hand and guided her gently through the construction barriers and bits of broken concrete surrounding the bus stop. Daisy was surprised and delighted by this act of . . . gallantry (the word didn't come readily to her) and with this word, which she thought she would never ascribe to Eddie, came another—tenderness. Yes, tenderness described the feeling she most often felt when she was with him. In that moment her estimation of Mr. Fixit soared.

She was glad it was a long block to the factory. It allowed for a longer conversation, for something in Eddie's manner told her he had something important to say. But instead, Eddie was unusually quiet. He walked along beside her with his hands in his pockets, occasionally clearing his throat. After a while Daisy, uncomfortable with the silence, stopped and faced him. "Is there something you want to tell me?" she asked.   Caught off guard by this direct question, Eddie stumbled, "Uh, yes, there is." Daisy waited impatiently.

"Well, why don't you just say it."

"I'm leaving Winner's at the end of the month. I've got a better job in Milverton and on the side I'm going to repair small motors and then maybe, I know it's a long shot, but just maybe I'll start my own business. Not right away, okay, but some day." It was out at last. He seemed relieved.

And I thought he wasn't ambitious, Daisy reproached herself. Why do I always underestimate people. "I don't know what to say. You surprise me. I am really pleased for you. Really."

"Daisy, I was wondering if you would . . . I mean do you think that we might ever . . . " Eddie never finished the sentence and Daisy never learned what he was going to say.

"Daisy, get in." The gleaming red Viper had stopped at the curb and the driver had rolled down his window. Ben leaned over the front seat and beckoned with his hand. "Come on," he repeated, smiling. "Hurry or you'll be late."

Daisy walked briskly to the car. She leaned against the door and said, "I don't want a lift. I'm talking to Eddie and I don't care if I'm late." Ben muttered and sped off, tires squealing and a large plume of exhaust fouling the morning air.

There was no more conversation after that. Daisy and Eddie parted at the employee's entrance without a word. Eddie didn't look back.

Daisy was confused as much by what Eddie had said as by what he hadn't. Was he going to ask me to marry him, she wondered. What would I have said? Do I love him? Her thoughts and emotions were in turmoil as she did what she'd been doing for over two years—press a button, pull a lever, and then start over again. She didn't mind the monotony. It gave her an opportunity to think. The heroine in the book she was reading had let her chance go by and it never came back. One chance. Only one.

Time passed slowly. At four o'clock the end of day horn sounded and all the whirring machinery stopped. Daisy gathered her things and hurried to the exit in the hope of seeing Eddie. As she punched her time card, she looked for his but it was missing. And even though it was raining, she went outside to the employee parking lot to see if Eddie's pickup was there. But it was gone. And he wasn't waiting for her at the gate either. Huddled under their umbrellas, Alma and Susan, two of her closest friends at the bakery, were waiting for a lift. "Did you hear what happened to Eddie?" Alma asked, as Daisy approached.

"No," Daisy replied.

"He was fired," Alma said as she collapsed her umbrella and with Susan got into a van that had suddenly pulled up. She rolled down the window and shouted, "Because of you."

"Fired because of me. It can't be. I don't understand. How?"

As the van pulled away, Alma shouted, "He had a fight with Ben. Eddie almost knocked him out. Got to go. I'll tell you about it tomorrow."

For a long while Daisy stood by the gate, hoping and praying Eddie might still come. But he didn't, and the light rain shower had turned into a downpour, and the wind had picked up and flung itself against her. Then, through the driving rain, the red Viper appeared and stopped at the curb. The door opened and Daisy got in. Not a word was said. She got out at the boarding house without saying goodbye and ran up the stairs to where Mrs. Longmore was standing at the door. The red Viper waited until Daisy had gone inside and closed the door before it disappeared into the mist.

"There's something for you in your room. I put it on the bed," said Mrs. Longmore. "It's from Eddie."

Daisy rushed up the stairs. On the bed was a box, unwrapped, but with a red bow on top. Daisy took the lid off and started to cry. In the box was the hat she had seen in Milverton. Also in the box was a note attached to a small bunch of forget-me-nots. It said: Sorry if I caused you any trouble. I'll write just as soon as I can give you all you deserve. Love, Eddie.

A year passed without a letter. On almost every weekend Daisy traveled to Milverton. At first she walked up and down the main street, wearing the hat Eddie had bought her, looking in restaurants and waiting outside the theatre where she and Eddie had gone to the movie. She inquired at the post office, poured through the phonebook and the Milverton newspapers looking for any information about Eddie's whereabouts. She walked through the factory district hoping to find the small motor repair shop Eddie said he had hoped to start up and visited the hospitals and the police station asking if anyone knew anything about him. Months became a year, then another and her visits to Milverton became fewer until they stopped altogether.

The bakery employees were stunned by the announcement and even more so by the photos on the front page. Nobody in Waynesborough could remember when the Courier ever printed such a lavish display and the rumor spread that the publisher must have been paid off. Alma glanced at Susan in total disbelief.

Sitting at the kitchen table with the Courier spread out before her, Mrs. Longmore felt anger rising in her throat. They lied to me. They lied to me. How could she be part of it, she asked, as she threw the newspaper on the floor.

> Mr. and Mrs. Ralph Winner are pleased to announce the marriage of their son, Ben Jason to Miss Daisy Elizabeth Yeats last Tuesday at the Bradford Golf and Country Club in Milverton. The newlyweds have left for their honeymoon in Europe as they plan to visit London, Paris and, especially, Rome. On their return Ben will assume the presidency of Winner's Bakery Inc. and Daisy Winner will head the Waynesborough Library Board and become President of Best Books Inc., a new company that will be established to encourage the sale of the best of literature at a reasonable price.

On the west coast a copy of the Waynesborough Courier lay on a desk in a leased factory where thirty-five men and women were busy repairing small motors. Beside the newspaper was an envelope. It was addressed to Miss Daisy Yeats.

As for the hat, every now and then Daisy takes the box out from a secret hiding-place, removes the lid, and gently lifts the hat out and holds it in her hands, remembering.

The
Outrageous Cannon

The ancient cannon did not go easily. It took four burly men from the Works Department to cart it off. Albert and I watched in silence from the steps of the school. Grunting and sweating, they pushed and pulled it across the grass and dragged it up a ramp onto the flatbed of a battered yellow truck. The truck shuddered and sagged under the cannon's dead weight. Afterwards, the men rested for a while, leaning against the side of the truck, smoking and clowning around. Then, as quickly as they had come, they left. One of them waved good-bye through the open window and yelled something we couldn't quite make out. As the truck pulled away from the curb, the cannon lurched backwards, straining on the ropes that lashed it to the platform.

As soon they were gone, Mr. Arthur, the school caretaker, hosed the pad down on which the cannon had stood. Soon the only remaining traces of the cannon were some dark smudges on wet concrete. Even those smudges are gone now, erased by the snow and rain. And schoolchildren play on the concrete pad unaware of the cannon and the event that changed my life forever.

The old cannon had guarded the entrance to General Gordon Public School for almost fifty years. It seemed perfectly harmless. For us it was just an oversized toy. Nobody in our gang ever imagined it had once fired in anger. But, in fact, it was one of the artillery pieces in the Anglo-Sudan War that had blown to smithereens the Madhi's desert warriors on the burning sands of the Sudan.

The school's namesake should have given us a clue as to its military pedigree. But, at the time, our knowledge of history was limited to stories of marauding bands of Vikings and merchant explorers in the fabulous kingdom of Kublai Khan. General Gordon meant nothing to us. It wasn't until much later we learned about the hero of Khartoum whose illustrious career was cut short by the Madhi on those same desert sands.

Unlike some of its companions in Gordon's ordnance, our cannon was not melted down to manufacture war medals. After Khartoum, Queen Victoria dispatched it across the ocean to inspire our loyalty to the Crown, a perpetual reminder of our glorious heritage. Strange, but none of our teachers ever talked about it in this way. They only warned us to keep off, or else. And we all knew what *or else* meant. But with its barrel stuffed with pitch and candy wrappers it didn't seem to pose any real threat. For us it was something to play on; something to help us while the tedious days of summer away.

That blistering summer day at the end of July was no exception. We stood around the cannon with our mouths agape. Plumstead was inching his way back along the barrel after executing a neat pirouette an inch or so from the muzzle. It was his sixteenth flawless crossing. Nobody in memory had piled up such a score. And now to our envy this newcomer from across the ocean was travelling backwards along that slippery slope. With a flourish Plumstead finished the dangerous maneuver at the point where the cannon's breech used to be and jumped down to the concrete pad. A wide grin lit up his all too handsome face.

At first, the only sound was the sucking in of our breath. Then, as one, in spite of ourselves, we shouted our hurrahs. Plumstead grinned some more and swaggered off, looking back only once. The grin had turned to a smirk.

For some the hurrahs quickly faded. Sides were taken, for and against this visitor from the home of the cannon. Sharp words were followed by pushing and shoving. The earlier bonhomie evaporated, replaced by sectarian rivalry. But even that quickly dissipated in the heat of the noontime sun. We broke up, some going off in search of their newfound hero, others doing the opposite.

That smirk was a declaration of war. We hurried across the schoolyard, kicking up dust as we went. As usual Harry took the lead. His long legs set a furious pace. Albert and I knew what he was thinking and where he was going. This wasn't the first crisis we had faced together. Plumstead had become the enemy. This war refugee with his uppity airs and strange way of speaking needed to be cut down to size. And, if Harry had his way, which he usually did, that was exactly what was going to happen. The only questions were how and when. So we hurried to the best place on earth for a council of war, the castle. No one went there at that time of the day except for an occasional stray dog looking for a scrap to eat.

It was not a real castle. It was the basement of an unfinished house, on a corner lot near the school. The builder had committed suicide so the house was left unfinished. By taking out every other cinder block along the top row, we had our castle. There we escaped the ever prying eyes of our other enemy—Grownups. And there we congregated Saturday nights for our weekly potato bake. Only Harry's followers were welcome. We even had our own initiation rite. In a mock ceremony, the initiate swore allegiance to King Harry and promised to obey his commands. Until that night no one took the initiation seriously. It was only a game like walking the cannon.

The council of war didn't go well at first. We started quarreling among ourselves as our sweaty arms and legs touched in the cramped space. And, when the shadow cast by the piece of cardboard over our heads shrank even smaller, we huddled closer together making things worse. Harry got more ill-tempered with each passing minute. We tried hard but we couldn't come up with any workable plan of revenge. We were beaten and we knew it. And in that steamy heat our resolve to get even was slowly but surely melting away.

Then a small miracle saved the day. Our cardboard roof collapsed and from the tangle of arms and legs Sally, a three-legged bitch, emerged and scuttled to the far end of the basement. There she turned and stared at us. When the shock wore off, we convulsed with laughter. Sally curled up in a patch of shade beside the basement wall and went to sleep.

Pushing the cardboard aside, Harry shot up and swept his long blond hair back in dramatic fashion. His mood had changed. Albert and I exchanged glances. Plumstead was definitely on his way down. And somehow that three-legged bitch figured in whatever scheme Harry had hit upon. As Harry vaulted over the basement wall, he shouted something about Damascus Light. This didn't mean anything to us but we were caught up in his buoyant mood and followed him over the wall. Whatever he had in mind, we were with him all the way.

We parted company at Harry's family's grocery store. With a smile and a wave of his hand he disappeared into the store without so much as a hint at what he was planning. All he would say was that we shouldn't miss the potato bake that night, not that we would have anyway. It was the one chance in the week not to go hungry.

On the way back to Albert's house we tried to connect the stray and Plumstead's fate, but we couldn't. Of one thing we were sure though, Harry would win in the end. He always did. But for some reason we felt uneasy.

The regulars were already at the castle when we arrived just after seven o'clock. Some were sitting along the basement wall at the front, talking. Others were behind the back wall smoking dried weeds wrapped in butcher's paper. Those who had chased after Plumstead in the morning stood around looking sheepish. It had the makings of an interesting potato bake.

Albert had brought some kindling wood and paper and I

had matches and some pieces of hardwood I had filched from a neighbor's woodshed. Harry was there too with a sack of potatoes from his father's store. He had also brought along a pound of butter in a stained paper bag. Everything seemed at this point remarkably ordinary. Albert nudged my arm. Maybe nothing was going to happen after all.

The preparations for the bake went smoothly. I scooped out a large shallow cavity in the sand in the middle of the basement and Harry positioned the potatoes in it. Albert covered them with a thin layer of sand and built the fire on top. When the kindling wood was blazing, I threw on the hardwood logs. All that was left was to wait.

Harry's behavior was extraordinary. He went around chatting with everybody, even Plumstead's admirers. Albert and I looked on in disbelief. Harry had gone soft and for a fleeting moment our respect for him faltered. Even Plumstead's gaggle were surprised by the unexpected goodwill Harry showered on them. The king of grudges, it seemed, was turning the other cheek. We wondered if this was what Harry meant by Damascus Light.

After one hour all that was left of the roaring fire were glowing embers and charred logs. It was time to sweep these away and get down to business. We waited for Harry's signal, but it didn't come. He was silent. For a long time he paced up and down, and then he got up onto the wall and looked down the street. Everybody began to grumble but Harry paid no attention. He was waiting for something. For what, we didn't know.

Soon the suspense was over. Two late arrivals showed up. One was Plumstead. The other, walking behind him in an awkward manner, was his cousin, Everest. The link between the three-legged bitch and Harry's scheme became a little clearer. Everest too had a deformity. His right leg was gigantic, like an elephant's, and covered in purple blotches. Everest was the fool of the neighborhood not only because of his deformity but also because he was dim-witted. Everyone laughed at him except Plumstead. From the first, he made it known he didn't want anyone making fun of his cousin. It was the kind of warning we all paid attention to, at least when Plumstead was around.

Harry sprang into action. He gave the long awaited signal and everyone scrambled to get to the head of the line. The potato bake had begun. Harry had brought extra potatoes, and with butter slathered on them they tasted better than ever. By the time we were finished eating it was almost dark. The troubles of the morning now seemed forgotten and the old camaraderie had returned.

It was then that Harry made the announcement. Two new members were to be initiated. He invited Plumstead to join him in the center of the basement. At first, Plumstead resisted but everyone encouraged him and he stepped forward. Harry picked up some cold ashes and sprinkled them lightly over the initiate. King Harry then issued his command. Here it comes, we thought, but we were wrong. "Run around the top of the basement wall." We were stunned. Harry had gone soft. He was a cream puff after all.

Everest was then called to the center. He was bubbling with excitement. He looked up at Harry worshipfully as King Harry performed the rite. He then issued his second command, "Walk the cannon." There was stunned silence again. Everest walk the cannon? It was impossible! The new initiate grinned foolishly. Yes, he was saying, I will walk the cannon. I will do anything Harry commands. Anything to be a regular. Then, a few moments later, gales of laughter broke out and no one laughed louder and longer than Everest himself.

Plumstead jumped down from the wall and placed himself between Harry and his cousin. The laughter stopped as the rivals faced each other. Plumstead shoved his smaller opponent to the ground and grabbed Everest's arm. Looking around menacingly, he helped his cousin over the wall and hurried him off down the street. When they were gone, the laughter began again and no one laughed harder than Harry. Plumstead's humiliation was sweet revenge. Who could be anyone's hero with a cousin like that. Everyone saw it clearly now. If there is something wrong with the one, there must also be something wrong with the other. Damascus Light, Harry called it.

Albert and I joined in the laughter. The thought of Everest walking the cannon, dragging his big leg behind him, was too funny to resist. Our faltering admiration for Harry rebounded. King Harry was still the best.

Before the evening ended, we celebrated Harry's victory with real cigarettes he had smuggled out of the store. It was an evening to remember after all.

Sometime in the early morning I was awakened by the sound of a siren. At first I thought I was only dreaming but the sound persisted. After a long while it stopped only to begin again a few minutes later. The next sound I heard was my name being called out. I got up and looked out the window into the yard below. Albert was standing there, looking up and calling for me to come down. I will never forget the look on his face. The bitter taste of the cigarette was still in my mouth as I pulled on my things and rushed downstairs. Albert was waiting on the back porch and when I opened the screen door he said, "Everest is dead."

Everest dead. At first I thought he must be joking. I closed the screen door and leaned against it. He tried to walk the cannon, Albert continued. He fell off and split his head open on the concrete. No one knew he had gone out until this morning until Plumstead found him there.

We sat together in silence on the porch steps. I remembered the look on Everest's face during the initiation. For a brief moment he had felt he was one of us.

Everything has changed. There is now a house where the unfinished basement used to be. The old General Gordon Public School building was torn down to make room for a modern one named after a school trustee. The new school looks out of place in the midst of worn out houses and dowdy high rise apartments. Harry's grocery store is gone too. In its place is a gas station. Harry was killed when his Spitfire crashed somewhere in Germany. Albert is gone too. He died on the beaches of Normandy. As for Plumstead, he went back home after the war. We never spoke again after that night.

Now I'm the principal of the school, and every day I look out of my office window at the place where the cannon used to be. And I remember.

The Lead Soldier

The telegram arrived in the late afternoon at the end of September in the third year of the war and my final year at West York High School. I had come home early from school because Mr. Palmer was in a bad mood. He was still angry about my decision not to play football that year.

You're the best damned quarterback in the county, he roared, and you've no reason not to play. I knew he was upset because I had never heard him swear before. He left the dressing room and without turning told me to go home. He didn't need my help. Besides, you might hurt your hands, he added with sarcasm, and slammed the door shut.

All the way home I argued with myself. I was determined to go to college, and if things turned out, I was going to be a doctor. I had the brains and I had the desire. If I could scrape the money together, I knew I could do it. Mr. Palmer was right about one thing. I wasn't going to take a chance I might injure my hands. Not for school. Not for Mr. Palmer. Not for anyone. I would help the team out, but that was it.

But something didn't feel right. Maybe I was fooling myself. I knew Mr. Palmer thought I was shooting too high. Sure you're smart, he once said, then checked himself and didn't finish what he was going to say.

I wheeled my bicycle into the driveway beside our modest house and just missed colliding with a Union Pacific messenger. Even with his cap and sunglasses I knew it was Tom. Tom had dropped out of school to take a job. Mr.

Hodges, Tom's father, had been reported missing in action in North Africa.

Tom decided to leave school last June to help the family out. There was bad blood between us and had been for most of high school. Tom wanted to be quarterback and thought I had used my influence with Mr. Palmer to thwart his ambition. I hadn't. He was big, but that was about it.

He braked too suddenly, swerved and toppled sideways. Clutching his pouch of telegrams, he crashed to the ground and slid along the soggy driveway until he hit the fence.

Before I could get off my bike to help, he had already struggled up and stood for a moment glaring at me. Swinging the pouch over his shoulder like a bandoleer, he let loose a string of obscenities and got back on his bicycle. You're a coward, he sneered, and don't think I'm going to forget it. I watched as he pedaled furiously down the street. Who says I'm a coward, I shouted after him. I'm not a coward. But Tom didn't look back. He turned the corner and was gone.

Trembling with anger, I put my bike in the garage and hurried through the backyard into the house. Mother was standing beside the kitchen counter carefully pouring paraffin wax over sweet-smelling relish in jars of varying shapes and sizes. At the sound of the door she turned and smiled. But behind the smile I saw something else, something that disturbed me. Lennie's coming, she said. Tomorrow. I knew then what it was. I picked up the telegram on the table which had only three words. Arriving home tomorrow. No mention of how and when, making it obvious he didn't want us to meet him. That could mean only one thing.

Lennie had been away for three years, seven months, and fourteen days. It was my chore to keep track and I took the job seriously, not only because it was a comfort to my mother and father, but because Lennie was the person I felt closest to. When the war began, he tried to join the navy but failed the medical exam. But Lennie was not a quitter. He found out that the air force needed gunners, particularly tail gunners, so he talked the recruitment officer into giving him a chance. We saw him for a week after that, then he was gone. First out west for training and then overseas, shooting and being shot at.

We received letters regularly at first. Though they were censored we could tell he was in the thick of things. Between tours he crisscrossed England, art portfolio under one arm and a girl, we suspect, under the other. And every letter asked for money. We never said no. Often I had to dip into my savings. Even so, we never could refuse Lennie anything.

Suddenly the letters stopped. Weeks passed without a word. Then they came. First a telegram informing us that Lennie was missing in action. A few weeks later, a chaplain wrote Lennie had been badly injured when their bomber had crashed at sea. He survived, while the rest of the crew perished, because the rear section of the plane had broken off. He was rescued after floating several days in the North Atlantic.

In a second letter, the chaplain said that Lennie's condition was improving but his injuries were serious, noting ominously, a terrible fire before the crash had left Lennie severely burned. We wrote for more information but heard nothing for six months. During that time I continued to mark off the days on the calendar, and our fears continued to mount. The Union Pacific telegram confirmed our fears were not unfounded.

Mother put her arms around me and though I tried not to, I wept. Of all the things Lennie was concerned about, his appearance was uppermost. He didn't smoke or drink or run around. Instead he ran and cycled and paddled. Even though he had only worked in a factory, he used what little money he had to dress well, not flashily, but smart; all the girls in the neighborhood would have killed to get a date with him. Yet all he really wanted to do was to draw and paint. And he was good. But now! I wept some more.

The telegram sparked a flurry of activity, partly because we wanted the homecoming to be memorable, but also to ease our own anxieties. Mother and I decided that everything had to be as it was the day Lennie left three years ago. The furniture had been rearranged at least a dozen times since then so we started by putting things back the best we could remember.

We made sure his room was exactly the way he left it—records, record player, old footstool he sometimes used as a drum, posters of Gene Krupa and Glen Miller, his alarm clock and the rocking chair he would rock in while sketching. Mother laid out his favorite cardigan, shirt, tie, shoes, pants, tie clip and cologne.

We laughed when we remembered how fussy he could be. How many times we had caught him studying himself in the mirror. You're a regular Beau Brummel, Mother would say. Beau who, he would always respond.

By the time Father came home, the furnishings were back just as they were when Lennie had left. There was only one thing we weren't sure about. For three years we had surrounded ourselves with Lennie's photos. When he began sending photos of himself and his buddies and the girls he had gone out with and the cathedrals he had been sketching, we displayed them everywhere. His handsome face always stood out no matter how many others there were in the photo. In the end, we decided to leave them in their places. Perhaps we were wrong about his injuries. Perhaps we were jumping to conclusions about the fire. Maybe, just maybe, he was alright after all.

Father tidied up the backyard and mother baked. I went down to the basement to the lead soldiers we had played with for hours since we were old enough to handle them. When Lennie went off to a real war, I lost interest in them and avoided going to the ping pong table where we had lined them up in majestic rows and battle formations.

Now they were in disarray, many toppled under the soft paws of a stray cat we had taken in for a while. Others were not with their comrades. Fusiliers were mixed in with

Grenadiers which in turn were scattered among the Horseguard and Light Horse. Drummer boys faced every which way and cannon the same. The tangle of foot and mounted soldiers spoke of months, if not years, of neglect. I knew Lennie would not be pleased.

By the end of the evening the tabletop no longer resembled the aftermath of a titanic battle. Every soldier and every piece of armament was in place, at the ready, facing the enemy proudly. Lennie would like it. I stood back for a while, remembering and was glad.

By midnight the house was as it had been. Father walked through its length, room by room, nodding his head with approval. Fine, fine he said in his quiet way, which had often rankled Lennie. He only admired men who were forceful, who spoke with authority—real leaders, according to him. Now that I think about it, I'm sure Lennie signed up to get away from home. He wanted to be with men he could look up to.

Once we argued about his disrespectful attitude and even scuffled a bit until Father pulled us apart. We never spoke about it again, but I thought a lot about it, and more so after Lennie joined up.

After a restless sleep I awoke to a misty autumn day. My dreams had been of massive, swirling clouds, dark and ominous. They swept around us, picking us up and taking us higher and higher, then dropping us like toys, yet we never touched the ground. I couldn't put Tom Hodges's accusation out of my mind and wondered if Mr. Palmer had anything to do with it. The chances of my injuring my hands were really not that great. I had already played four seasons and nothing had happened to them. Was there some other reason, I wondered, a reason I didn't want to admit, not even to myself?

A light rain began to fall. It streaked the window pane and I watched the droplets as they ran their jagged paths down the glass. I tried to remember when it was I decided not to play football. And, as near as I could place the decision, it was after we received the chaplain's second letter. That was in the spring. In one of his letters Lennie had written about tempting fate. Every time we get back safe, he wrote, the next time we might not be so lucky. Maybe that was it. Maybe I didn't want to tempt fate. I knew I wasn't a coward. I wasn't afraid of getting hurt. But I was afraid that my luck would run out. All of a sudden I felt at peace. More than I had felt for a long while.

I skipped the afternoon classes and rushed home. Mother had arranged some red, white and blue bunting on the verandah and put out a flag. Inside, the fragrance of baking mingled with the scent of roses brought in from the garden, the last of the summer harvest. I looked out the window and watched Mother carefully choosing gourds and squashes and cucumbers to make up a centerpiece for the table and I couldn't help but smile. I would always remember her that way. I called out to her and she turned and smiled at me. And, for a moment, there was some real happiness in her eyes.

Father will soon be home, she called out. The foreman had given him the afternoon off. He hadn't asked, and never would, but Mr. Bridges heard Lennie was coming home. Give him a big hug for me and tell him he's a real hero. When Father recounted the foreman's remarks, he seemed embarrassed. I can't remember Father ever hugging Lennie.

I wandered through the house and stayed awhile in the living room. On the mantle a rose separated Lennie's photo from Father's. Father looked smart in his infantryman uniform. He had come home from the First War unscathed and I often think Lennie was resentful that Father hadn't been injured. Whenever we played with the lead soldiers he would say this one must be Father. And it was always one of the soldiers out of the center of the action.

Lennie also resented the way Father would never talk about the war. Maybe, I once said, Father feels guilty that he came home without a scratch when so many of his friends had died. Lennie only laughed. Warriors should not be silent and they shouldn't feel guilty either. Warriors should tell their sons about war. After all, it's war that makes men what they are, he exclaimed.

When Father came home, he seemed quieter than usual. He puttered about the garden, doing the same things over and over again. Mother and I looked on in silence, trying to figure out if he was thinking about what he would do when Lennie arrived. Later we found out he was passed over for a promotion he'd been promised for over a year. Father had poured his heart and soul into the assembly line job and more than once been cited most valuable employee. He was told in the end he wasn't a leader. He never spoke about the job again.

After supper we listened to the radio. The Allies had landed in Normandy and victory, the announcer said, was at hand. No details were given about casualties or about the landing itself. Father turned the radio off after the news. He was in no mood to listen to the patter of Jack Benny and George Burns, so we turned to reading and listening to records. Vera Lynn was Father's favorite and by the time we had played We'll Meet Again about a dozen times, we began to wonder if Lennie was coming home after all.

Shortly before 10 o'clock a car stopped in front of the house. Moments later we heard it drive off again. Mother got up and looked out the window, then ran to the front door. We followed and went outside and stood on the verandah. Lennie walked slowly up the path. In the pale moonlight he seemed like an apparition. Perhaps it wasn't Lennie. The figure seemed so small. It wasn't until he reached the stairs that he looked up. It wasn't Lennie. At least it wasn't the Lennie who had left three years before. If I had passed him on the street, I wouldn't have recognized him. His face was covered with hideous scars. It had been destroyed. His nose was only a stub. No surgeon's skills could restore it. Mother gasped, then caught herself and rushed down the steps and gathered Lennie in her arms. They both wept as we watched in silence, too stunned to move.

Father stayed where he was. There would be no hug. He watched helplessly until the moment he might have acted was gone. I hesitated too, but only for a moment longer. Then I ran down the stairs and put my arms around them both and wept uncontrollably.

The shock we experienced remained with us for the rest of the evening. Lennie sat in a chair in the darkest corner of the living room. It was difficult for us to have eye contact with one another. We didn't talk about the war. We talked about how the neighborhood had changed and other safe topics. But soon Lennie said he was feeling tired and went to his room. He put out the light almost immediately. Mother knocked on the door of his bedroom and asked if he needed anything. He said no, everything was fine. Father also went to bed early. He was on the early shift and proceeded to walk up the stairs. I had never seen him look so old. In fact, it was the first time I had ever thought of my father as being old.

Mother put away the baking and other things. I sat by the kitchen table, too tired to go to bed, and we talked softly. Why did God allow such things she asked. She had prayed every day—not one day went by without a prayer. She turned and looked at me, why, she said, why. I had no explanation.

I remembered what Lennie had written about his luck running out and maybe that is the explanation. Life is just luck, good luck, bad luck, nothing more. I said nothing. Instead, I put my arms around her and said don't cry. But none of us had any tears left. Later, as I tossed and turned in bed, I thought of a verse from Isaiah 52 the pastor had used as the subject of his sermon the week before. His face was more marred than any man's.

The weeks following passed quickly and without event. Lennie was like a stranger living in our house. He rarely left his room, not even for meals. Mother would leave a tray outside the bedroom door and sometimes it stayed there untouched. The football season ended but it didn't matter. We were not in the finals and Mr. Palmer wasn't talking to me, not even in science class. Once or twice I tried to break the ice but he rebuffed me. From time to time the accusation that I was to blame for the team's loss was cruelly passed along to me. Many times I revisited the thought that maybe Tom Hodges was right. I am a coward.

Things began to change at home a few weeks before Christmas. The tray was not left outside the door very often now and Mother was humming to herself again the way she used to. Once or twice I heard the record player and late at night a radio broadcast. Then, one night as I was studying for the Christmas exams, Lennie came to my room and sat on the bed. We talked about school and he asked me what my plans were for the next year. I lied. I said I would probably get a job. He got up and as he left the room said I hope you're not thinking of joining up.

A few days later he joined us in the living room after supper. The Prime Minister of Great Britain was talking over the radio and telling us that Hitler and his Nazi gang were almost defeated and the world would soon be rid of them. The Allies were victorious everywhere now and the long, dark road was almost at an end. Lennie listened passively and before we could say anything he left the room. Father got up from his chair to follow, but Lennie had already gone back to his bedroom and shut the door. It wasn't until the next week that I heard the record player and the muted sound of drumsticks as they beat upon his ottoman.

On the Sunday morning of Christmas week I heard Lennie pacing up and down in his room. I knocked on the door and asked if he wanted anything. He opened the door and for the first time since he had come home he tried to smile. It was a grotesque smile through twisted lips and I felt sick. He reached out and put his hand on my shoulder. I know how you must feel, he said, and please don't try to hide it from me. It's easier that way. Let's go down to the basement. I haven't seen the soldiers for a long while.

We stood beside the table in silence, each lost in his own thoughts and wondering what the other was thinking. I noticed for the first time that none of the soldiers on that table was wounded, disfigured or maimed. In their colorful uniforms they looked resplendent and invulnerable. No matter how many times we had knocked them over, over the years, they remained the same. They're just as I remembered them was all Lennie said. Let's go for a walk.

I still remember how I trembled as I put on my heavy boots and buttoned my jacket. I waited on the verandah and when he didn't come out at first I was sure he had changed his mind, and for a moment, just a moment, I was glad. But then the front door opened.

Dressed in his uniform he stepped out into the swirling snow. I let him lead the way and was not surprised when he headed for the park where we used to skate. On a rink, made by neighbors, young people skated to the tune of Skater's Waltz. Do they still play lacrosse in the park, Lennie asked. Yes, I said, and always to the tune of Roll Out the Barrel. He laughed and I laughed with him. A band that sounds like Harry James is playing tomorrow night at the Palais Royale, he said. Do you want to go? Sure, I said. Though truth be known, I didn't. As we turned to leave the park, someone changed the record. Bing Crosby's voice flooded the park. That's a good song, Lennie said. The boys liked it over there.

The dance hall was lit up. Red and blue light from the string of Christmas lights around the entrance and along the eaves reflected off the newly fallen snow. Inside the Palais Royale hundreds of eager fans waited noisily for the bandleader to come out.

Lennie and I slipped in unnoticed and stood in the shadows at the back of the hall. I looked around nervously hoping there wouldn't be anyone I knew. I wasn't ashamed of Lennie. It just felt awkward. I had always been proud of him. While he was overseas I boasted about how smart he looked in a uniform. I was still proud, but in a different way, deeper and more personal, something I couldn't quite explain. I turned and looked at him. His eyes had a look of disappointment, even disgust, or perhaps sadness.

Are these the zoot suiters we've been hearing about, he asked. Before I could answer, the band leader appeared on the stage and the crowd went wild. The leader smiled a handsome smile and blew the sweetest trumpet sounds I've ever heard. The dance floor quickly filled with gyrating couples who abandoned themselves to the swing music. Lennie relaxed. He loved dancing and had won a number of amateur contests. He leaned against the wall, closing his eyes. For the first time that evening I relaxed too and was glad we had come. Lennie was healing. Things weren't so bad after all.

You have the monster with you tonight, the voice said out of the darkness. I looked around. There beside me was Tom Hodges. He answered my puzzled expression. You know, he smirked, Frankenstein's monster. In an army uniform, too. Tom nudged his companion and they both laughed. The other one sneered, "Some date. Is the great quarterback running out of luck?"

Lennie opened his eyes and looked at the pair. They were dressed in zoot suits with long chains that dangled down to their knees. Tom covered his face with his hands in mock horror. I thought boy scouts knew how to play with matches, he said, or did you rub the sticks too much. I tensed and was ready to strike but Lennie put his hand on my arm and restrained me.

Let's go, he said quietly. Good idea, the other one said. You might just scare the girls. They laughed and by this time others had joined them and were staring at Lennie. Suddenly, the music stopped and the lights went on and it seemed at that moment everyone in the dance hall was looking at us. Lennie put on his cap and walked toward the exit. Don't go Scarface, one of Tom's friend's shouted after us. Lennie turned and faced him and in that brief moment I felt ashamed.

As the door closed behind us, the sound of a trumpet led the band in a dreamy fox trot. Snow was falling steadily and through broken clouds a full moon shone bright and cold. We walked slowly through the almost empty parking lot toward the streetcar stop. Coward. The word exploded like a howitzer shell behind us and with the same shock. I turned. Standing a few feet away was Tom Hodges and his friends. We've got a few things to settle, Tom called out. I stopped and faced them. Come on, Lennie said. I've had enough fighting. But I knew I couldn't. It wasn't even so much that they had made a fool of Lennie. It was because at that moment I remembered the expression on Mr. Palmer's face whenever he looked at me. It was a look of contempt or maybe worse, pity.

I don't remember much of what happened next. All I can remember is searing pain, then darkness, then Lennie's voice and the tears on his scarred cheeks. I'm sorry, he said. He put his arm around my shoulders and helped me to my feet. I couldn't move my right arm or clench my fist. And I never would again.

I awoke after midnight to a sound I didn't recognize at first. It was only after I heard my mother's voice calling to me to come downstairs that I did. Father was working the midnight shift to earn extra money for what was to have been the best Christmas celebration since Lennie had gone away. The lead soldiers were scattered across the table with Lennie's head resting among them. A thin river of blood trickled across his scarred cheek. There would be no Christmas celebration.

After the war ended, we moved out West to my uncle's farm. It had been neglected for years and despite our best efforts we could not bring it back. With my useless right arm and hand I was more of a burden than a help. My father lost his will to live and died of a broken heart. His dying words were, I never told Lennie that I loved him. Mother struggled too, but hung on a while longer as she knew I needed her. When the road that ran past our house became a highway, we opened a gas station and things began to get a little better. Mother added a gift shop and called it The Lead Soldier.

Often, late at night, when the North Star is high in the heavens, the gas pumps are locked, and Mrs. Alesworth who looks after the gift shop has gone, I sit on the porch and think about luck and fate and free will and God's will and wonder how things would have turned out if I had become a doctor and Lennie had lived.

The
Vacuous Widow

I sharpened my pencil, and with a sigh made one more attempt to finish my article on the poet, Robert Frost, for the New England Literary Society Journal.

Every four years New Hampshire looms like a thousand pound gorilla over presidential politics. But the Granite State has an even greater claim to fame than helping select the most powerful leader of the Western World. For ten years in its south-east corner, one of America's most celebrated poets turned soil and rock and husbandry and neighbors into songs which still live in people's hearts a hundred years later. A president of the United States and a prime minister of India lived their lives by these incandescent lines ...

A knock on the door interrupted this syrupy paean to Robert Frost. It was the third interruption in as many hours. Not again, I groaned, and put my pencil down. I was beginning to regret my choice of Emily's Bed and Breakfast. On only a colleague's say-so, I had booked a room for the entire summer and, with a remarkable lack of foresight, paid in advance. That was my first mistake.

A more serious mistake was revealing why I had come to the Town of Exeter in the first place. It seems many of the town's elite have distant cousins who remember hearing about New England's favorite son when the poet was farming in nearby Derry. None of these would-be contributors, with their quaint but unreliable hand-me-downs, had added a scintilla to my small store of Frostian trivia, but all had managed to put me behind a week or two.

At this rate I would not be lounging around on Cape Cod after all. The parsimonious National Endowment for the Arts grant would only stretch so far. It was an act of murder, however, that snuffed out any vagabond thought I had of fishing for a blue off Provincetown. But I am getting ahead of myself.

Had I known what was beyond the door, I would have put down my pencil with less irritation and more alacrity. Standing slightly behind Mrs. Fairclough in the narrow hallway was a young woman in her mid-to-late twenties. In today's threadbare parlance she was a definite ten. Perfect hair, perfect face, perfect teeth, perfect smile. And the coolest, greyest eyes I have ever seen. I decided then and there a short break from my research was in order. After all, The National Endowment expected its recipients to reach out to the community (how did the application put it) in meaningful ways.

"I'm really sorry to bother you again, Professor Clemson," Mrs. Fairclough began, "but . . ."

"No need to apologize, Mrs. Fairclough," I broke in. "In fact, I was just about to break off my writing when you knocked."

"I'm so glad to hear that. The last time I was here I felt you were a little annoyed by the interruption."

"Not at all, not at all. I'm always delighted to meet someone who might be able to contribute to my work. I have come to Exeter, as I mentioned before, simply to learn. Now perhaps you would introduce me."

"Of course, Professor Clemson. This is Althea Conroy, niece of our Superintendent of Schools, Dr. Stubbins."

"I'm very pleased to meet you, Althea," I said with more conviction than I had with the dozen or so other visitors Mrs. Fairclough had brought to my room previously.

My first thought was that Miss Conroy might be one of

those nitpicking high school teachers who delight in dissecting poetry until it dies a slow and painful death—etherized upon a table, as one of Frost's rivals penned in another connection. But when she spoke there was something about her voice which assured me I was mistaken. The intonation was definitely more lyrical than pedantic.

"I believe you know Professor Evans, Dr. Clemson," Althea said.

"Martin Evans? Yes, of course. We were graduate students together at NYU. He teaches at Amherst now, doesn't he?"

"Yes. He's my supervisor there. He suggested I should talk to you about my thesis."

How could I refuse? Martin always was the luckiest of devils, I thought to myself, even though I knew the inference was indelicate. And if I continued to harbor such corrupting sentiments, the Endowment would revoke my grant if it ever found out. It was Mrs. Fairclough who rescued me from this moral lapse.

"We can't stand here in the hallway talking. Why don't you continue your conversation on the verandah. I'll go and squeeze some lemons. Nothing better than cold lemonade on a sultry day."

On the way to the verandah one of the other guests, Mrs. Peabody, a proper Bostonian matron from the Back Bay, confronted Mrs. Fairclough. She complained about the mattress. "It was lumpy and uncomfortable." She hoped something could be done about it. Soon.

Mrs. Fairclough motioned for us to go on. "Make yourselves comfortable. I'll bring the lemonade shortly."

The screened-in verandah with its enormous ceiling fans was the coolest place in Emily's B & B. Fortunately for us, Miss Conroy and I had the verandah to ourselves as the other guests, a rambunctious family from Florida, had gone off for the day. We settled down comfortably on the wicker rocking chairs for what I hoped would be a long and pleasant conversation.

"Tell me about your thesis," I began, hoping I might learn something useful for my own labor of love. I am, of course, unalterably opposed to any and all forms of plagiarism, particularly from the work of students, and always give credit via footnote to the origin of anything I borrow and weave into the texture of my own findings and reflections.

"I'm trying to put something together on Frost's years at Derry," she said. "About those early years, those difficult years when everything seemed to be conspiring against his dream of becoming a poet."

"What a remarkable coincidence," I said with a smile. "I'm also researching those early years in hopes of ferreting out the roots of Frost's poetic genius. Yes, a remarkable coincidence indeed."

"Maybe I can be of help, Dr. Clemson. In 1937 my maternal grandfather had many long discussions with Frost at the Breadloaf Conference. I have his diaries and I'm using them as my primary source. They're filled with anecdotes which have never been published before."

"At Breadloaf in '37. Very interesting. And these anecdotes are not in any publication, you say."

"No, not one. Professor Evans and I have scoured everything ever written about Frost. There isn't one mention of them anywhere."

"Well, then, I think you might really be on to something. Perhaps you would like to share some of these anecdotes."

"Certainly. Would you like to read the diaries?"

"Well, yes. I might just be able to find time to read at least some of them. But enough about me. How can I help you with your thesis?"

"Professor, I'm not really here to talk about my thesis."

"You're not," I said, perplexed.

"No, it was just a pretext. I'm sorry. I need your help with something else."

Just then, Mrs. Fairclough arrived with the lemonade, and not a moment too soon. I was dumbfounded by Miss Conroy's totally unexpected revelation and needed a brief hiatus to absorb it.

"There, now. I hope this will refresh you. Just call if you need anything else. I've got a lumpy guest, correction, a lumpy mattress to attend to." Mrs. Fairclough chuckled and went on her way.

As I took a sip of the lemonade, I observed Miss Conroy and thought I had never seen a more beautiful young woman. However I quickly put the thought out of my mind and chose my words with care. "You were saying, Miss Conroy."

"Please call me Althea, Professor Clemson. Al, really. Everyone calls me Al." She hesitated for a minute before continuing. She too was choosing her words with care. "My uncle, not Dr. Stubbins, my other uncle, his brother-in-law, died six weeks ago." Those greyest of eyes filled with tears.

"I'm sorry to hear that. My condolences, Althea. I mean, Al. I'm not sure how I can be of help, but if there is anything useful I . . . " My quandary was deepening by the minute. How I, a total stranger, could be of any service to a family in grief I could not imagine. I have had no courses in pastoral counselling and in fact do not believe counselling of any sort is helpful. Probably the opposite is closer to the truth.

"Professor, I believe my uncle was murdered."

"Murdered! I don't understand. You mean your uncle's death is being investigated by the police. Or . . . "

"That's the problem. It isn't. It's been ruled accidental. But I know it wasn't an accident. It wasn't."

"I don't know what to say. Why do you think he was murdered? No, don't answer that. I really shouldn't get involved, Al. Surely you must realize that I would like to help, but . . . " I shrugged and gulped down a large swallow of lemonade. Again, I was rescued by Mrs. Fairclough who, without our knowing, was standing nearby.

"Telephone call, Al," she said. "Your aunt. I'll take the glasses away. Can I get you anything else, Professor? Maybe a cup of tea? Coffee, perhaps?" I was just now beginning to realize what a solicitous woman Mrs. Fairclough was. It put Emily's B & B in a more favorable light.

"Are you alright, Al? Is anything wrong?" She put her arm around the young woman's shoulders. "There, there. I know you're still upset about your uncle's death. You'd better take the call from your Aunt Elizabeth. She's worried about you."

Althea's reaction was puzzling. She shrank from Mrs. Fairclough's touch and left the verandah in a manner which can only be described as rude. I felt like apologizing to Emily (from this point on I began to address Mrs. Fairclough by her given name at her request) but thought better of it. I hadn't the faintest idea of what was going on.

"Althea's not been the same since her uncle's death. She's upset, poor thing. I think she might be heading for a nervous breakdown. I know her Aunt Elizabeth thinks so."

"Is Aunt Elizabeth the widow of the deceased?"

"Yes. Elizabeth is Dr. Stubbins' sister. Elizabeth's husband was Augustus Boone, a fine man he was. Yes, a very fine man. A lawyer and a good one, honest, I mean. And you know how rare that is, particularly in New Hampshire."

"How did Mr. Boone die?" I was hoping Emily was going to say by cardiac arrest.

"He fell down a flight of stairs and broke his neck. A terrible accident, just terrible. Everyone in Exeter was shocked by his death. We all hoped he'd run for public office. For senator or governor, well, something like that. Not that everyone exactly loved Augustus. He was . . . how should I put it . . . he was, I guess the word is . . . hot-headed, yes, hot-headed. Goodness, I shouldn't be speaking ill of the dead. You'll have to forgive me, Professor,"

When Althea returned, she seemed more distraught than before. "Professor Clemson, I'm going to run along now. I'll be in touch, if that's okay with you. Perhaps we could meet tomorrow morning. Could we? We could go over to Derry." Her look was so full of hope I knew I must cave in and help.

"Why yes . . . shall we say ten. Your thesis sounds very

interesting, and I will do all I can to help you solve the . . . the mystery." Emily Fairclough shot a questioning look in my direction. She was about to say something but changed her mind. "The mystery of Robert Frost's poetic genius, I mean. Yes, the origin of poetry is a mysterious process . . . as mysterious as the origin of life itself." I stopped. Even I could not keep up such ridiculous prattle.

From the steps of the verandah I watched her go, remembering what Althea must have been implying about another set of steps. She turned, waved and got in her car. I was still waving when she turned the corner and disappeared. Emily disappeared too. She had spotted the Bostonian matron cycling up the path from her shopping in town.

I measured out the remains of the day with coffee spoons and an interior monologue about the desiderata of life. What flaw in my personality makes me so vulnerable to the "drowning cat" syndrome, I asked myself, not really certain I wanted an answer. She shouts, Murder, and I come running. Could it be, after all, not a personality flaw but some dysfunction lodged in my genetic code somehow. The possibility that my rashness was because of a defective gene made me feel better. I finally slipped off into a restless sleep. The dream repeated itself over and over. A long staircase reached into heaven like Jacob's ladder and a man kept missing most of the rungs on his way down.

When I awoke, I noticed a plain, unmarked envelope had been slipped under my door. Inside the envelope were two clippings: an obituary announcement and a news article from the town paper. Not surprisingly, the untimely passing of Augustus Boone in his fifty-third year was lamented in both. Prominent Exeter lawyer, amateur water colorist and philanthropist has tragically passed away. Augustus Boone was indeed, in Emily's words, a fine man. Son of both Amherst and Harvard. Helicopter pilot. Decorated Vietnam veteran. Self-made millionaire. Tireless advocate of the poor and downtrodden. Fundraiser for the GOP. (Could this be a contradiction, I wondered?) Town selectman. School board chairman.

The Medical Examiner concluded that a scatter rug at the top of the stairs contributed to Augustus Boone's fatal accident. Over five hundred mourners from across the country attended the funeral service. The Governor of New Hampshire read the eulogy. No mention of his being hot-headed. I put the clippings back into the envelope and sat down on the edge of the bed. How am I going to talk Althea out of the bizarre notion that her uncle was murdered? I had until ten o'clock the next day to untie that Gordian knot.

At exactly ten o'clock a car horn sounded. I closed my notebook and slipped an elastic around the pile of file cards I was using to record what few findings I had on the roots of Robert Frost's genius. The Gordian knot, however, remained firmly intact.

"Professor Clemson, Althea's here," Emily called up the stairs. "It looks like rain. You'd better take an umbrella if you have one. If you haven't, there's a spare one on the verandah."

"I'll be right down, Emily," I said without enthusiasm. Tramping around a farm in pouring rain in search of something as elusive as a poet's inspiration was a Don Quixote gambit, okay for an ambitious graduate student no doubt, but no longer necessary for a fully tenured professor who was set for life. As I looked down the stairs I wondered how it was possible for a person to break his neck tumbling down such a short distance. If he were pushed violently, perhaps. By the time I reached the bottom of the stairs the rain began. All I could think of was mud.

"It's not a very good day for a ride in the country," said Emily, the proprietress.

"Well, Emily, scholarship is a stern taskmaster. We're off to Derry. Two tramps in mud time, so to speak. I'll borrow that umbrella you offered."

Mrs. Peabody was sitting alone at the far end of the verandah. Our eyes met for a brief moment, during which something was communicated that would haunt me the rest of the day and longer.

"I thought we might run over to Derry but I don't think we should go today, Professor Clemson," Althea said, as I squeezed with difficulty into a low bucket seat in an even lower sports car. I just managed to haul the umbrella aboard and close the door before the car leaped ahead. "Frost's old homestead will be just a patch of mud. We could go later in the week. Is that alright with you?"

It was a delicious proposal. "That's a sensible suggestion, Althea." (I abhor all things mutilated, especially names) "But the rain certainly would give us a better idea of what Frost had to put up with."

"Exactly. Well, perhaps on another occasion." I settled back and watched the wipers swoosh the drizzle away. For a long moment the silence was filled with Nino Rota's chilling theme music from the old Godfather movie. It made a gloomy day gloomier. I tried to recall whether it was raining or snowing the night they shot Don Corleone. Snowing, I decided. "I got your envelope with the clippings," I said to break the silence.

"Envelope?" she said, glancing at me with surprise.

"Yes, the envelope you slipped under my door."

"I didn't leave you an envelope. What clippings?"

"About your uncle's death. You didn't leave them?"

"No, but I think I know who did." Althea's voice had lost its lyricism. "It was probably Mrs. Fairclough, Professor. I'm not the only one in Exeter who thinks my uncle's death was not accidental. In fact, I'm certain Emily is spreading a rumor that my Aunt Elizabeth is involved. She's a very treacherous person."

"Emily? Treacherous? I can't believe it."

"People in small towns can be just as cruel, even more so, than those in the big city, Professor. I don't know exactly why but Emily has hated my Aunt Elizabeth for many years. She's said the most malicious things about my aunt and uncle.

About their marriage, I mean, hurtful things I don't care to repeat."

The rain stopped as suddenly as it had begun. Althea pulled over to the curb in front of a muffin shop. "Would you like a coffee?" she said. "You won't find any better in New Hampshire." She slid out of the car easily and waited for me as I wrested myself from the bottomless bucket.

A couple of septuagenarians playing checkers looked up as we passed by. "Hi, Miss Conroy," said the one who was obviously winning. "Sorry to hear about your uncle's accident. He was a real fine man. Do you know he got me the job driving the school bus? Asked Dr. Stubbins, he did. Yep, he was real fine." The old man lowered his voice. "There's some ugly rumors going 'round, Miss. Real ugly. I'm sorry. No one has the right to talk about your aunt that way. She's the salt of the earth. I don't want to presume but if there's anything I can do, I mean anything, you only have to ask. I might be helpful." He smiled and returned to the game. "I've got ya," he said as his checker skipped across the board.

Althea placed her hand lightly on the old man's shoulder. "Thanks, Todd. I'll keep your offer in mind. Is Mrs. Harper feeling better?"

"I'm afraid not. She's not going to make it. We've had a good life together so now we're just taking it a day at a time." At that moment, winning the game was no longer on his mind. "I guess I'd better be getting back home," he said to his companion and got up and left.

"Was it a good marriage?" I said as we planted ourselves at a secluded table where no one could listen to our conversation.

"A good marriage?" Althea frowned and looked unpretty.

"Your aunt and uncle. Did they have a good marriage, like the Harpers?" It wasn't until much later that I realized that I had asked the fundamental question. At the time I was only trying to find out what the nature of the rumors flying around Exeter could be.

"How do you take your coffee, Professor?" It was with uncommon abruptness.

"If it is as good as you say, black."

"A muffin?"

"Yes . . . blueberry if it's available."

Althea returned with the coffee and muffin. She played with the spoon, turning it over and over on the paper serviette, but said nothing. I have a low tolerance for conversational silence.

"Here's a quiz, Al" (For the moment I suspended my rule never to mutilate a name). "Quote the first verse of Frost's The Bearer of Evil Tidings."

Without hesitation, she repeated the lines. Her frown, then, became a faint smile. She stopped turning the spoon over and looked up. "I'm truly sorry, Professor. Forgive my petulance. It's just that Aunt Elizabeth and Augustus have been so good to me. I couldn't do what I'm doing if they hadn't been so generous for so long. Anything that hurts them hurts me."

"Forgiven. Now tell me this. Why have you enlisted my help? Apart from being a fan of detective stories, I have no investigative credentials. At least none to investigate a possible murder. I don't even wear a trench coat like a bona fide P.I.. So why me? Tell me now."

"Well, I felt I couldn't ask Professor Evans. And there's really no one in Exeter I can confide in. I'm not sure who I can trust. When Professor Evans suggested I talk to you about my thesis, well, I thought you were a godsend. Someone who knows no one in town, who knows nothing about my uncle's death, who wants to know the truth about things, who would be objective. I guess that about sums up my thinking."

"Fair enough. Okay, now that I'm on your side, you're going to have to be honest with me. Even when it means being a bearer of bad news."

"Yes, you're right, of course. From now on I'll be as forthright as I can, really I will. It was not a good marriage. I'm not sure why. My aunt married Augustus just a week before he left for Vietnam. Something happened between then and when he came back two years later. The marriage had died, at least that's what my mother has said."

"Why did it die?"

"I'm not certain but I think there was someone else."

"Now back to Emily Fairclough. Why do you think she hates . . . your word remember . . . your aunt Elizabeth?"

"I wish I knew, Dr. Clemson."

"Okay, tell me then about Emily. About her background. Anything. How does she know your aunt, for example? I mean apart from living in the same town."

"They went to school together, all the way from elementary through high school. At one time people used to think of them as sisters. The dark one was Emily and the blond one, Elizabeth. Emily wasn't as attractive as my aunt but she was more popular, especially with the boys. She was a terrific athlete, and smarter than Aunt Liza. But my aunt came from a better family. In Exeter, family pedigree means everything. After college Emily taught English at Exeter High School and married Tom Fairclough. Tom was a local dentist and a drunk. A car crash got him before his liver gave out. After Emily retired from teaching, she opened the bed and breakfast. That's about all. "

"How does Augustus fit into the picture?"

"He was the son of Judge Boone. The Boone's were very wealthy, particularly on his mother's side. Top drawer family. Augustus was every girl's dream. You've read the clippings?" I nodded. "Well, he was everything they wrote about and more." Those greyest of eyes filled with tears. I hadn't the heart to probe any further.

"We can stop if you like."

"No, I'm just being silly."

"Tell me what you know about your uncle's death."

"It happened on a Wednesday about nine-thirty in the evening. That was the first of May. My aunt was out. She was taking Auburn for a walk and—"

"Who is Auburn?"

"I'm sorry. Auburn's their dachshund."

"Okay. Continue."

"My aunt came back about half an hour later and found Augustus in the hallway at the bottom of the stairs. She called for help and the paramedics came but there was no sign of life. The inquest ruled it an accidental death. That's about it, Professor."

"The scatter rug at the top of the stairs. Tell me about it."

"That's the strangest thing. I'm certain there was no scatter rug at the top of the stairs. My aunt was very careful about things like that. I lived there for about five years, at one time, and there was never a rug of any sort on the hallway floor. Never."

"That is strange. And your aunt never questioned the police findings. "

"Come to think of it, she never did."

"You're convinced your uncle was murdered."

"Yes."

"Not just because of the rumors."

"I know it's only a feeling. But I'm certain."

"You realize that your aunt is a prime suspect."

"My aunt?"

"Yes. I don't know what her alibi is but police usually suspect a family member. You said she was walking the dog. Well, someone probably saw her, which would put her in the clear."

Althea became crestfallen. "No one remembers seeing her," she said. "You don't really think . . ." She couldn't bring herself to say it.

"No, I don't. But if you want us to go through with this covert investigation, everyone including your aunt is a suspect."

"Including me?" she said.

"Yes, including you. Now do you really want us to continue? "

"Yes, I do. I know I wasn't involved and I'm certain Aunt Liza wasn't either. So . . . if you're willing . . . "

"I'll do what I can. I hope you won't be disappointed. You were right about the coffee. Best I've tasted anywhere. Why don't you show me around town. New England towns have always fascinated me. They're so . . ."

"Predictable," Althea offered with a smile.

"I wasn't quite thinking of that, but it will do for now. Shall we go?"

An hour later Althea dropped me off in front of Emily's. She promised to come by later with the diaries. We chatted for a few minutes under the watchful eyes of Emily and Mrs. Peabody who were sitting together on the verandah. Later, I began to wonder what, if anything, these two had in common.

"Did you get to Derry?" Emily called out as I crossed the verandah.

"Not exactly. But we did tour Exeter. Wonderful. Just wonderful. I love the towns in New England. They're so . . . so quaint. Thanks for the use of the umbrella. Good-day ladies. My work beckons."

I hurried up the stairs and entered my cozy room. (The rooms at Emily's are not numbered. Each has its own name. Mine is called Paddington Station.) On the floor inside the door was another plain, unmarked envelope. The neatly folded paper inside had a name on it. Vincent Dolce. I turned the slip of paper over but there was nothing except the name, a name I recognized but couldn't place at that moment. The handwriting was definitely feminine and schoolmarmish.

For a long while I lay on the bed trying to remember how I knew the name Vincent Dolce but all I could remember was a dictum I had learned at school. One of St. Augustine's utterances. To him who does what in him lies, God will not deny His grace. I devoutly hoped the saint (even though he was a bit of a rogue) knew what he was talking about. I was on a slippery slope with a gaping abyss not too far off.

One thought haunted me. What if the rumor was true?

What if Althea's aunt was more than the prime suspect? What if? A sour marriage, a tempestuous argument perhaps, a violent push, impulsive, not premeditated. A scatter rug at the top of the stairs which was never there before. An evening walk no one witnessed. Ugly rumors around town. But what would trigger such a murderous reaction? I suddenly realized where I had seen Vincent Dolce's name. It was on the back of the news article about Augustus in the town paper.

Only bits and pieces of the article appeared on the clipping. Exeter's own Vincent Dolce, successful author and playwright, had apparently just completed some lectures sponsored by the town's Book Society. (I had never heard of Vincent Dolce the writer but perhaps he produces more modern stuff) The rest was cut off.

Why would Emily, if it were her, point me to this particular person? It was obvious she had listened to our conversation and was taking an uncommon interest in my participation in Althea's surmise about Augustus's death. Was she being treacherous or helpful I wondered as I returned the clipping to the envelope and put it in the desk drawer. And what was her motive in saying malicious things about the Boone's marriage?

"Professor. Telephone call." It was Emily's voice from the bottom of the stairs. "Don't be too long, I'm expecting a call."

The voice at the other end was unfamiliar. The caller began hesitantly but soon regained her composure.

"Professor Clemson, this is Elizabeth Boone calling. I hope I'm not taking you away from your work. But Althea has spoken so much about you, I thought you wouldn't mind if I called."

"Not at all, Mrs. Boone. You've called at the right moment. I was taking a short break." The voice was not unlike Althea's. Only a little more mature, huskier.

"I'm inviting a few friends and some members of the Book Society for a late dinner. Would you join us if you are free? I know it's short notice but I thought you wouldn't mind." There was that hesitation in her voice once more. Was it lack of confidence or lack of sincerity? That I couldn't tell.

Ordinarily, I would have declined the invitation. For sociability I adhere strictly to Thoreau's formula. One chair for solitude. Two for company. Three for society. Dinner parties with strangers are particularly wearisome. But I wanted to see that lethal staircase for myself. How a man like Augustus could break his neck in a tumble down some stairs seemed impossible. Besides, I had to meet Aunt Liza and look her over.

"Yes, I'm free this evening. Thank you very much for the invitation. There's nothing I enjoy more than meeting others of a kindred spirit." Kindred spirit, I thought to myself. What an absurd thing to say!

"Eight o'clock, then. Althea will come for you. I'm looking forward to meeting you at last. Goodbye Professor, and dress is informal. "

Dress is informal. What did that mean, I wondered, as I hung up the phone. I quickly reviewed my wardrobe and decided I had nothing else but informal. Already I was having second thoughts.

Althea called by in the late afternoon with the diaries. She confirmed she would come by just before eight o'clock and dashed off to meet Professor Evans. "He wants to see me. Says he has some information. See you later. Dress is informal." That expression again. Where is my dress code manual when I need it?

The diaries were pure gold. I had wasted hours sifting through the detritus of a hundred counterfeit scribblers but here was the real thing. Panning for a few small gold nuggets (I hoped Althea wouldn't mind my filching a trifle or two from this mother lode) consumed the rest of the afternoon. A quid pro quo, I thought, as I entered the anecdotes neatly on my file cards, and if I managed to solve the murder (if such it was) . . . a Faustian bargain indeed.

But all the time a name was trying to reach the surface of

my consciousness. It was an irritant I didn't need when my research was at last bringing within reach the Cranberry Highway and the pleasures of sand, sea and sky on the Cape. I slogged on until the chiming of the grandfather clock in the hallway and the blast of a car horn announced the dinner hour. Ah yes, an evening with the Book Society. At least my dress would be informal as there was no time to change into anything else.

Althea was unusually quiet. Enquiries about her tête-à-tête with the good professor from Amherst were met with evasion. Even my inquiry about the evening's other guests was met with a shrug. I gave up. We rode in silence.

Harper! Yes, Harper! That's the name that had been trying to surface. But why his name, I wondered. Why the old man with the dying wife? The question went unanswered as we arrived at the Boone's colonial mansion.

As it turned out, I was the most informally dressed guest by far. Disregarding my unorthodox habiliments, Elizabeth Boone introduced me to the literati of Exeter. Among them Vincent Dolce strode on his platform shoes like Gulliver among the Lilliputians. Dolce had an oleaginous charm that attracted and repulsed at the same time. He claimed he had read my recent article on T.S. Eliot in the Harvard Literary Review. A rather good try, he said, damning with faint praise. I discovered before the evening was out that that was his specialty.

But it wasn't the author of soft porn (at least I assumed this was his genre), nor the gaggle of guests that occupied me. Rather, it was the spiral staircase which curved gracefully from the downstairs hallway to the second floor. It seemed too delicate to be lethal. So fair a lady could not be a murderess, as one medieval poet put it.

Dinner chez Boone was too French for an uninterrupted flow of digestion. The beef too rare, the platitudes overdone. Dolce regaled his admiring bog with anecdotes about his meteoric rise from obscurity. I was astonished by Elizabeth

Boone's reaction to this bombast. She hung onto the troubadour's words like a disciple to the last testament of a dying saint. Somewhere between the sorbet and the liqueur Althea excused herself. A headache, she claimed. Dr. Stubbins will drive you home, she whispered in passing. This time it was I who shrugged.

After one more monologue from Exeter's gift to the world of pulp fiction, Elizabeth Boone suggested I might like to look at some of her late husband's first editions. In my time I have perused more than enough first editions, but as Augustus's study was upstairs, I accepted the invitation with enthusiasm.

The study was cavernous and replete with the works of some of America's giants. Augustus had discriminating taste which I had come to realize was not shared by his lovely wife. Oils of Judge Boone and his forebears looked down gloomily from the paneled walls. On shelves and tabletops framed photographs of friends and wartime buddies joined the crowd of silent onlookers.

One photo, in particular, caught my attention. A handsome young pilot standing in front of a helicopter, and an equally handsome young man in civilian clothes, both smiling, relaxed, arms interlocked. What caught my attention was the glass. It was broken and there were still shards in the picture frame. Why wasn't the glass replaced, I wondered, as I examined the Melville and Crane and Twain first editions.

Elizabeth Boone chatted amicably about her husband's collection of miniature soldiers and his remarkably good water colors. She seemed strangely detached from her husband's death, as if he had only been a distant acquaintance.

Fortunately, as our chit-chat began to sputter out, Dr. Stubbins appeared. He was taking his leave. A report on a recent gun incident in one of the schools required his attention. As we left the study, I looked for any sign of a scatter rug in the vicinity of the stairs. There was none. Nor were there any obvious marks on the stairs or rails where, presumably, Augustus had met his untimely demise.

"A blow-hard. Writes potboilers only fit for trailer park trash," Dr. Stubbins commented as we drove away. This was his brusque assessment of Vincent Dolce. "I don't understand why Elizabeth puts up with him, but she's almost as vacuous as he is. When poor Augustus learned Vince had returned to Exeter, he was apoplectic. There was bad blood between them. Over Elizabeth. Goes back a long way. "

Dr. Stubbin's candor was surprising. He dropped the subject and began talking about school violence. Retirement, he said, was looking better all the time. "It's the Democrats. Soft on crime. Now if Nixon had only burned those tapes everything would be different." He sighed. "Camelot. What a sick joke!"

I stayed awake most of the night trying to convince myself that Elizabeth Boone was not a murderess. Shallow, definitely; impulsive, probably; homicidal, unlikely. And yet, if there had been a terrible row, I could guess the trigger. Vincent Dolce, literary hack, potboiler producer.

The question that bothered me was—Where was she that night? No one had seen her walking Auburn. And where was Vincent? Augustus was hot-headed, according to Emily, and had a grudge against his possible rival. Could it be . . . that Vince Dolce and Augustus . . . quarreled . . . I finally fell into a fitful sleep.

It was after ten when I awoke with a throbbing headache. Emily had an inflexible rule about breakfast. Service between seven and nine only. It didn't matter because I wasn't hungry anyway, and in any event had another eatery in mind. I greeted Mrs. Peabody who was heading out on her bicycle for wherever it was she went every day, rain or shine. I'm not really a leg man but I noticed how unusually powerful her legs were as she pedaled down the street. Unlike the previous occasion, she avoided direct eye contact. She just fluttered her right hand in recognition of my morning felicitation. Strange I thought, then dismissed the incident. At that moment I had bigger fish to fry.

The Paul Revere Muffin Shop had its usual coterie of retirees enjoying the highlight of their day. Todd Harper was not among them. His checker companion was sitting alone by the window. He was studying a checkerboard on the table, anticipating his next game plan. When I slid onto the bench across from him, he glanced at me. "Will Mr. Harper be along today do you think?" I said.

"Maybe," he said. His eyes held suspicion.

"I'm Althea Conroy's friend. Do you remember I was with her yesterday? Mr. Harper spoke to her."

The old man looked me over and recognition slowly dawned. "I remember. You're the professor staying at Emily's place." He smiled. He had a victim. "Do you play checkers?"

"Yes, but not very well." The truth is I play checkers very well indeed. In fact, my formula is almost unbeatable, particularly if I get the first move. But today I had no intention of winning.

"Go ahead then. Move first." Marvin Boyce was almost salivating as I made a disastrous first move. "You're no expert," he said as he maneuvered his checker in for the kill. Five wins later he was just warming up when Todd Harper appeared. "'We have a real professional here today," Marvin said with a chuckle.

"You're Miss Conroy's friend," Todd Harper said. "'You were here yesterday, weren't you?"

"Yes. I was hoping we might be able to talk. About Althea and her aunt." I watched his reaction slowly change from suspicion to caution. "Did Miss Conroy send you?"

"No, not really. But she would approve. I know that. I won't keep you long. Really. Just a question or two."

"I'll only be a few minutes, Marvin," he said. "Keep the board warm."

"Well," he said as we sat down away from the others. He was waiting for me to make the first move.

"I'm worried about Althea and her aunt. About the rumors. I'm trying to help them but I don't have much to work on. If you know anything at all that might help Mrs. Boone, well, I would appreciate it. I know they would too."

Todd Harper nodded. He was thinking. "Did you beat him?" He jerked his thumb in the direction of Marvin.

"No, I didn't."

"Hmmm." He nodded some more. He was still thinking it over. "You're a stranger in Exeter. We usually don't confide in strangers." He continued to turn the matter over in his mind. "Do you think Marvin's a good player?"

"No, I don't."

Todd smiled. It was the right answer. "What do you want to know?"

"I'm not sure. Anything you know about the night of the accident. Anything. Even things you might have heard about Mr. Boone's death."

"I was there that evening. Not in the house, mind you. I had brought a small gift for Mr. Boone. Some golf balls. For helping me get the bus job. I'm not doing it anymore. Not since my wife took ill. Well, when I arrived at the house, Mrs. Boone was coming out. She was going to take Auburn for a walk. She asked me if I wouldn't mind taking care of the little fellow for an hour or so. Well, Auburn was from our litter and me and the missus had taken care of him when the Boone's were away. So I didn't mind."

"What time was that?"

"Let me see. About eight-thirty. Yes, just a little before eight-thirty."

"You're certain it was that early."

"Yes. I was at the hospital until eight and drove right to the Boone's place. Maybe it was a tad earlier than eight-thirty. Well, as I was putting Auburn in the truck, a car came by and Mrs. Boone got in."

"Did you see the driver?"

"No. I've seen the car about town though, but I don't know who owns it."

"Anything else?"

"Auburn got out through the truck window and chased after the car. I got him and as I was coming back I saw someone, a woman I think, going up the front walk."

"Are you certain it was a woman?"

Todd nodded.

"Would you recognize her if you saw her again?"

Todd grimaced. "Maybe. I'm not sure. My eyesight's not so good anymore. The golden years they say. Don't you believe it."

"Try to remember."

Todd closed his eyes. When he opened them, he was thinking about something else altogether. "I don't know. It was raining that night. Not much. Just a sprinkle. The woman had an umbrella. I'd recognize the umbrella. Least I think I would."

"Describe the umbrella, Mr. Harper."

"Lemme see. It was big, bigger than most umbrellas, and it had stripes, very wide stripes. Red and white, I think."

"When did you bring Auburn back?"

"Around ten thirty."

"There must have been a lot of activity going on."

"Yes. Lots of police. An ambulance. Neighbors were standing around outside. A lot of things going on."

"And you dropped Auburn off."

"Yes. In the front yard. He ran off into the house."

"Did anyone ask you questions?"

"Nope."

"At any time after that night? At the inquest?" Todd shook his head.

"And you never volunteered any information?"

"Never did. None of my business."

Marvin tapped his friend's shoulder. "You said you'd only be a few minutes. The board's real warm now."

Todd got up from the table. "I hope I've been of help. Mrs. Boone's a fine lady. She doesn't deserve to be talked about. People should mind their own business." He put his arm around Marvin's shoulder. "Well, old friend, are you ready for a beating? This fellow here says you're the best checker player he's ever met." Todd turned and winked.

"I'm sorry, Mr. Harper, but there's one more question I'd like to ask," I said.

"For a professor you're sure full of apologies. We've got a saying around here—if you can't bark with the big dogs, get off the porch. Say your say." He had the steadiest gaze of any man I have ever met.

"Could the person you saw . . . the person with the umbrella . . . could that have been Emily Fairclough?"

"Maybe yes, maybe no, the umbrella, you see, got in the way. But I'm glad you asked. Emily's the busybody who's been spreading the rumors. Tell her from me she'd better stop or we'll find a way of making her stop."

"You've been a real help, Mr. Harper. Thanks."

"Don't mention it. And remember what I said about barking with the big dogs."

To this day I don't know what Todd Harper meant by this homespun expression. Presumably he meant that there were other players, big players, in the events surrounding Augustus's death. Could there be a political connection, I wondered. It seemed implausible. Maybe Todd Harper was starting a rumor of his own.

The short list of suspects was getting shorter. If Todd Harper's story was true, then Elizabeth's alibi ruled her out. Who she was with and where she went, however, were still open questions. If Vince Dolce was the driver of the car—a real possibility—then he too had to be crossed off. Only one suspect was left, but could Emily have done it?

By the time I left the muffin shop, I was leaning toward the accidental death explanation. Augustus was a large man, a veteran, apparently in good form, hardly a push-over for a woman. Besides, the woman (if it wasn't Emily) was probably just dropping something off. A brief or a file. Why make something sinister out of this trivial incident? On the other hand, if Augustus was dead by nine-thirty, then she might have been the last person to see him alive. I looked around for a public phone. I knew I was kidding myself. Who hath deceived thee so often as thyself? Ben Franklin, stay out of this. But the venerable Franklin could not stay out. The woman with the umbrella was a plausible suspect. In fact, the only one on a very short list.

It was a tearful Althea that picked up the phone. She tried to disguise her emotions but failed. Why women cry is one of the great mysteries of life. It's unnerving. "I'll call back," I said. "Later today, if that's okay with you."

"I must see you, Dr. Clemson. Where are you?"

"At the Paul Revere Muffin Shop."

"Please stay there. I'll be by in fifteen minutes. I must talk to you."

"Okay. I'll wait outside. Take your time." I wanted to add, please leave the tears behind, but couldn't bring myself to say it. A sharp rap on the window near where I was standing turned my head. Todd Harper mouthed the words, That car I told you about. It just went that way. I turned quickly in the direction he indicated and caught a glimpse of a silver RV. The RV, I mouthed back. Todd nodded his head. At that moment Althea pulled up to the curb. I waved good-bye to the old men who seemed not to notice. They were already too engrossed in their checker game.

"We could drive over to Derry," said Althea. A skilful application of makeup covered the stain of tears, but I learned the truth of the saying that crying makes the eye more bright and tender.

"Sure, why not. It's time I surveyed that hallowed ground."

We drove in silence until my irrational fear of lapsed conversation got the better of me. "You seemed upset yesterday," I said. "Do you mind me asking why?"

"No, not really. That's what I want to talk to you about, but I don't know where to begin."

"Try at the beginning."

"Professor Evans is in town for a few days. He's staying at a friend's place. You remember I told you he had some information for me. Well, it wasn't really information, as it turned out."

"What then?"

"I'm not sure whether it was advice or a warning. I'm still at the point of tears when I think about it."

"That doesn't sound like the Martin Evans I knew."

"I know. I can't understand it. I've never known him to be so intemperate before. He gave me a tongue lashing. He told me I was meddling in things I shouldn't be. And that I shouldn't involve you in this foolish enterprise. In fact, he said if I continued I would have to find another supervisor for my thesis. He wasn't going to waste his time with someone who was more interested in fiction than in biography."

"A nasty thing to say. What a strange reaction! I can hardly believe it. Was he referring to your uncle's death?"

"Yes. I don't know. Maybe. He might be right. Do you think we should give up?"

"That's entirely up to you. But first, here are the facts. Your aunt was not walking Auburn that night. And it wasn't nine o'clock when she left the house. It was about eight-thirty. She gave him to Todd Harper to take care of and went off in a silver RV."

"Vincent Dolce drives a silver RV."

"I thought so. Well, at least your aunt is in the clear. Vincent Dolce, too. Harper saw a woman with a large umbrella with red and wipe stripes heading toward the front door of the house about the same time as the RV drove away. That umbrella sounds like the one I borrowed from Emily the other day. Was it Emily? In Harper's words, maybe yes, maybe no. Ergo, we've just scrubbed two suspects from the lineup and now there is only one. Shall I continue?"

"Yes, please do. I'm so relieved Aunt Elizabeth's not involved. I don't know why she lied. Well I guess I do. I was suspicious Vincent Dolce was the other man. At least my mother hinted as much. But the woman Todd saw, if it wasn't Emily, who?

"That is the sixty-four billion dollar question. Harper told no one about what he saw that evening. So we'll probably never know unless the mystery woman, assuming it was a woman, comes forward, and why should she. If it was Emily, she becomes the prime suspect. How we could prove anything I can't imagine. Game over it seems."

"No, it's not. I don't care what Professor Evans does. I'll find another supervisor. This is not meddling." Those greyest of eyes harbored defiance, not tears, now.

"Turn around then. I want to check something out at Emily's. It's just a hunch."

"You don't want to see the Derry farm?"

"Of course, I do. But later." I was being economical with the truth, as politicians say. I had not the slightest interest in visiting the farm. Field work is definitely not my cup of tea. I prefer to read about things. That way I'm seldom disappointed.

Emily was sunning on the verandah when we pulled into the driveway. "Wish me luck," I said, heaving myself out of the bucket seat. "I wish you'd get a bigger car. Preferably a Land Rover." Althea held up crossed-fingers.

"You're going to be as red as a lobster," I said, hoping to get from there to the more mundane subject of murder. Emily had been napping in the sun. Her handsome face had a pinkish glow. She raised herself on one elbow and smiled. I hadn't thought of her before as particularly beautiful but she most certainly was, in an Irish sort of way. Was she someone Augustus might have been interested in at one time? Or more probably the other way round. Next to love the sweetest thing is hate. I wondered how Longfellow knew.

"Lobster red. I hope not. I detest red." Emily moved out of the sunlight and swung her legs over the side of the chaise.

"You do?"

"I certainly do. I wouldn't be seen dead wearing red."

"What about the red and white umbrella?"

Emily laughed. "The spare umbrella? That's a leftover from one of the guests. But why are you so interested in it? If you've become so attached, it's yours." Emily got up and opened the screen door. "It's you who's been out in the sun too long. I'll bring you some iced tea." Through the screen door, she added, "You look bewildered. I hope it's nothing I've said." She laughed some more.

I was bewildered. I had lost another suspect. Elizabeth Boone gone. Vincent Dolce gone. Emily Fairclough gone. The secret was still sitting in the middle and taunting me. I decided it was time to taunt back. Emily provided the opening. She put the iced tea on the table and sat down across from me. "Well, was it something I said?"

"Yes, kind of. Emily, do you think Augustus Boone's death was an accident?"

She soothed her sunburnt cheek with the cold glass. "No I don't. Augustus was murdered."

"You think Elizabeth was involved."

"Yes, I do. She's nothing more than a floozy." She spat the words out with vehemence. "Augustus was too good for her. I've lost count of the men she's been running around with. Even before Augustus got back from Vietnam she had at least two lovers. She's a tramp."

"That doesn't make her a murderess."

"Maybe not, but it sure does give her motive. You've met Vince Dolce. He's the latest, and was the earliest too. Since he came back to Exeter, well, you figure it out."

"I'm almost certain Elizabeth was not directly involved. Indirectly, I'm not so certain. But she wasn't there when Augustus fell down the stairs." I resisted revealing where I thought Elizabeth was, at least for the moment.

"You mean pushed down the stairs, don't you? "

"Maybe. But I don't know. Not for sure. Todd Harper saw a woman entering the house that night. About an hour before the accident. The woman had a red and white umbrella with her. Maybe the spare one you loaned me. Emily, who were your guests on that Wednesday in May? You keep a guest register, don't you?"

"I'll fetch it," Emily said. "But I think I already know who she was."

"Don't bother fetching the register, Emily. The woman with the umbrella was me." Mrs. Peabody opened the screen door and stepped out onto the verandah. "Forgive me for listening to your conversation. I usually don't eavesdrop."

This time it was Emily who was bewildered. "You . . . Roberta, you were at the house that night."

"Yes I was. May I sit down?"

"Please sit here Mrs. Peabody."

"Thank you, Dr. Clemson. Many times I wanted to talk to you, but each time I lost my nerve. I'm glad you found out. I want to tell the whole story."

"You don't have to say anything to us, Mrs. Peabody. Really. It's none of our business. I have only been helping Althea to dispel rumors that her aunt Elizabeth was to blame for Mr. Boone's death. I think I've done that now." I shot a withering glance at Emily who looked away.

"It's better if I have my say, Dr. Clemson. It'll feel better to get it off my chest." Her voice was soft, almost inaudible. "Augustus and I fell in love in Vietnam. I was there for several months with my husband who was part of a Washington mission. I won't go into details but it wasn't just a frivolous romance. We knew that divorce was out of the question so we agreed to stop seeing one another."

"Mrs. Peabody, you don't—"

"Please, let me continue. We did see one another over the years. Not often. And we wrote occasionally. I don't think Elizabeth knew and Ronald, my husband, didn't either. At the beginning of May Ronald went to Washington and I was to join him." Mrs. Peabody's voice faded for a moment, but she went on. "I have an illness. Serious, they say, but you know how doctors exaggerate. Well, foolishly, I wanted to tell

Augustus, face to face, not in a letter or by phone. So I drove up to Exeter, hoping to see him, even for a few minutes. That night I went over to the house and waited for a while. When Elizabeth left, I went in." Her eyes filled with tears and she stopped. "I'm sorry."

This time it was Emily who intervened. "Roberta, please, this is too painful. Don't feel you must go on."

"I'm alright Emily. Augustus and I talked for a few minutes. But I couldn't tell him that this was probably the last time we would see one another. I didn't think it was fair. To upset him, I mean. He gave me a framed photograph of himself and Ronald when they first met in Vietnam. I dropped it and the glass broke. Well, he said he would have the glass replaced and bring it over to Emily's the next day. We could talk further then, he said. About changes he wanted to make. I think he meant about his marriage. He was terribly distraught. Well, it was difficult being together like that so I said I'd better leave. He wanted to drive me back to Emily's but there was someone waiting for him downstairs."

Someone waiting downstairs. Perhaps, at last, the secret was beginning to leave the center of the circle. The remark did not pass unnoticed by Emily either. She glanced at me as if to say, what do you make of that?

Mrs. Peabody continued her story. Her voice was stronger now as she regained her composure. "I went back to Emily's and packed my things. I returned to Boston and the next day joined my husband in Baltimore. There were tests and things there. We returned home just after the first of May. It was then I learned about Augustus. A friend . . . a mutual friend told me he had died." She took a deep breath. "I suppose you're both wondering why I came back to Exeter. I just wanted to be near him."

Hadn't the Biblical poet said that love is stronger than death. There was silence for several minutes. Mrs. Peabody was one suspect I didn't mind losing. Emily reached across the table and covered Roberta's hand with her own. It was an act of tenderness I didn't think Emily was capable of. I wished Althea had been there. She might have changed her opinion about her aunt's antagonist. I was reluctant to intrude upon this poignant moment but I had to ask the question which was on my mind, and I'm sure on Emily's too.

"Mrs. Peabody, I have just one or two questions. Did you see whoever it was waiting downstairs?"

"Yes, I did."

"Could you describe the person? It is rather important."

"He was a tall, good looking man. In his mid-forties I would think. A President Kennedy look alike, but with salt and pepper hair. One other thing. When I passed the door of the living room, he got up from the chair and walked across the room. I think he was limping. At least, that was the impression I had."

"Thank you very much, Mrs. Peabody. I know how difficult it has been for you to tell us these personal things. Will you be staying in Exeter?"

"Just until tomorrow afternoon, Dr. Clemson. I want to go to the graveside once more."

"Yes, I understand. Well, I sincerely hope your health will improve. I'm very glad I've met you even though the circumstances haven't been the best. If I'm not being too personal, I think Augustus was a very fortunate man, indeed, to have known someone like you."

As I left the verandah, Emily and Roberta were sharing memories of the man they had both loved. Augustus had been doubly fortunate. Why he had settled on a flighty woman like Elizabeth when he obviously attracted better women was a mystery. A character defect perhaps. We all have them. It was a rather gloomy thought. I had one more thing to do before I panned for a few more gold nuggets in the diaries.

Althea was not home when I called so I left a message. It was evening before she returned the call. She had spent the day at the hospital. Mrs. Harper had died. Todd was broken up over it, almost suicidal. I explained what I wanted her to do, with no questions asked. You may have to deceive like Mother Eve but do it anyway. Don't let me down, I said, because this is our last kick at the can.

At exactly eleven o'clock the following morning the three of us, Emily, Roberta, and myself, were sitting on the verandah as I had arranged. Althea and her passenger wheeled into the driveway. I got up and went to meet them as they left the car. "It's been a long time. Too long," I said. "But you're looking as fit as ever. Come and meet the owner of the best bed and breakfast in New Hampshire."

The two men, one of them with a noticeable limp, first admired the colorful borders of the front garden. Their animated conversation was punctured with laughter as they talked about things past. Althea, not sure what was happening, waited at the bottom of the stairs. "That's him," Mrs. Peabody said. "That's the man."

Emily got up and whispered to Althea, "Who's your friend?"

"Professor Evans," Althea said. "He's my thesis supervisor."

....

The Argonaut Motel in East Sandwich on the Cape has a better view than Emily's but is not half as charming. My file cards are stowed away and I have caught more than my share of bluefish. Exeter is buzzing with truths, half-truths, and outright rumors about the demise of Augustus Boone. The police are embarrassed as they try to explain their way out of the mess. Martin Evans was there that evening. He was besotted by Elizabeth's empty charms. Unlucky for him, he was also an honorable man and hoped to engage Augustus in a reasonable dialogue about his intentions. Reasonable dialogue about Elizabeth was not Augustus's forte. When he threatened the ill-starred lover and went up to his study to choose something from his arsenal, the feckless professor pursued, stumbled at the top of the stairs, unbalanced

Augustus and sent him crashing down the stairs to his untimely end. Manslaughter. That is yet to be determined.

Elizabeth is not out of the woods yet. Her participation in this fateful event remains unclear. Vincent Dolce was not and never was Elizabeth's lover. His distractions were otherwise. In fact, this otherwise was the reason he left Exeter when he was still young. The last time I saw Todd Harper he was still playing checkers at the Paul Revere Muffin Shop. As for Mrs. Peabody, she was rushed to Boston General and is not expected to survive her illness. Emily is thinking of franchising her bed and breakfast operation, starting in Vermont and Maine. I am now Althea's thesis supervisor, thanks to the intervention of the graduate dean who needs my support for a large research grant he's after.

Like Martin Evans, my intentions are honorable as they concern Althea. So the National Organization for Women need not fear that I will in any way take advantage of the power relationship between supervisor and supervised.

I will, however, be expected to spend an appropriate amount of time at UMass Amherst. Maybe the National Endowment for the Arts will provide another grant, this time to discover the roots of Emily Dickinson's poetic genius. Hopefully, no one in the beautiful town of Amherst has murder on his mind.

The
War Casualty

The twenty-fourth of May is the Queen's birthday, if we don't get a holiday, we'll all run away. We used to chant this rhyme as a kind of incantation to ensure that the holiday appeared as it was supposed to. For me, it meant a late breakfast with oatmeal cakes and hot scones and jam and even a cup of tea in honor of good Queen Victoria. Then, we were off to the annual School Fair with its games and prizes and still later to a dazzling fireworks display which filled the night sky with wonder and our nostrils with the smell of smoldering punk. The twenty-fourth of May was magical and not to be denied us.

Until that twenty-fourth, I never knew anyone who had run away. It seemed to me out of the question. Where would you run to? And what could be so bad that you would leave home for some unknown destination? Running away was just part of a rhyme. It was only an idle threat, never to be taken seriously. But on that twenty-fourth someone did run away, but not because the holiday celebration in the Queen's honor had been cancelled.

It was because of the war. One by one the men teachers enlisted in the army and left the school. Soon only one remained—Cecil Smythe, sometimes known as Captain Smythe, his rank in the First World War, the principal and the only male teacher left on the large staff at Wellington Public School. Wounded in the right leg by a shell burst, Mr. Smythe walked with a limp on good days, and on bad days he leaned heavily on a cane with a silver handle. With the arrival of another world war, he took to wearing his service ribbons pinned to his handkerchief pocket. On some occasions, he even wore his army uniform, still smelling of mothballs.

One day, at the beginning of the school year, he called all the senior boys together. Wellington Public School is going to have a cadet corps, he announced proudly, and all the senior boys are going to be in it. There'll be no shirkers. He leaned heavily on his cane as he met our eyes and stared us down. No shirkers, he said. England still expects her sons to do their duty.

Within a week there were drills after school on the playground. At first, we used broom handles for rifles but soon we all had wooden rifles manufactured by the manual training teacher at a neighboring school. Because that September was terribly hot, Mr. Smythe added stretcher bearers, who carried off those who fainted.

And, as we marched up and down, he was ever on the lookout for the most promising cadet. Mr. Smythe had borrowed a uniform from the high school principal and the best one of us would have the honor of wearing it. By the beginning of October, he had identified his drill sergeant.

Maurice Brownstone enjoyed playing at soldiers more than any of us. He was the toughest senior, and a year older than the rest of us because of a birthday in December, kindergarten admission regulations, and a failed year. When he stood erect, as he liked to do, he was a head taller than anyone else and only an inch shorter than Mr. Smythe himself. Anyone seeing him in his khaki uniform could easily have mistaken him for an enlistee. As his instinct for soldiering blossomed under Mr. Smythe's guidance, Maurice was transformed almost overnight from a fifteen-year old to a full grown man. He bristled with confidence. He was ready to take charge, ready to lead, ready to do his duty.

For many months he did take charge. Whenever Mr. Smythe was out of the school, Maurice was waiting for us on

the playground. He was dressed proudly in his uniform with
sergeant stripes on his sleeves, with smart gaiters folded just
right, polished boots and a leather swagger stick. For a while
we ragged him until he learned to stare us down the way Mr.
Smythe did. When the autumn months passed, the gymnasium
became our drill hall and the marching routines became even
more professional. By springtime, we were almost enjoying
ourselves and the hectoring of Maurice had stopped. He had
by this time won our grudging admiration. We all had to
admit that Maurice Brownstone was a fine sergeant even if
none of us had met a real one.

But it was not only on the playground and in the
gymnasium that the call to arms was heard at Wellington
Public School. We marched into school and out of school to
the strains of the Colonel Bogey March. Morning exercises
were embellished with prayers and hymns for those in peril on
the land and in the sky and on the sea. Mr. Smythe hung a
huge world map in the hallway beside his office under red,
white and blue bunting. Tiny Union Jacks on pins marked the
places where our boys were fighting the Nazis and the sons of
Nippon. And, from time to time, he would take the whole
arithmetic class to explain how he would win the war. Once a
month we assembled in the gym to hear a guest speaker tell us
what we could do to speed up V-E Day.

At the February assembly, Maurice's father was the guest
speaker. He was a graduate of Wellington School but hadn't
gone on to high school. For a time he was an apprentice
electrician but soon went on the pogey. Then the war came
along and rescued him. Now he was sitting there on the
platform beside the principal and the teachers. Corporal
Browntone looked uncomfortable. He fidgeted on the chair
and every now and then wiped his hands with a soiled
handkerchief. More than once he licked his lips and stared up
at the gym ceiling. After a lengthy introduction which didn't
fit the Mr. Brownstone we all knew, Mr. Smythe sat down
and nodded to the guest speaker to take his place at the

podium. A long, awkward silence followed. We nudged one another as we tried without complete success to suppress a giggle.

Corporal Brownstone shifted his gaze from the ceiling to his polished boots. His face reddened and beads of sweat formed on his forehead. He dipped into his tunic pocket and took out a piece of crumpled paper and studied it but otherwise did not move. Finally, Mr. Smythe leaned over and whispered something in his ear. It must have been a stern command because Corporal Brownstone got up immediately and strode to the podium. He gazed around at the assembled student body and stammered a few words without referring to the piece of paper in his hand. He said he didn't really want to fight but had to. The country wanted him to fight and he would do it. And he would do his best too. He sure would. Then he made a joke or tried to. It took him almost six months to earn his corporal stripes but Maurice got sergeant stripes in four weeks. The joke fell flat. Only the teachers laughed and that half-heartedly. I shot a glance at Maurice who was looking straight ahead. There was a tear on his face which he brushed away with a swipe of his hand.

At the end of the assembly, Miss McClelland who had just been made acting vice-principal announced that school would be dismissed early in honor of the guest speaker. We all shouted a hurrah which was quickly silenced and we were sent out of the gym to the sound of Land of Hope and Glory. Maurice's father fled from the platform and ducked out the nearest exit. We never saw him again. Within a few weeks he was shipped overseas to somewhere where the Union Jack was flying on the map beside the principal's office. His name was added to the Honor Role of teachers and graduates who were serving in the Kings service.

It was a few weeks after the Brownstone assembly that Mr. Smythe announced a new project to raise money for the troops. By the twenty-fourth of May, Victoria Day, the school would raise five hundred dollars to donate to the Red Cross to buy cigarettes for our soldiers at the front. Tickets were to be sold for three events. An oratory contest to which parents and friends of the school would be invited. A school dance on a Friday evening for both parents and students of the senior classes featuring the music of Glen Miller. And most important, a display of the marching routines of the Wellington cadet corps under the direction of drill sergeant Maurice Brownstone. After much consultation with the parents' committee, the price for tickets was struck at two dollars. Mr. Smythe reminded us over the PA system that the fate of our way of life rested on the success of even small ventures. We were all expected to pitch in. There were to be no slackers.

I didn't go to the dance. No one went from my family. Dancing when there was a war on didn't seem right to my father. I didn't fare much better in the oratorical contest. Strictly speaking, it wasn't an oratorical contest at all. Mr. Smythe gave each of us an excerpt from a speech given by the British Prime Minister and asked us to read it in his office, with Miss McCelland hovering behind. They chose three of the best readers to compete with three of the best readers from a neighboring school. I was not chosen. I had done reasonably well but Mr. Smythe said I was disqualified because I had read corpse instead of Corps. I stayed away from the contest and so did the rest of my family. We'll boycott it, my father said.

The last event before the twenty-fourth was the marching of the cadets. We put on a splendid show to a cheering crowd of parents and neighbors. Mr. Smythe was bursting with pride and took the occasion to reminisce about the Great War and the bravery of the soldiers whose valiant deeds would forever be enshrined in all our memories. Even though it wasn't Remembrance Day one of the teachers recited In Flanders Fields and a high school student played Taps rather uncertainly. He missed the last note altogether and Mr. Smythe grimaced.

Each day we watched the red crêpe paper on the cardboard thermometer beside the world map rise slowly toward the top and the five hundred dollar goal. But with only a week to go before Victoria Day the red column stalled. The target was short by over seventy dollars. Coat hangers and six-quart fruit baskets and even milk bottles were collected and sold to the dry cleaners, corner stores and dairies. The red column began to move again. But it was the Home and School bake sale which put us over the top. We all breathed a sigh of relief. Our boys, as Mr. Smythe always called them, would get their cigarettes after all.

At the very height of his success Maurice began to fall apart. We still practiced marching three times a week but now that the show was over our hearts were no longer in it. Maurice became irritable and many stopped going to the practices. Those of us who kept going began hectoring Maurice again which made matters even worse. More than once Mr. Smythe dressed us down for not taking things seriously. Wars are lost and won because of lack of discipline was his standard line, but his rants were losing their effect. We were no longer prepared to accept Maurice's moodiness. Even the war itself was becoming a bit boring.

Miss McClelland was determined to leave her mark as acting vice-principal. She knew if she didn't, and the war ended soon, she would be back to teaching fulltime. Not interested in the goings-on of the cadet corps she began to search for a project to call her own. The project she was searching for was, in fact, next to the principal's office. The stock room hadn't been tended to in months. Miss McClelland pounced on the opportunity to make her own contribution to the war effort. Good housekeeping was also a way to strike a blow against the common enemy.

Three weeks before the twenty-fourth of May, just before Monday morning recess, she asked five of us to stay behind. She had something important for us to do. You will put the stockroom in order, she said. You will sort, count, label and shelve every pencil, pen nib, ink bottle, eraser, piece of chalk, paper clip, chalk brush and everything else. This was important, as important as the cadet corps. And, for that reason, starting today there will be no more practice drills until the job is done. To our surprise she even put Maurice in charge. You can go to recess now, she said with a smile, and walked into Mr. Smythe's office. Later we learned from the caretaker there had been a holy row, but Miss McClelland would not back down.

After school we assembled outside the stockroom door. Mr. Smythe walked past us with a scowl but didn't say anything, even though Maurice tried to get his attention. Miss McClelland had a look of satisfaction on her face as she opened the door and ushered us into a room about half the size of a classroom. Everything was in disarray. The spit-and-polish image cultivated by Mr. Smythe collapsed in that airless space. Putting the school on a war footing apparently did not apply to school supplies. Maurice shook his head in disappointment. His hero had let him down. Going over her instructions to us once again, Miss McClelland handed a record book to me and said, "Don't miss anything." At first Maurice seemed overwhelmed, but like the good drill sergeant he was, within an hour we were a going concern and what seemed at first impossible now seemed manageable after all.

I was surprised by the number of things that were needed to keep a school running. By the end of the week the job was finished. Miss McClelland reported the miracle to Mr. Smythe and he inspected the room with grudging admiration. He found fault with a few things, ordering the rearrangement of scribblers and mimeograph paper. He also insisted that the hectograph be restored to its proper place. When he left, Miss McClelland told us not to bother. I can still remember the huge smile on her not unhandsome face.

We returned to marching and drilling with renewed enthusiasm in anticipation of the Victoria Day celebration. We were intent on repeating our successful display, this time with a real colonel to review us, along with some people from the Red Cross. Mr. Smythe was once again in a good mood, however Maurice was becoming more on edge. Rumors were going around that he had taken things from the stockroom and I partly believed them. Twice during the week of cleaning I had to change the number of items in the record book when I went back to check the things on the shelves. The stock was short three or four boxes of pen nibs and erasers and some other things including a tin of condensed milk. At the time I was sure I had made a mistake in the records so I didn't think much about it. Also, my puzzlement didn't have time to grow into suspicion because it was baseball season again and I wanted to be outside with the others. By the end of the weekend, I had put the idea completely out of my mind.

A surprise awaited our return to school on the Monday morning before the Victoria Day holiday. We had just settled down for our penmanship lesson when Miss McClelland called out five names and asked us to report to the principal's office. She had hinted earlier that our efforts to put the stock room in order would not go unrewarded. As we filed out of the classroom, we wondered what Mr. Smythe had in store for us. Maybe he's going to give us the afternoon off, I whispered to Maurice, who just shrugged his shoulders.

When we entered the office, Mr. Smythe was standing by the window and looking out into the schoolyard. For a long time he remained motionless. When he eventually turned, the expression on his face told us not to expect a reward. He leaned upon his cane and said nothing. He glared at us with disdain. "One of you is a thief," he said. My heart sank. I wanted to look at Maurice but I dared not. As his eyes searched out mine, I froze. I knew my suspicion had been right after all. For the first time in my life, I felt terror even though I had done nothing wrong.

"One of you is a thief," he repeated. "Thievery is always despicable but in wartime it is unforgivable. It undermines the war effort and aids the enemy." He said other things too, harsher things, but I was too frightened to remember them. Then Mr. Smythe read out the stolen items. Two boxes of pen nibs. Five pen holders. A box of pencils. A box of paper clips. A tin of condensed milk. An unspecified number of No. 14 envelopes. Miss McClelland was sure of these but there could be other missing items.

He looked coldly at each of us in turn. "You can be certain I will find out the truth. Each will be interviewed separately. You will tell the truth even if that means reporting on someone else. If, at the end of the interviews, the thief has not confessed or been revealed, you will all be punished equally." Mr. Smythe reached behind him and picked-up a leather strap from his desktop. "This is not an idle threat," he continued. My hands grew clammy. I felt like being sick.

We waited out in the hallway for our turn. The questioning did not take long. I was called in first. Did you steal any of the items on the list or any other item? Do you know for certain if anyone else had stolen anything? Were you suspicious of anyone and who was that individual? I clenched my fists so tight my fingernails dug into the palms of my hands. I did remember something. I remembered Maurice's furtive actions when he thought we weren't paying attention and how he always stayed behind when we left. But why would anyone steal pen nibs and a tin of condensed milk? If Maurice needed anything, why didn't he ask one of us? Why did he have to take these things and get us all in trouble? It wasn't fair.

Mr. Smythe put his cold hand under my chin and raised my face to his. He repeated the questions again, very slowly this time. I shook my head to signify I hadn't stolen anything. I shook my head again that I didn't know for sure that anyone else had taken anything. And, no, I wasn't suspicious of anyone. He smiled and dismissed me. I knew he didn't believe me. I'll be talking to you again, he said, and pointed his cane at the door. The way he looked at me made the hairs on the back of my neck stand up. I knew then that I was a coward. I would be no good in the army and I hoped the war would be over before I grew up. I joined the others along the wall and tried not to look at them. Maurice glanced at me and I tried to reassure him by my expression that I hadn't given him away, not yet.

Maurice was the last to be interviewed. He had worn the King's uniform so he couldn't be a thief. He was in the office the shortest time of us all and soon joined us again. As the clock in the outer office ticked off the long minutes, we thought about the strap and wondered how many strokes we'd get. No one dared to speak or whisper.

Each one wondered what the others had said. If no one told the rumors about Maurice, we would all be punished. It was the first time for me and I was certain I couldn't take it without tears. I couldn't imagine what would be worse. The pain of the strapping or the humiliation of being called a sissy.

The dismissal bell rang and pupils and teachers filed past us. Our classmates sniggered as they went by and some of them tapped one hand against the other and grinned. Only Maurice reacted with defiance and with an implied threat that he would get even. But it was to be an idle threat.

When everyone else was gone, and the Colonel Bogey March came to a scratchy end, Mr. Smythe emerged from his office and stood in front of us. Miss McClelland stayed by the door. She looked pale and even frightened a little. When the punishment was meted out, she would be the witness. She would have to inspect our hands before to make sure there were no cuts or bruises, keep a record of the number of strokes and inspect our hands afterwards to make sure there was no unusual bruising. This was also a first for her and for a fleeting moment I felt sorry for her.

Mr. Smythe seemed to take forever choosing his words. It was not wrong, he began, to report on someone who had committed a crime. Truth was the first casualty of war and he was gratified that someone had the courage to tell the truth. Misplaced loyalty in wartime was dangerous because it wasted time and time was as much an enemy as the enemy themselves. After he dealt with the offender, he went on, there would be further investigations. Some knew things but withheld what they knew. He looked in my direction then dismissed us all except Maurice.

At first I was so overwhelmed with relief that I failed to realize what had happened. Then it dawned on me. Someone had told on Maurice because I was sure Maurice had not confessed. One of us was a snitch. A coward. This realization was almost as devastating as the thought of being strapped. I looked back as I walked away and watched Maurice disappear inside the principal's office. Why did he do it? Who gave him away? Would he think I was the one? What was going to happen to him now? All of these questions and a hundred more pounded in my head as I ran home. That night I didn't want any supper. I just wanted to be left alone in my room. Later, I fell into an uneasy sleep with Maurice's eyes staring at me.

The twenty-second of May was a glorious spring day. When I got to the schoolyard, nothing had changed. The girls were still skipping double Dutch or playing red rover. The boys were flipping bottle tops and playing handball and workup baseball. Teachers were prowling about. I looked for the others but they were nowhere to be found. Only Maurice was there, leaning against the fence all by himself. He was looking straight ahead but not really seeing anything or anyone. I wanted to go and tell him I wasn't the one, but I couldn't. I didn't want to look into his eyes and see the look of contempt. So instead I went to the baseball diamond and pretended to be watching. For the rest of the day I kept to myself and didn't say a word to the others who finally showed up after morning recess.

Mr. Smythe was waiting for us in the classroom when we got back after lunch. His voice had an edge to it. All the boys in the cadet corps were to report to the gymnasium after school. No excuses. He left, unsmiling. Miss McClelland started the lesson but stopped and told us to take our spelling texts and copy out the words twice. She stayed at her desk for almost all the rest of the afternoon.

After school we assembled in the gym. Maurice was the only one who didn't show up. By now everyone knew about the theft and our sergeant's part in this infamous affair. Not a few of the boys were gleeful about Maurice's downfall and I found myself joining in on their malicious remarks. It was not long before Mr. Smythe entered with Maurice walking stiffly behind him like a prisoner heading for the gallows. Maurice was not in uniform which told me this meeting was not about our display of marching routines. We formed up quickly and stood at attention. I glanced at Maurice briefly and was glad he looked back without any discernible animosity.

Leaning on his cane, Mr. Smythe cleared his throat and began to speak in that precise manner of his which I now found increasingly irritating. Maurice has disgraced the school, his fellow cadets and himself by stealing school supplies, he said slowly. Wartime meant sacrifice and heroism, not deceit and dishonesty. Discipline was all-important and punishment must be swift if it was to be effective. Maurice would no longer be a member of the Wellington Public School cadet corps.

Mr. Smythe turned to Maurice who stood unsmiling and unrepentant. Would he like to apologize to his fellows, asked Captain Smythe. Maurice said nothing. He shook his head negatively instead. But I noticed he was holding back his tears just as he had when his father had come to the February assembly and made a fool of himself.

As soon as we were dismissed, everyone scattered as quickly as possible, avoiding Mr. Smythe and particularly the cashiered drill sergeant. I was about to turn away too but Maurice blocked my way. He told me he knew who had snitched on him, then suddenly broke off and ran out of the gym. I followed, but he was too fast. I last saw him running down the street, but not towards home. I remembered the last thing he said—It doesn't matter anymore. For a long time I stood planted on the sidewalk, wondering what he meant. It didn't matter anymore.

Next morning I was surprised to see Mrs. Brownstone standing outside the principal's office. She looked terrible— worried, frail and tired. Miss McClelland was trying to comfort her and as we filed past she put her arms around the younger woman and guided her into the office foyer. Moments later Mr. Smythe announced over the PA that anyone who had seen or spoken to Maurice Brownstone after school on the previous day should come at once to the office. I raised my hand and Miss McClelland hurried me out of the room. Once again I found myself standing in the corridor. For a while I stared at the map of the world with its Union Jacks flying stiffly on their little pins. The flags had not moved much since Mr. Smythe put the map on the wall and I wondered if that meant the war was going badly. Mr. Smythe had said the boys over there would be moving those flags speedily on every front, just wait and see.

Soon I was sitting on a chair between Mrs. Brownstone and a police officer. I told Mr. Smythe what I knew. That I had seen Maurice after we had been dismissed and that he had run down the street but away from home. When encouraged to remember anything else, I remembered what he'd said. It didn't matter anymore. When pressed further for an explanation, I said I didn't know what he meant by it.

The police officer took down some notes on a small black pad while Mrs. Brownstone sobbed quietly.

Did I know where Maurice might have run to, the police officer asked gently. Where did the boys go, for example, to have a smoke without getting caught? I looked at Mr. Smythe and he nodded that I might answer, but I couldn't. I really didn't know where they went and I felt ashamed I didn't know. The police officer said it was okay I didn't know and he smiled. He put the black pad into his tunic pocket and stood up. If I remembered anything else, no matter how small, I was to tell the principal. Other boys were quizzed too, but no one was willing to give any information, not even the one who snitched on Maurice.

Later, I did remember something. The boys often went to the bend in the river beneath the trestle bridge. I never saw them smoking there but they liked to swim and fool around and collect apples from the orchard nearby. It would be a good place to hide. Not long afterwards I was in a police car winding our way down a dirt track leading to the river. We bumped across a rough field and stopped not far from where the river bends as it flows under the high trestle. The river was widest there and spring rain had swollen it so that it was running fast. Mrs. Brownstone got out of the car and ran to the river's marshy bank and then along to one of the concrete supports for the iron girders of the bridge.

We ran after her but she ran faster. By the time we reached her, she was cradling Maurice's broken body in her arms. He was lying half in and half out of the water. One leg was twisted grotesquely under the other and he was delirious. As I looked up, a train passed across the bridge, its whistle blowing a warning.

We marched on the twenty-fourth of May in the afternoon at the annual School Fair. Colonel Hardcastle, the high school principal, congratulated us on a fine showing. He said how impressed he was, particularly as our drill sergeant was unable to attend because of ill health and he wished him a speedy recovery. You'll make good soldiers when the time comes but the war will be over soon, he went on. I'm sure of that. Discipline's important, though, even in times of peace, so your efforts are not in vain. No, not in the least. Those coming on to high school will find that discipline tops the list of my expectations. A quick salute and he was gone. The lady from the Red Cross gushed over the gift of five hundred dollars, and if we wanted the boys over there to have cigarettes then that is what they would have. Even little people, she said, could contribute to the war effort.

Mr. Smythe was dressed in his uniform with service

medals and all. He made a long-winded speech about boys becoming men when they put on a uniform. The day was hot. By the time he had finished the stretcher bearers had unceremoniously carted off two of the fallen. Miss McCelland thanked everyone for making the day so successful and officially opened the Victoria Day festivities. Let the fun begin, she said with forced laughter.

As soon as I could I slipped away and ran over to the Brownstone's small house. It wasn't much more than a shack. As I carefully walked up the broken porch steps, I realized for the first time how poor they were. I knocked once softly, half hoping no one was home, and wondering why I had come at all. As I was about to turn away, the front door opened a crack. Mrs. Brownstone recognized me and said to wait. In a few minutes, she stepped out onto the porch. She smiled weakly and said, "I'm sorry I can't invite you in." We stood there together, not saying anything. A baby's cries filled the empty background. Is that why Maurice took the tin of condensed milk, I wondered. "I must go back and look after the baby. I'm glad you came around," she said . "Maurice had his leg amputated last night but he'll get better in a few weeks or months. Now he's a casualty just like his dad." She closed the door behind her. I left but not to go back to the fair.

After Victoria Day, everything returned to normal at school. Mr. Smythe added a note to Corporal Brownstone's name beside the world map where the Union Jacks were still flying. It said: Wounded in Action.

The Gift

My story may begin like that Dickens novel of long ago, but that was fiction. This is my story. It was a time of giving and receiving. It was a time of hope and expectation. It was a time of happiness and love. And I believed it was my time.

Milverton City was never part of my dream. For me it was always the city of last resort. Growing up on a farm, I often dreamed of far away places like New York and Los Angeles, and even farther away places like London, Paris and Rome. The walls of my childhood bedroom were a picture gallery of destinations where I hoped to live someday. But, in the end, I settled on Milverton, a small uncelebrated city on the banks of the muddy Milver River. Why there? Because it was only a small bus fare away and I was told apartments on Bradford Street were cheap.

On its welcome sign on Route 29, in weather-faded letters, was the city's motto: Where Dreams Come True. I wondered if that would be true for me. Three months after my arrival, I thought I had found the answer in an unexpected visitor. Carl Steven was like a gift from God.

It was possibly naive to think that anything good would come from Carl's promise. It was, after all, only the promise of a promise. But the circumstances were so out of the ordinary that I began to wonder if God's ways were as mysterious as the poet claimed. After so many disappointments, I had come to believe my prayers were like undelivered letters, lost among the stars with all the others.

But now, I was ready to take a chance. I had even made the sign of the cross, a thing Catholics do to get special attention I was told and should never do because it was only superstition. Then I closed my eyes, crossed my fingers and prayed.

Father in Heaven,

Forgive me, but he came for help and it was like a gift because I was so unhappy and he has given me a reason to live. I feel really terrible because I know You are disappointed in me but I hope You will understand and help us find the right way, maybe even together, and Father, even though Carl is not a believer in the Way, he is so childlike and has been wishing for snow for Christmas, could You, it's such a small thing to ask.

Amen

It was later, after midnight, on the day before Christmas when part of my prayer was answered. Weeks of mild weather had lulled us into the false belief that autumn would go on forever. But the temperature dipped suddenly below freezing and it began to snow gently, at first, and then with fury. By early morning it lay knee-deep across the city.

I was awakened from a troubled sleep by a scraping sound as though something heavy was being dragged across the floor overhead, followed by a door slamming, then laughter and footsteps on the stairs. Through the fog of slowly returning awareness, I vaguely remembered Tara, the tenant on the third floor, telling me that she and Tina, her girlfriend, were catching the 5:30 bus to Columbus. Hope we don't wake you up, Willow, but then you know what we're like. I opened my eyes and glanced at my watch. The tiny hands, glowing green in the dark, told me it was five o'clock.

Wake up, wake up and get out of bed . . . the devil's keeping you from the good Lord's work. From childhood I had heard this refrain. I knew it was sinful to waste time staying in bed, but that morning I didn't care. I needed time to think about how everything had changed since Carl had come into my life. Turning quietly onto my side, I peered through the darkness across the small living room toward the bedroom where he was asleep. It was a dream come true, as on the Milverton welcome sign, and in stories I secretly used to read about the handsome prince who rescues the young unloved maiden from her misery and they live happily ever after. Can it really be happening to me, I wondered. I was still fantasizing about the promise Carl said he would make after I got home from work when the sound of the alarm under my pillow nudged me back to reality. Once again I glanced at my watch. Now I had to hurry. I couldn't be sure the six o'clock bus would wait for me again.

I sat up and slipped quietly off the sofa and into my slippers. I folded the flannel sheets and the quilt Grandma Hanson had made for my hope chest, then stuffed them and the pillow into an overflowing cupboard. Everything must be left tidy. Carl liked it that way. A place for everything and everything in its place was the way he put it when he first came. I knew he was right. It was something my father used to say. Maybe that's why I like him so much, I told myself, as I carefully smoothed out the wrinkles left on the sofa's seat cushions from my tossing and turning during the night.

The smell of stale pipe smoke hung in the air. I had told Carl, as firmly as I dared, about the house rule—no smoking or you're out—but he had insisted on smoking anyway. Listen to me, listen carefully, old lady Lockerby means cigarettes, he said with a dismissive wave of his hand. Don't you worry. I'll have a talk with her in the morning. I knew it was pointless to argue. Besides, the evening had been going so well and just maybe my life was now moving in a new direction where the rules I had grown up with and slavishly followed all my life no longer applied. The thought of being free, free to be myself, free to do what I wanted, made me feel giddy. Is this what love does to you, I wondered, frees you from all the things that make you unhappy? But in my heart I wondered if it could ever be. Could twenty-eight years of baggage disappear overnight? If so, it would be the Christmas gift I would cherish for the rest of my life.

The giddiness soon passed but not the smell of pipe smoke. I moved quietly across the living room to the mullioned window that overlooked the street and parted the heavy green velvet drapes. I raised the window sash and looked out. Snowflakes drifted through the open window. They landed on my brow and nose and lips, melting and sending tiny cold streams down my cheeks. It made me feel clean and alive and happy. I smiled and breathed in the cold, fresh air. Thank You, thank You, Lord. It was going to be a white Christmas after all.

For the first time in a long while Bradford Street seemed to glow in the fading light of the low hanging moon. Maybe this is an omen of good things to come, I told myself. Just maybe things are going to work out at last. How many times on a wintry morning on the farm I had prayed for something I couldn't really understand but felt instinctively—something out there, waiting for me. I lowered the sash, propped up the window with the pewter mug Carl had used for an ashtray and closed the drapes. And, in the light of the red and blue and white bulbs twinkling on the tiny Christmas tree in the corner of the room, I got ready for work.

My morning routines were timed to the second. Putting on my makeup took more time now. Carl liked a woman to look natural, don't paint your face, he said, you're not Ophelia. So I chose the softest color of lipstick, applying it sparingly and with greater care. My thick, auburn hair, I brushed, pulled it back tight, and tied it with a green ribbon. I slipped into the store uniform, cream blouse with the Steven's logo on the pocket and navy slacks. Glancing in the mirror, I frowned.

Why wasn't I born pretty, I asked myself. It was a question I had asked myself often over the years.

Before I left the small bathroom, I made sure that everything was placed exactly the way Carl liked it—towels straightened, hand soap centered in the soap dish, shower curtains closed, and nothing left around the hand basin. It was good to have someone who cared about such things. On the farm I hadn't the time, but now I was with someone who did care. It somehow made me feel worthwhile.

Just after midnight, I had set the table with the dishes we had bought from a fashionable boutique in a trendy area by the canal. They were outrageously expensive, wiping out almost all the savings I had put aside for a summer holiday. But Carl was right. They were perfect for the holiday season. I knew he would be pleased. As I was placing a sprig of holly on the plate, I debated whether or not to leave a note. Would he think I'm being foolish, I wondered. He didn't like people who were gauche and didn't know the proper thing to do. You've got to be decisive, more confident, you're so unsure of yourself, he had teased when we were shopping for a sofa for me to sleep on. But was I really that way, I wondered? I decided finally he probably knew me better than I knew myself. I put a green candle in a holder and a wreath of holly around it, and thought how wonderful the table looked. I'll do it. I'll leave a note. On a sheet of writing paper with the store logo on it, I wrote in my best handwriting a short note:

Carl,

I'll be late tonight. It's a double shift so I won't be home until about eight. I'm really curious about the promise you have in mind. I have a surprise for you. It's snowing. If you go out, dress warmly. I've left a book of poems. I hope you like them. They're my favorites.

Willow

I put my navy pea coat and winter boots on and wrapped a wool scarf around my head. At the door I stopped for one last glance around the room. Nothing was out of place. This was going to be the best Christmas ever.

Even though it was already past 6:00, Bus 39 Downtown was waiting at the corners of Bradford and Aylmer. Great plumes of exhaust billowed into the brittle morning air, turning the pristine snow nearby into sooty gray. Breathless, I plodded through the heavy snow and reached the bus door which unexpectedly swung open. Bradley Hunter, the bus driver, stood in the doorway with his hand outstretched. He helped me over the snow bank turned up by the plow. "You're late again," he said with a smile. "If you keep this up, you're going to get me fired." I returned the smile and said I was sorry. "Apology accepted because I'm in a Christmas mood. Remember what we talked about," he said as I stopped by the fare box. "I will," I promised and hurried by.

I closed my eyes and rested my head against the window. I thought about the journey I had taken from the farm to Milverton. Everyone had warned me I was taking a risk, that I would be sorry in the end, that at twenty-eight I was past the time for such a change, that I was certain to fail. But I had proved them wrong. I have never been happier than I am right now. I have a good job, a promotion, and there was Carl too.

The bus stopped suddenly and I opened my eyes, catching for a brief moment my reflection in the window. I'm not attractive, I said to myself. I was puzzled by the bus driver's interest in me. We had met once by chance at the market by the river and had coffee. He surprised me by telling me he had been a fighter pilot, and after the war an airline pilot, but he gave up flying for a less demanding job so he could have what he valued most, time to read, write and think about things. I remember how embarrassed he became because he thought he was talking too much about himself. But he was interesting and I wished he had kept on talking. We promised to meet for coffee again sometime but then Carl came into my life and I put it out of my mind.

As the bus passed slowly by the gaily decorated houses, a thought which kept rising to the surface nudged its way into my consciousness. Why me? Why had Carl come to me? At the store he hadn't even noticed me, never spoke to me except when he had to, and even then was always curt, almost rude. He lavished his attention on Betty and seemed even more involved with Jasmine. They used to joke that I'd never get a promotion when the boss's nephew was so down on me. I put his indifference, if not outright hostility, to the fact I was too shy to chat him up like the others, and thinking about it now, perhaps he thought I sided with Eddie and some others who thought he was an offensive snob, who got the manager's job because he was the owner's nephew. Maybe it wasn't Carl's fault after all but my own. I wasn't friendly and he mistook my diffidence for dislike. Yes, that must be it. I was wrong. That's why he came to me and not the others.

The bus turned onto Main Street with difficulty. Caught in its headlights was the notice board of the Alliance Church on the corner. Besides the usual Christmas wishes there was a Bible verse, part of it hidden by a dollop of snow. I had memorized it in Sunday school and was given a pencil with the verse inscribed in gold letters. I treasured that pencil and took it with me to school and showed it off with pride. But now the verse sent a chill down my spine. "Be sure your sin will find you out." I hadn't thought about sin very much since coming to Milverton, hadn't gone to church except for a couple of times, and if Carl hadn't come, I wouldn't have thought about praying either. But I knew right then I was sinning, no matter how I tried to deny it. It wasn't right to have Carl living with me, although he hadn't so much as held my hand. The appearance of it was wrong. Even though Mrs. Lockerby seemed to believe the story that Carl was a cousin—my first lie ever—she looked at me differently from then on. Also, Tara winked and gave me a knowing smile as she passed by.

But it was unfair for anyone to think I was doing something wrong. I tried to remember how it was that Carl ended up staying with me. I went over each detail, putting them in order. I was standing outside my door, turning the key in the lock when Mrs. Lockerby called up from downstairs. You have a visitor, she said. Before I had finished turning the key Carl was standing beside me, smiling. I was surprised and uncomfortable, and didn't know what to say when he invited me for a walk. It was a Saturday and I was going out anyway so it seemed alright. We walked along the river and chatted though he did most of the talking. He was upset that his uncle had fired him, accused him of theft, and was angry that Mr. Steven wouldn't listen to his side of the story.

That's how it started. I felt sorry for him because at home I was often accused of doing things and nobody listened to my explanation. And then after a while, we just began to talk about nicer things. He asked a lot of things about myself and said how he always admired me because I was such a good worker and wasn't silly like the other girls. You were always serious, he said. I like that in a girl. We looked in store windows and stopped for apple cider and cake. Soon we were laughing and he said he was glad I wasn't serious all the time.

We walked back to my house and he didn't ask to come in. I was glad he didn't. But, as he was leaving, he said he didn't have anywhere to go for Christmas. He had given up his flat because he had run out of money. I don't suppose you could put me up for a few days, he said and laughed. No, it was too much to ask. Then I said, well, if it's only for a few days, I don't mind.

That's how it started. I wasn't thinking. I felt sorry for him. Yes, I felt I was doing something Christian. Wasn't that what Christmas is about? It wasn't wrong. It wasn't sinful. It was the right thing to do even if it looked wrong. I was sure of it.

"Willow," a familiar voice said, "a penny for your thoughts."

Beth Marchant was manager of the Fine Linen & Things boutique next door to Steven's. Sitting down on the bus beside me, she smiled as she brushed the snow from her coat. "You were lost in thought. It must be man trouble."

I tried to ignore the remark but it unsettled me. I turned and smiled but said nothing.

"How is dear Mr. Steven?" she continued.

"Fine, I guess. I don't have much contact with him. He's real busy at this time of year."

"Of course, we're all busy. Is his nephew busy too?"

"Well, yes. I'm sure he is." I wanted to take the reply back but it was too late.

"Why that's funny. I heard he was fired for stealing from the store." Beth paused. She knew she had caught me in a lie. She was toying with me. "Well, was he?"

"Yes he was but Mr. Steven has asked us not to talk about it. It's a family matter. I don't want to say anything." It was my turn to pause. "You can understand, can't you?"

"Were you at the Spice & Cider Shoppe the other day?"

"No, I don't think so," I replied. Another lie.

"Strange. I thought I saw you there with Mr. Steven's nephew, Carl. That's his name, isn't it?"

I felt a cold chill pass over me. I can't remember what I said next but I know I stumbled over the words and sounded unconvincing. The rest of the journey passed in silence. I looked out the window without seeing anything. I was frightened. What would Mr. Steven do if he found out about Carl and me. Beth pretended to be looking through a fashion magazine, turning each page triumphantly. Not a word passed between us as we walked toward our stores. As we parted, she said, "Be seeing you. Please give my regards to Mr. Steven. And Carl, too, if you happen to see him. Merry Christmas." She smiled mischievously and vanished inside the boutique.

Eddie Blackburn was standing outside Steven's smoking. He opened the door and with a gallant gesture waved me through. I was still trembling and he noticed but mistook the reason, thinking it was because the morning was so cold.

"This terrible weather will discourage shopping," he said dolefully, flicking his unfinished cigarette away. Eddie was Mr. Gloom personified. We were all dumbfounded when Mr. Steven made him floor manager after Carl left. But now I was too preoccupied with my own troubled thoughts to say anything in reply and hurried to the staff room. I put my coat and purse in the locker, glanced in the mirror, and took a deep breath. I loosened my hair and touched up my lipstick. Mr. Steven liked his cashiers to look anything but drab. Bad for business he said. Smart, everybody's got to look smart. In spite of my encounter with Beth, I was determined to make it through the day and hurry home to Carl. If the worst happened, we could go away together. Perhaps, he would go to the farm. It was mine now and we could work it or maybe sell it. The thought turned my mind to Carl's promise. Whatever could it be, I wondered. I must get through the day.

Eddie was wrong about the weather discouraging shoppers. They came in droves. By the middle of the morning my legs were tired and I kept glancing at my watch. The other cashiers had already taken their break. Five minutes before I was to take mine, Eddie placed a note from Mr. Steven on my counter. I picked it up and read it. It said, come up to my office during your break. My hand shook as I folded the note and slipped it into my pocket. Maybe Beth had already spoken to Mr. Steven. The couple minutes until I could close my counter seemed like an eternity now.

Mr. Steven's office always smelled of cinnamon. The few times I had been there I tried to discover the source but today I was too worried to even to notice. I stood there, shivering and speechless. Should I say something, I thought, but what?

"Is there a problem, Miss Hanson?" Mr. Steven seemed more perplexed than annoyed.

"No, sir." My voice was barely audible.

"Good. Now, the reason I asked you to come up."

Mr. Steven reached for a tissue from a box on his desk. He snorted into it and threw the crumpled tissue into a wastebasket.

He cleared his throat and continued. "When I promoted you to head cashier, I knew I was taking a chance. The other cashiers didn't like it one bit but I knew you were the best of the bunch. You're quick, accurate, polite, never complain and yet you're no pushover with the customers either. In other words, you're everything I want in an employee. If Betty and Jasmine leave as a result, then so be it." He tapped the desktop gently with his forefinger that was crowned with a large, fake diamond ring he had won in a poker game in Las Vegas.

The phone rang. Mr. Steven gestured with his hand for me to sit down on the leather chair next to the desk.

I liked Mr. Steven. He was a big man with an even bigger voice. He intimidated me but I knew his bark was worse than his bite. I sank into the chair and said, Thanks Lord, under my breath. I shut Mr. Steven out as he spoke to the caller. It was probably the new woman in his life, as his voice had become unusually dulcet. Could it be Beth Marchant, I wondered. I know she used to hang around the store and make all kinds of excuses to talk to him. Curious now, I listened as closely as I could for hints as to the identity of the caller, but the conversation was intimate and carefully guarded. Given Mr. Steven's remarks about my promotion, my thoughts turned to the possibility I had not been doing enough. That worried me.

The call ended. Mr. Steven took off his glasses and laid them on a large ledger book which every now and then he had been glancing at. It wasn't Beth after all. Of that I was certain.

Once more he cleared his voice and wiped his lips with a tissue.

"I'm telling you this in strictest confidence. We're in trouble, big trouble, if we don't make today, Boxing Day and the rest of the week the best days of the year. You've got to keep the customers moving quickly through the checkout. You can do it and you can be an example to the others. I'm not saying you're not doing it now, but don't cave in." The phone rang again, but this time he ignored it. He wanted me to say something and became impatient. "Well," he said, "you looked awfully pale when you first came in. Don't get sick on me, please."

"I won't cave in, Mr. Steven. Thank you for trusting in me. I'll keep them moving. I really will. Can I go back now?" I got up from the chair. Once more I smelled the cinnamon fragrance and my legs no longer felt tired. I looked at my watch. Six hours, just six hours more and I'll know what Carl's thinking about. The thought gave me a warm rush. Mr. Steven went back to his ledger, and with a brief wave of his hand dismissed me.

Back at the checkout, the lines were long and most of the customers looked annoyed. I whispered to Jasmine and Betty, "The boss wants us to keep the customers moving. And he means it." Their facial expressions said in response, don't bother us, you got the promotion. As I returned to my station, I noticed Mr. Steven looking down from his office window. He didn't look pleased.

"You seem so happy, you must be in love," said Enid Cuomo, who often visited the store to chat. She told me once I was the daughter she would have liked to have had if things had been different. She was married only a week when her husband went overseas to fight in the war and was killed in action. Sometimes she left a small gift, inexpensive but sweet.

I liked her, in return, and often thought she was the kind of mother I would have liked to have had, but never did. I smiled. I was sure I was blushing. There's a surprise waiting for me at home was all I could say.

"Well, I hope it's a wonderful one. You deserve the very best. Merry Christmas." Mrs. Cuomo picked up her small parcel and left the store.

The hours flew by. Near the end of the day Eddie announced over the PA that the store was closing in 10 minutes and dimmed the lights for a couple of seconds. The harried stragglers hurried to the counters and were soon outside in the crisp, starry night.

Jasmine and Betty quickly emptied their cash drawers, put the money into canvas bags and left the bags on my counter. Laughing, they chorused their good-byes and said hope your surprise is a good one. They blew a sneering kiss and hurried outside. Through the open door a gust of wind blew a cloud of snowflakes into the store.

I was tidying the counter, putting gift wrap and bags away, when Eddie stopped by to chat on his way up to Mr. Steven's office. I knew he liked me. But even though he was a good floor manager and had been more attentive to me than Carl, I never took to him. Mr. Uncool, Betty and Jasmine called him behind his back.

"Would you like to go out for a coffee?" he asked. "After the sales meeting."

I was surprised by the invitation. He had never asked me out before. There was at time when I would have liked to go out for a coffee but not now, not with Carl waiting for me at home. I smiled and begged off. Eddie looked disappointed. I didn't want to hurt his feelings so I said maybe another time. I shared Betty and Jasmine's opinion that he was too ordinary, and now my hopes were on someone who was truly extraordinary.

Eddie was not deterred. "Now that I'm floor manager, I thought, well, I thought we could be more than just Steven's employees. You know, I'm still thinking about Carl. I know Betty and Jasmine thought he was Mr. Right but why did he steal. Him with his MBA and being Mr. Steven's nephew, you'd think he wasn't so dumb. Well, his stupidity is my luck. I wouldn't trade places with him for anything."

Mr. Steven's booming voice from above ended Eddie's tirade. It hurt to hear him speak so disparagingly about Carl and confirmed my dislike of Eddie. There would be no going out for coffee, ever.

I quickly put on my coat and winter boots, carried the cash bags to the Business Manager's office, and left the store. It felt good to be outside in the cold air and to feel the snowflakes on my face. As I waited at the bus stop for the No. 9 Bus Uptown, I tried to stop thinking about Eddie's irresponsible talk about Carl. Carl wasn't stupid. Mr. Steven treated him miserably even though he had tripled the store's profits. Anyway, he only took things that weren't selling. Carl wasn't like anyone she had ever known before. Yes he was different, but he was good and honest about things that really mattered.

I was surprised Bradley was still driving the bus. "I've come to take you home. Special delivery courtesy of Milverton Transport," he said. When I attempted to put the fare in the box, he covered it with his hand. "This one's on me." He smiled. "You look tired."

"It's been a long day." I sat down on the seat behind him. "You've had a long day too."

"Well, everyone else has someone to go home to so I volunteered to take another shift," There was no self-pity in his voice.

No. 9 bus lurched to a stop at the corner of Aylmer and Bradford. "Merry Christmas," I said, "and thanks for everything."

"I hope you have the best Christmas ever," Bradley said. He was about to say something else but changed his mind. "See you on Boxing Day."

I got off the bus and in spite of the slippery sidewalk ran all the way to 90 Bradford. Carl would be waiting for me there and at last I would know the surprise. For the first time in my life I was feeling really happy. Mrs. Cuomo was right. I was in love. I felt almost delirious at the thought. I hurried up the porch stairs and fumbled as I put the key in the lock. There were delicious Christmas fragrances in the hallway. It reminded me of those early Christmases on the farm when Mom was still alive. Thank you, Lord, for Christmas, especially for this Christmas.

My heart was bursting with expectation as I turned the key in the lock. But the door was unlocked and partly open. I stepped inside the apartment. The winking blue lights on the small artificial evergreen I had bought with Carl shone dimly in the darkened room.

"Carl," I called. I put down my purse and key on the table inside the door and switched on the table lamp. On the little oak table my mother had given me a dozen years before was a long stem rose in a wine bottle. Beside the vase was a sheet of paper and a key. I picked up the paper and read the scribbled note.

Willow,

It's been really fun during the past few days but I've got to move on now. I've got big plans for my life and I don't need any baggage to hold me back. I'm sure someone like you understands. I'm heading south and don't expect to be back soon unless uncle leaves me a packet in his will. You need someone like Mr. Plain. I know he's sweet on you. When I get settled, I'll send the hundred you loaned me. And when I arrive wherever I'm going, I'll return your luggage. Have a good Christmas.

Carl

P.S. I'm not too fond of poetry.

I read the note over and over again, trying to take it in. I looked at the paper rose in the vase and began to laugh. Nothing seemed real. Nothing made sense. Was it a joke, I wondered. I knew Carl liked to tease me, as he often did during the past few days. This must be a joke. He must be hiding in the bedroom. The surprise must be in the bedroom.

It had to be. I kicked off my snow boots and took off my pea jacket and threw it over the back of a chair.

"Carl, where are you? Please come out. Stop teasing me," I pleaded. "I'm really tired."

I switched on the bedroom light. The closet door was ajar. My clothes were pushed to one side and my only suitcase was gone. I closed the door and turned out the light. I was only baggage, I thought, only baggage. I wanted to cry, but no tears came. Don't waste your tears on disappointments, my mother used to tell me, you won't have enough to go around.

There was still a little left in the bottle of wine I had brought to the apartment the night before. The winking lights on the Christmas tree threw a spider web shadow on Carl's note. From down below, laughter and strains of Christmas music drifted up the stairs. The wine had a bitter taste. I gulped it down anyway then washed the glass in the kitchen sink where the night before we had talked about our future together. We're a good team, you and me, Carl said. You wash up and I like to watch. We had laughed and laughed.

I dried the glass and returned it to the cupboard. A place for everything and everything in its place. Carl liked it that way. Now everything seemed like being in a dream.

I curled up on the sofa bed I had bought on credit to make the apartment more comfortable when Carl moved in. He had good taste and chose one I never would have thought of. We'll take it with us. We'll have only the best, only the best for someone like you. Carl was like that. Always thinking big. I liked that. I wanted to love someone who thought big.

I was drifting off to sleep when there was a knock at the door. At first I didn't stir but the knocking persisted. When I had collected my thoughts, my heart started to race. It's Carl, I thought, he's come back.

"I hope I didn't wake you, Willow," said Mrs. Lockerby. She stood on the landing with a shoe box tied with a red ribbon in her hands.

"That's okay, Mrs. Lockerby," I said. "Is there something you need?"

"Willow, that nice bus driver, I think his name is Bradley, came here a few minutes ago. He asked me to give this to you. I asked him to come in but he said he didn't want to bother you on Christmas Eve. I hope you like it."

"Thank you, Mrs. Lockerby. I'm sure I will. Merry Christmas."

"Are you not feeling well, Willow?"

"No. I'm just tired."

"I saw your cousin leave. I guess he's going home for Christmas."

"Yes, he's gone."

"Would you like to come join us?"

"Thanks but I think I'll turn in early. It's been a busy day at the store."

"Well, if you change your mind, come down. Hope our noisy celebrations don't disturb you. Merry Christmas, Willow."

Tucked under the red ribbon was a note.

Willow,

Remember you once mentioned that one of the things you missed about the farm was the cat you had to leave behind. Well, I hope you don't mind my presuming to fill the gap with this little gift. I've cleared it with Mrs. Lockerby so I hope it's okay with you too. I'm not taking the holiday off so maybe I might see you tomorrow. Probably just a foolish thought. Merry Christmas, Willow.

Ever your faithful bus driver

Inside the box was a black kitten with a white star between its ears curled up asleep in the corner. Suddenly it opened its eyes and looked up. Then I cried.

The Letter

The preacher was persuasive, his voice soothing and hypnotic. He had taken my measure and knew I was vulnerable. He said, "You're feverish. We must take the temperature of your soul," which left me wondering—was I to be part of the *we* in this preposterous undertaking. My impulse was to tell him what I was thinking, that he was a charlatan and a fool if he believed anyone had a soul, and that he had neither the wit nor the means to take my soul's temperature.

I was angry with myself for arranging to meet with him and was about to leave when he said, "If you want to leave, do so." But for some reason I didn't. He had a peculiar hold on me that I couldn't shake. He was playing with my mind and somehow had convinced me that despite his unctuous nonsense he might penetrate this shell of deception that I was hiding under, and lessen the pain. The pain I had endured for so long. While tapping his finger on an open Bible, and not letting my eyes stray from his, he declared, "The truth shall set you free."

I wanted desperately to believe I had finally found someone who could rescue me from the demons of self-reproach, self-loathing and self-destruction that tormented me. And for a time, the preacher's bit of pious flummery worked. I felt relief and well-being, but it was short-lived. The arrival of a letter shattered what had been, after all, only a delusion. I should have known better. Knowing the truth doesn't set you free. It only provokes the demons and they return with a vengeance.

....

The letter was lying beside the morning newspaper on the porch. When I picked it up, I immediately felt unease, verging on panic. There was no postage or return address, only the name I used to go by. Whoever had delivered the envelope was gone. Had it been a windy day, the letter would have blown away and the truth it contained vanished with it. I sometimes wish it had.

I carried the envelope to my small study and laid it on the desk. For a long while I couldn't bring myself to open it. I just stared at the name I hardly recognized anymore, wondering who had penetrated the veil of secrecy I had so meticulously constructed. From the Thomas Albert Hoskins of my birth, I had become Carman Petrillo, reviewer of books from an undisclosed location in the West. I had, until now, been certain I had erased both the name and the past that went with it. Now I wasn't so sure.

When at last curiosity overcame the dread of what I might find, I opened it. To my astonishment, it contained an obituary from The London Times and a handwritten note on letterhead for Colonel Harold Twining, Commandant, Melrose Military College.

I recognized the looping handwriting immediately. In an instant thirty years melted away. Harold, or Hal, had been one corner of a triangle of friendship forged in the passion of youth.

I thought you should know, he wrote. I hope it's over now. It's been too long, Tom. It's time for healing.

The death notice was brief. But in those few lines was a stunning revelation that awoke the fury of the demons. I read it over and over. With each new reading, a dark chapter in my life returned more clearly, a chapter that could have no ending, not even with the passing of the one who had shared that chapter with me.

....

Not many school teachers are memorable. Over time, the remembrance of names, faces, and personalities fade, they become shadows in a half-lighted gallery. There are, however, exceptions to this dismal rule. My Latin teacher was one of them.

In my mind's eye I can still see him, standing in front of the class, leaning slightly forward on his crutches. He was once a handsome young man, now with a face scarred by machine gun fire and legs that were no longer his own. Surprisingly, despite his war wounds, he was more vibrant than most of his peers at Silberson High School.

Robert Smythe was one-of-a-kind in other ways too—an expat with an Oxford pedigree and a veteran of the RAF who had received the Distinguished Flying Cross, one of Britain's highest military honors. For four years he had battled the enemy in the skies over France and yet never spoke about his war service or his injuries. Even as the editor of the high school newspaper, I could not persuade him to tell his story.

In the end I surmised it was too painful. Even though everyone encouraged me to, I stopped asking, not wanting to participate in morbid curiosity. He was a war hero, the bravest person we had ever known. That was enough. Besides, I was certain he would tell us eventually.

There was something else about him that piqued our interest. Why had he turned to teaching, and more specifically, why had he come to Silberson, a small city school in a county not known for trusting strangers or teachers, particularly intelligent ones? And he was clever, far above his fellow teachers in intellect and knowledge. It didn't make sense. But he was evasive and only smiled, sadly, as I remember it now, when I interviewed him for a news article about the approaching second great war.

It was our final year at Silberson. Hal and I were

inseparable, passionate, religious, arrogant, and romantic. Jealous of our unique friendship, we wouldn't allow anyone into our company.

Among other things, we loved the study of Latin. Miss Trimble, our Latin teacher with her rumpled purple dress and red wooden beads, had retired at last. We had spent three long years with her, conjugating nouns and verbs and translating long passages of text with only a dictionary as our guide. She, unfortunately, had the uncanny knack of making a dead language even deadlier.

Mr. Smythe on the other hand was someone who made Latin sing and showed us how meaningful the ancient texts could be. As the clouds of war darkened, we traveled with Roman legions through Gaul, the Gaul Mr. Smythe knew intimately. We witnessed the brutality of a well-oiled killing machine led by a ruthless commander who took no prisoners and seemed to find pleasure in butchering whoever stood in his way—men, women, children, the aged and the infirm. Was Caesar a brilliant general or a psychopath-wanton killer? Was any war justified? Did the pursuit of empire inevitably lead to bloodshed? We talked about these things and learned Latin at the same time. And, as our love for studying Latin grew, we came to believe in war less.

There was nothing glorious about war, nothing Kiplingnesque, nothing glamorous. Its horrible consequences became more and more repugnant to Hal and me. And we did not keep our feelings to ourselves. We wrote editorials in the school newspaper denouncing war . . . that is, until Principal Evans ordered us to stop. He wanted an end to the "rubbish" that dishonored the men and women who fought and died to defend our way of life.

As winter turned into spring, Hal and I were labeled pacifists by some and unpatriotic cowards by others. Even Mr. Smythe urged us to calm our rhetoric because he thought we were unwilling to hear the other side of the argument.

Everyone in our school was pro-war. We did finally get

one convert, John Kuzmich. We hardly knew him, even though he had been a classmate for three years. We knew his father was a prominent doctor and chairman of the school board, and his mother, Ethel, was a former combat nurse in France. John himself was a cipher. But, under Mr. Smythe's tutelage, he started to come alive. Mr. Smythe's unusual, almost fatherly, attention was the reason. John began to soar above us in Latin and much else. We were of two minds about this. We didn't like the fact that we had to share Mr. Smythe's attention, yet at the same time, we appreciated John's skill and mastery of our favorite subject.

Soon, Hal and I invited John to join our anti-war cause and a triangle of comradeship was formed. The three of us were fierce public debaters, winning all our arguments. But once again Principal Evans stepped in, this time with a school suspension, and this time approved by John's father, Dr. Kuzmich.

We stopped promoting our ideas about war in school, not because of the suspension, however, but because of a warning delivered to Mr. Smythe. "Stop inciting students or hand in your resignation," said the letter from Dr. Kuzmich. So we stopped.

But off school property we became pamphleteers, producing and distributing the *Three Against War* bulletin. We attracted some admirers but far more detractors. And more attacks. We were branded cowards.

Spring came early that year. Under an unusually hot sun the snow and ice melted and our thoughts turned to a familiar haunt. It was under a railway bridge where a small stream gleamed in the sunlight. Hal and I would retreat there to lick our wounds and commiserate when things were going badly. We invited John to join us one Saturday. That day we read Virgil's Eclogues and came upon the lines: "Smile for the birth of the boy, the blessed boy for whom they will beat their swords into ploughshares, for whom the golden race will rise, the whole world new." We decided, then and there, to prove we were not cowards and show our bravery by rushing the train.

Rushing the train was a kind of rite de passage for Silberson High School seniors. You waited until the train passed the old elm tree and then ran as fast as you could ahead of the train across the bridge. We put three small stones in a bag, one grey and two white. The whites would rush the train and the grey would take a photo. John and I drew white stones. Hal, the grey. We chose a date and then sat awhile, talking and arguing about who was the greatest Roman poet— Ovid, Virgil or Catullus. We laughed and smoked and sometimes remained silent, breathing in the beauty of that spring day.

The following Saturday we met again but this time on the bridge. John and I watched Hal as he made his way across and took up his position at the far end with his camera. He smiled and waved and shouted something we couldn't make out, but we waved back and said, "Make sure we're smiling." We then listened for the sound of the train. It was right on time. We waited until it reached the elm, then we began to run. I went ahead with John following. The railway ties were wet and slippery from a mixture of oil and rain and running was not easy. I didn't look back until Hal began shouting and waving frantically. I turned. John had stumbled and was trying to get up. The train was already on the bridge and I panicked. I thought John would get up so I didn't go back to help, instead I kept running. When I reached safety, I turned and saw the train bearing down. It was then we knew John wouldn't make it. He paused, looked at us and jumped. We found him lying in the stream, his leg grotesquely twisted and his eyes closed. In his hand was the white stone.

They were waiting for Hal and me at the hospital. Dr. Kuzmich was pacing up and down. Ethel Kuzmich sat with her head bowed. Mr. Smythe sat across from her, his face pale and eyes moist. Bertha Trimble, the deadly Latin teacher, with her beads like strings of cranberries, beside him. Principal

Evans scowled as we entered. Police Officer Robinson was leaning against the wall. We said little, sat down, and waited.

The surgeon approached us near midnight. From the look on his face, it was clear he was not bringing good news. They tried but couldn't save the leg, and his left hand would no longer be useable. He will recover, but it will take time. Dr. Kuzmich held his wife's hand, a mixture of relief and pain in their eyes as they looked at one another. It will take time, the surgeon said again as he turned away.

Hal and I were given a strong warning, but not charged. We returned to school when the suspension was over. Everything had changed, even Mr. Smythe. The weeks passed slowly. My father and mother seemed to grow old as summer disappeared and the world exploded. Hal and I joined up—I went to the air force, he to the army. We didn't see each other, as we waited for our orders. My only consolation was Virgil's hope that someday a golden race would rise and with it a whole new world.

As I flew across France, I thought of Mr. Smythe and hoped that what I was doing might make up for the grief I had caused, for my arrogance and for my recklessness. I didn't care what happened to me and took chances which paradoxically earned me recognition I didn't deserve or necessarily want.

When the war ended, I returned to Silberson only once, to visit my father's grave and to gather up the few things I had left behind. I saw Mr. Smythe but didn't approach him. I couldn't. Instead, I left a brief note at the school office, wishing him well and telling him of my plan to make a new life out west. I didn't try to see John either. It was cowardly but I wasn't sure he would want to see me again.

....

The revelation in the obituary confirmed I had made the right choice. I could not imagine how either Mr. Smythe or

John could ever have forgiven me given what I knew now about their true relationship. The death notice read:

> Yesterday, at the Oxford University Hospital, Dr. John Kuzmich, distinguished Professor of Classical Studies, passed away from complications arising from an injury sustained in his youth. Professor Kuzmich was predeceased by his father, Mr. Robert Smythe, DFC, OBE, also a graduate of the University, and his mother, Ethel.

The Homecoming

Officer: Stand easy, Corporal. Well, you stopped them. A company of SS fanatics and a panzer unit. Incredible. And without air support! Those Krauts thought they were invincible. But you used your head. You did a damn, fine job. You and Rivet, both of you pulled off a miracle. Yes, a miracle.

Corporal: Thank you, sir.

Officer: I've mentioned you in my dispatch to HQ and recommended a decoration and field promotion. You deserve both.

Corporal: Thank you, sir. And Pvt. Rivet?

Officer: Rivet, too. And Price . . . your hand? Your leg? Not too much pain, I hope.

Corporal: No, sir. Not too much.

Officer: Good, good. I'm sorry about the others. We've lost some fine boys. Yes, some very fine boys. Especially Sergeant Boyce. Well, you'll soon be on your way home. It's Ashworth, isn't it? I've got an aunt in Milverton. She often talks about Ashworth. Says if anything ever changed there, the world would stop revolving, and means it as a compliment. You're very lucky. That's what this war's been all about. Making sure the things we believe in last. That's why you've been fighting. For Ashworth and a way of life unmatched by any other place on earth.

Corporal: Yes, sir. I know, sir. Ashworth's like that.

Officer: You're a brave, smart young man, a credit to the

Company and I'm not being patronizing when I say it was an honor serving with you. You deserve the best.

Corporal: Can I say something, sir?

Officer: Of course.

Corporal: Well, sir, we did what we did because we knew you really cared about us, but some of the officers . . . well, they were different and we didn't try as hard, but when you were with us we weren't as scared.

Officer: Yes, I understand. Good, good. Well, yes. That's all, Corporal. Dismissed.

. . . .

Who said war doesn't change anything. It changes everything. In war, it seems, there are no victors, only victims, and when the battlefield of smoke and death finally sleeps another battlefield more terrible awakes, the battlefield of the heart and the mind.

. . . .

The S.S. Celestine was once a luxury liner, one of Bright Star's most opulent—fodder for the bragging rights of the smart set on both sides of the pond. For the discriminating traveler, said Black's 1936 travel guidebook, a triumph in comfort, gourmet dining and sophisticated entertainment. With its passenger list of the royal and the rich, it cruised the Mediterranean summers and the Caribbean winters, visiting all the hot spots where the elite play their games of indiscretion and intrigue and, if they play the game well, become even richer and more celebrated. Then the war came and the War Office commandeered the liner for official business. Report to Belfast for refitting without delay was the terse communiqué. The war effort needed troop carriers for deadly convoy routes.

Now the Celestine, still draped in camouflage grey and pitted by enemy gunfire, fore and aft, sails from Southampton.

Once in open waters it turns west, away from its old playground. Its speed is leisurely and its course no longer furtive. Its mission has changed, as has its passengers. They crowd the decks, some on stretchers, many walking wounded, not a few have scars that don't show. They are a different elite—veterans of a bloody conflict. They are homeward bound.

Near the bow, leaning against the railing, admiring the scarlet sunset, a young sergeant with a shock of blond, tangled hair and deeply-tanned face, aged beyond its years, catches a fine spray. Even though he knows his homecoming will be bittersweet, it was thoughts of home that kept him going during the toughest time of the war. Soon he turns and limps back to where an even younger soldier is lying on a stretcher. He stops and lights a cigarette and places it between his comrade's crooked lips. They exchange a weary smile and know what each is thinking. So many left behind.

The war was over at last. The threat of a dark age more hellish than in the past was lifted. The job was done. The troops were coming home. Throughout the country, church bells rang out in ecstatic anticipation. Crowds of people thronged the streets, singing, dancing and reveling. Strangers hugged and kissed. Veterans were hoisted onto shoulders and paraded about, while fighter planes frolicked in the sunlit heavens above. Red, white and blue streamers and confetti drifted down from windows and from the tops of buildings. Children, scampering about and shouting, played outdoors without fear from the sky. Radio waves crackled with a bewildering array of up to the minute announcements and pronouncements. Car horns blared, and for the first time in years, street lamps shone throughout the night. It was a time of celebration.

....

But, while peace was breaking out almost everywhere else

in the world, in the town of Ashworth a quiet insurgency was under way. The insurgents' target: an antique ordinance.

> *Under no circumstances, no matter how felicitous or propitious, shall the train station, given to the town by the generosity of the god-fearing Ashworth family, whose ancestors, with God's help and guidance, founded our most favored town, be sullied by adornments of any kind.*
> —By order of the Town Council, Ordinance No. 337 in the Year of our Lord, 1869.

A band of plucky war widows said to 'blazes' with the ordinance. One night, just before dawn, they draped bunting and hung banners all around the train station, turning it into a victory shrine. Our husbands won't be coming home but others will, they said, and we're going to make sure they get the best homecoming possible. Everyone in town cheered them on and donated ribbons and bows and lilac boughs. Under a front page photo of the widows in the Ashworth Chronicle, Editor Thomas Lear crooned: Our old Victorian-style station has had a facelift. It's about time. Hurrah! Welcome home, boys. That was May 7th 1945, V-E day.

By the fall, however, the bunting and banners were faded, some in tatters. Everyone was appalled. On the banner attached to the bunting, the V in Victory had disappeared altogether. The stationmaster implored the town council to provide funds to restore it and all the other festive decorations, but was rebuffed. Economy trumps patriotism was Henry Crimson, the Town Clerk's, curt reply. But when the veteran's association roared its displeasure, he had an abrupt change of heart. Three additional flags will be provided out of the council funds to be used at the stationmaster's discretion, he wrote, and cautioned such flags need to be returned in good condition after a reasonable interval.

....

It was unusual for the train to stop in Ashworth mid-week. Almost everyone gets off in Milverton now that a dozen munitions factories with rows of wartime housing had grown it into a city and overtaken its nearby rival, leaving Ashworth dispirited and in decline. But on that Wednesday afternoon, late October 1945, the train did stop in the Ashworth Station and a soldier stepped onto the platform. He had no luggage except for an army kit bag. As he passed the tattered Welcome Home & Thanks for the Victory banner with its missing V, he paused for a moment and smiled ruefully. No one greeted him, not even Aubrey Sitwell the stationmaster, who was more curious than ever now about new arrivals because there were so few of them. But he was busy writing a letter to the town council arguing for five new flags.

It was certain the soldier was no stranger for he walked, albeit with a noticeable limp, directly to where a taxi was parked behind the station out of view of the arrival's platform. Waiting there, smoking a cigarette and leaning against a vehicle out of the gangster era, was an elderly man with a grizzled beard, dressed in civvies with a row of service ribbons pinned to the breast pocket of his rumpled jacket. By the number of cigarette butts scattered on the ground, he had been there for some time. As the younger man approached, the taxi driver sprang to attention and playfully saluted. "Sergeant Harold Price, I presume. Welcome home," saying the latter with an exaggerated bow.

"At ease, Private Second Class Tom Harcourt or should that be First Class." The two men embraced briefly and laughed. It was a private joke. Harold tossed his kit bag onto the back seat of the taxi and sat down beside the driver. He leaned back and closed his eyes. Home at last. Thank you Lord, he murmured, as he exhaled softly and settled down.

Gunfire? In Ashworth? Harold ducked and with his one useable hand clutched the bottom of the car seat. A well-known sound. A gut-wrenching fear. The survival instinct. After a moment he realized it couldn't be, not in Ashworth. He stopped panicking, but only slowly unwound, saying sorry about making a fool of himself. For a long while he turned his face away and stared out the window. The trembling had ceased, and he finally released his grip on the car seat, but his face was damp with sweat.

Tom flung the door open and raced across the parking lot to where the gun-like reports had come from. There, a haulage truck was idling with black exhaust fouling the air. Tom pounded on its window and shouted at the driver, "Farmer, why don't you get that wreck off the road?" The driver, startled, rolled down his window, brandished his fist and shouted, "Clear off or you'll get more than you bargained for." Then, with the sound of grating metal and a cloud of smoke, the truck rolled to the edge of the parking lot. Farmer poked his head out again, made an obscene gesture, and shouted, "You're a crazy old fool, Tom. I like you better when you're drunk." His laughter could be heard above the coughing of the motor as the truck lumbered down the lane, away from the station.

Breathless and red-faced, Tom returned to the taxi and got in. He was still shaking with anger. "Sorry! You, sorry? Making a fool of yourself? What the hell! After all you've been through." Tom put his hand reassuringly on Harold's shoulder. "Let's get out of here," he said, pulling away from the platform. "What's this town coming to. It's coming apart at the seams."

Getting up from his chair in a hurry, the stationmaster upset a small bottle of ink, spilling its contents across the letter. He swore under his breath, shook his head in annoyance and went out to the parking lot.

"What's all the shouting about?" he asked, waving at Tom.

Tom pulled the taxi over to the stationmaster and rolled down his window. "I'm mad as hell, Aubrey. Why doesn't Farmer fix that truck? All it does is backfire and belch smoke.

It shouldn't be on the road."

"'Cos he's broke just like everybody else around here. Besides, missus Farmer's expecting."

"Again? Hasn't he got better things to do? And Aubrey, the bunting looks like hell. Why don't you do something about it? It's a disgrace."

The stationmaster shrugged his shoulders.

"I'm doing my best." Then, as an afterthought, "You know Clerk Crimson. Nothing will change while he's in charge." He wiped his face with a handkerchief and removed his glasses. "Is that you, Hal?" he said, peering into the taxi. "We heard you were coming. Why didn't you tell us when? We could have met you on the platform."

Harold got out and stood beside the open door. He took off his cap and stood stiffly at attention. "I knew you'd be busy, sir, and I didn't want to bother you."

"You look awfully thin, Hal," Aubrey said. "How's the leg?"

"It's ok. It wasn't much," said Harold.

"And your hand?"

Harold just shrugged his shoulders. "It's ok, too."

"Are those sergeant stripes on your sleeve?"

"Yes sir, they are. But I really don't deserve them."

"Nonsense. You're a hero. Old Lear's going to publish your story in the Chronicle as soon as he can get a hold of you. Ashworth hasn't produced a hero in a long while."

"I only did what I had to, Mr. Sitwell, and I wasn't alone. The real heroes are the ones we left behind," said Harold.

"Yes, yes, but you're a hero just the same. And the town won't forget it either. You've made us proud. I won't be the least bit surprised if you don't have a street named after you. And we're going to have a ticker-tape parade right down Main Street, just you see. Yes, and I'm going to see the mayor about it. And I'll ask Dr. Holland about the high school marching band too. You're a celebrity, Hal."

"Thank you sir, but please don't. I don't want any fuss. I

just want to get back to normal."

Tom raced the motor and called out to Harold. "Let's get going. Aubrey's just an old windbag."

Harold paid no attention. He liked the stationmaster who had hired him when no one else would.

"Sorry about your mother's passing. She was a fine woman. If anyone deserves to be called a saint, it was her. That's for sure."

"Yes, she was. Thank you, sir, for saying so."

"Will you be staying long? In Ashworth I mean. After all, the . . . " The stationmaster changed his mind and didn't finish his thought. Instead, he fidgeted with his glasses and put them back on.

"Yes sir, for a while at least. There'll be things to do about the house and so on." Harold knew what the stationmaster was hinting at. "And it's okay about Betty. We were too young, I guess. I'm sure she's better off without me."

"Say, would you like your old job back? Your bike's still here. I can't pay the same 'cause there's not much business anymore."

Harold hesitated. "That's very nice of you, sir, but I'm not sure I'd be any good now, my hand and my leg . . . I hope you understand."

"Come on Harold, get back in the car," Tom said.

"You'll come by for a chat real soon. I know we can figure something out," the stationmaster said. "It'll be like the old days."

"Yes sir, I will. Once I get settled. Goodbye, Mr. Sitwell." Harold got back into the taxi. "Well, let's go."

"Where to?" Tom asked.

"St. Margaret's cemetery," Harold answered.

"Yes, St. Margaret's," Tom said knowingly.

In the distance a church spire towered over the town. Its cross aflame in a sudden burst of afternoon sunlight.

. . . .

"I joined up, Mom," Harold said. "Army. The air force won't take me. I failed the vision test. Is that rhubarb you're doing down?"

"Yes. There's a rhubarb pie in the oven." Sarah Price wiped her hands on her apron and leaned against the kitchen counter for support. The gnawing pain had returned and with it the bitter taste which made her nauseous.

"Are you okay, Mom?" said Harold

"I'm fine. Just a little tired." Sarah finished pouring the rhubarb preserve into the Mason jars and left them to cool. She already knew Harold had been to the recruiting office. Thelma Clark, one of the clerks, had phoned her as soon as Harold had left. Harold has a heart murmur, Thelma said, and really shouldn't be in the army. Make sure you ask him about it. Besides, he lied about his age, Thelma said as she rang off.

"Tell me all about it," Sarah said, sitting down at the kitchen table.

"You know I wanted to be a flyer like Dad but the examiner said my vision wasn't good enough, though I think they just didn't want me. So I went over to the army, had my medical, and that was that."

"Was the examiner Dr. Siegel?"

"Yes."

"What did he say?"

"Well, he said I have a heart murmur and didn't have to join the army and probably shouldn't. He said soldiers depend on one another and if you're not completely fit you'll just be a burden. But Sergeant Billings said a lot of recruits have heart murmurs and it doesn't really matter."

"Harold, I know you want to join up but you aren't really old enough and if you have a heart condition maybe you should wait and help out in some other way."

"It's too late, Mom. I've signed the papers and everything. I have to go. You would know that better than anybody. And all my buddies have already joined and they aren't much older than me."

Sarah reached across the table and took hold of Harold's hand. "I won't stop you if that's what you really want. You're so much like your father. It's just that he didn't come . . . but no, I mustn't think about it."

"Mom, there's something else, something I have to do. Sergeant Billings says I have about two weeks before I leave for boot camp. Betty and I have been talking things over and she wants to get married before I leave. I know it's sudden but we are serious and, well, if I shouldn't come back . . . " Harold squeezed Sarah's hand beseechingly.

"Married. But really, Harold, if you will be leaving in two weeks and you don't know when you'll be back, is it fair to Betty?"

"But Mom, it's her idea. She says she'll wait for me no matter what. She loves me, Mom. And I can support her now with my army pay and maybe you could help out too. Please Mom, I love her. Please say it's okay. She's already told her Mom and she says it's okay with her. You like Betty, don't you?"

"Yes, of course I do. But Harold, you're both so young and you might be making a terrible mistake that you'll regret. I don't know."

"But you were Betty's age and didn't you marry Dad a week before he went overseas?"

The pain was there again but this time it was different—a pain with tears. Sarah was looking at Harold but she was seeing someone else and the memories flooded back.

"Mr. Sitwell says he owes me some back pay and Tom will drive us up to his cabin at the lake. All Betty needs is a new dress, not expensive, just something pretty to be married in, something she can go dancing in afterwards when I'm not here. I don't want her to stop having fun. Her mom can't help, but you will, won't you? And I'll pay you back."

. . . .

"I don't understand. When I left, Farmer had four moving vans and at least ten employees. How come he's broke now?"

"Because of the competition. He was doing okay when he was moving people and things to Milverton, but business dried up and the guys in Milverton got all the army contracts. They got spare parts for their trucks and tires too, even extra gas rations. Farmer got the boot."

"It just doesn't seem right, Tom. Was Mr. Sitwell joking when he said everyone in Ashworth is broke?" asked Harold.

"Hal, we'll drive along Main Street so you can see for yourself. Ashworth survived the '29 crash but not the war. In war, some win and some lose, and we lost big time."

. . . .

"I love Main Street, Hal, don't you?" said Betty squeezing his hand. "It must be one of the most prettiest streets in the world. No wonder so many visitors come here." She pulled Hal over to Foyles Jewelry window and looked in. "I'll never ever get tired of window shopping. Never, never, never. But one day I'm going to stop window shopping and buy everything I see. Isn't that the most gorgeous ring, Hal? If you join the army, I'll marry you."

"That's no reason to join up," said Harold.

"Maybe not, but I will."

"Anyway, when I do, I'll be gone just like that. Remember Andy and Judd. They were gone in about two weeks and never came back once. I just can't get married and disappear. It wouldn't be right."

"I wouldn't mind. Come on. We've talked about getting married so let's do it, unless you've changed your mind."

"Your Mom won't let you."

"Sure she will. She keeps saying it's time for me to move out."

"I don't know, Betty. My Mom . . . she's . . . well . . . she probably won't like it."

"Doesn't she like me? I guess I'm not good enough for the Price family."

"It's not that, Betty. She thinks we're too young."

"You told me she was my age when she got married. And didn't your dad go off and leave her just like you might have to."

"But if we got married and I went away, what would you do to have fun. You like dancing, going out to parties and things. I don't want you to sit around doing nothing. You wouldn't like it."

"I won't sit around doing nothing. Honest, I won't. If I thought you wouldn't mind, I'll go out and have fun while I wait for you to come back. See, now you don't have an excuse not to. Besides, other boys look at me just the way you do, so you'd better grab it while it's still on the shelf. Let's go to Lucy's Dress Shoppe. I'll need at least a new dress to get married in and to go dancing. And what's next door. The army recruitment center."

"Betty, what if I didn't come back. What then?"

"I'd still be young. I guess I'd have to find another guy."

"Sometimes I wonder why I love you so much. But I do. I was going to join up anyway so I guess we might as well get married. But you have to promise me one thing."

"What?"

"You'll wait until you're sure I'm not coming back."

"Promise. Cross my heart. Now I'll look at some dresses while you keep your promise."

....

"You remember, Hal, when Main Street was called Million Dollar Road. Look at it now."

Tom drove slowly, ignoring the cars following him whose drivers were honking their horns before pulling out from behind and passing. "I'm cruising for passengers," Tom would call out occasionally as they passed.

Harold looked out the window, remembering how things used to be, bewildered by the way the war had swept away so many memories. Perhaps it was the dreariness of the afternoon but everything, including the storefronts and the people walking along the street, seemed shabby. Even during the height of the Depression Main Street buzzed with activity: delivery men rushing in and out of stores; shoppers of all shapes and sizes bustling home with their parcels; mothers pushing strollers, their kids laughing; couples strolling hand in hand; young people hanging out at the drug store; and old men sitting on the benches under trees that Mayor Billings had planted years before to fulfill a campaign promise to turn Main Street into the Champs-Elysees, not that many in town had ever been to Paris and therefore couldn't know how inapt the comparison was. Billings had never been to Paris himself but he was determined to make Ashworth the Paris on the muddy Milvern River or die in the attempt which, unfortunately, happened. Outdoor concerts on Saturday night. Buskers entertaining at all times of the day.

"Foyles has gone?" asked Harold.

"Oh, yes," said Tom. "Yep, gone to Milverton. McCurdy's and Mooney's gone too. Only one gift shop left. Remember the antique places that brought so many visitors. Gone. Just second-hand places now and junk shops. Sidewalk cafes no more. Only Oliver's, and all the good restaurants have left too. Ashworth isn't quite the Paris I remember."

"Lucy's Dress Shoppe?" asked Harold.

"Yep," said Tom. "One of the first to go."

As they approached the end of Main Street, For Sale signs appeared more frequently in store windows and a couple of storefronts were boarded up. A brown paper shopping bag rolled along the street like tumbleweed. And the Tivoli Movie House, where he had taken Betty on their first date, was closed indefinitely.

"Betty lives in Milverton now," Harold said matter-offactly.

"Yep," Tom said.

"Alone?"

"Do you really want to know?"

"Yes, kinda."

"She's with Cedric."

"Oh, I thought he was somewhere in the South Pacific."

"No, he didn't join up. Didn't have to. He worked for Maxwell's Munitions. You know how he was always tinkering with machinery. Well, he invented some gadget to speed up production, so he got a deferral and went on to make some more gadgets and more improvements. He's got patents on the gadgets and looks like he's going to be a very wealthy young man. Talk about being lucky."

Harold fell silent. He remembered Betty saying that some day she would stop window shopping and buy everything she wanted. He looked down at his useless hand, scarred and twisted. Not good for anything. He was glad she was living with Cedric and can now have everything she wanted. He could still hear her voice, a voice that made his heart pound. I'll wait for you until I'm sure you're not coming back. Cross my heart. Promise. Her promise meant very little. One week at the lake was all she had had in mind.

"I'm real sorry," said Tom. "Your Mom was right all along about her. You're better off. Get a divorce and move on. You're lucky she's out of your life."

"Tom, I still love her," said Harold. "Probably always will. But I'll get a divorce so she can marry Cedric if that's what she wants."

"Marry Cedric. Fat chance. He'll never marry Betty. He's got bigger fish to fry. I hear he's already running around with one of Maxwell's daughters, a stunner so they say. Betty's threatening to harm herself and that's the only thing keeping them together. In the end, you can bet your last dollar Betty will accept a big payout and play her game somewhere else. That's what I think."

"Don't be too hard on her, Tom. She never had it easy. Get her address and I'll write to her. I owe her that much. No matter what has happened, she's still my wife and I don't want any harm to come to her. I wish I weren't so useless now when she really needs me."

"Hal, it's none of my business and I'll only say this one thing. Betty was always a taker, not a giver, so don't feel sorry for her and don't talk ever again about you being useless. That's an order, Sergeant Price."

………………..

"Mommy, did daddy fly too high?"

"I don't know what you mean."

"When he went to heaven. You told me he was flying when he went to heaven and that's why I have never seen him except in a picture."

"Oh, yes. I guess you could say he flew too high."

"Well, when is he coming back."

"When someone goes to heaven, he can't come back. But one day, if you're good, you'll go to heaven and see him. He can see everything you do and he loves you very much."

"If you can't never leave heaven when you want to, then I don't want to go there. Never."

………………..

"Do you want me to wait," said Tom,

"No, I'll walk. I'm not sure how long I'll be."

"Okay. I'll drop your kit bag at the house. You'll find everything shipshape, with lots of food in the ice box. I'll come by later. Oh, I've been sorting out the mail, throwing out all the junk and putting what you might want to look at in a box. It's on the table. Looks like a storm's heading this way so don't get caught. I'll leave the key under the mat."

"Hey, don't baby me. I'm not an invalid. Thanks Tom for

everything. Now get going. Don't you have any other fares?"

Harold waited until the taxi was out of sight before he turned and walked up the gravel driveway to St. Margaret's cemetery. Circling high above, a flight of sunward-sailing geese trumpeted their farewell as oak leaves, dry and sere, crackled under foot. As he neared the entrance, he realized the iron gate with its beautifully wrought angels at prayer was missing. Was this another casualty of the war, he wondered. For a moment, he stopped and glanced about, searching for the exact spot where as a boy he used to sprawl on the grass, while his mother Sarah would sketch the angels nearby, all the while telling fantastic stories about these divine creatures. Watching her there, all golden in the sunlight, and listening to her gentle voice, he remembered asking her, do angels die, and when she answered, no, angels live forever, he had said, mommy, then you'll live forever too. I wasn't there when she needed me, he reproached himself. I failed her. I failed my angel.

"Harold Price." The voice came from a young woman, standing a few feet away, her long auburn hair tossing in the wind.

"Yes, I'm Harold Price."

"I'm sorry if I disturbed you just then. Please forgive me."

"Have we met?" said Harold.

"No. My name's Amy Thornton. I knew your mother. You're wondering how I knew who you are. Mr. Sitwell said you had come home and thought you would probably go to St. Margaret's first. I thought that too."

"You knew my Mother."

"Yes, first as her nurse at Milverton General. I only knew her for six weeks but for me those six weeks were like a lifetime. My mother died when I was a child and I guess I had always been searching for someone I imagined my mother must have been like. I found that person in Sarah."

"Were you with her when she passed away?"

"Yes."

"Did she suffer greatly?"

"Yes, but she bore the suffering with amazing courage. She was a remarkable woman. And all she thought about was you. You filled her thoughts right to the end."

"Were you going to the grave site?"

"Yes. I promised Sarah I would come on my days off and tend to the grave until you came back. It's a promise I found easy to keep."

"It's getting darker. We'll have to hurry before it rains. Do you live here in Ashworth?"

"I grew up in Croydon but recently moved to Milverton when the job opened up at the General."

"It seems like everyone's moving there. Did you come by train today?"

"No. I drove."

"Oh, but then you just happened to drop by the train station."

"Not exactly. Aubrey Sitwell is one of those distant cousins twice-removed and just about every week I've been checking with him about whether you had arrived. That's another promise I made to Sarah."

"Can I call you Amy?"

"I wish you would. I feel I know you just about as well as anyone I have known all my life. So you won't mind if I call you Harold."

"I'm glad you found me, Amy. There's so much I want to know about Mom while I was away. I guess I feel guilty. I should have known she wasn't well. I shouldn't have joined up. I didn't have to, you know. I was selfish. And I did something real stupid just before I left."

"I'm glad I found you too. I'm not exactly a praying person but lately I've been praying real hard. I so wanted to keep my promises to Sarah. I'll never be able to tell you how much she has enriched my life. Saved it really."

"There's so much I want to know."

"Then we'll have to get together soon. I can come on most

Wednesday's. Right now my life leaves lots of room for going over past things."

"I would like that. The past is all I have too."

....

"I met Amy Thornton at St. Margaret's. She told me you took care of everything, even the funeral expenses. I can't thank you enough, Tom, and I will try to repay you. It will take time, but I will."

"Hal, you know I loved Sarah. She only thought of me as a friend but she was far more than that to me. As for you, you've repaid me a thousand times just by being you. Yes, you've made mistakes, but you're honest, kind and true and you're like the son I never had, so you don't owe me a thing. As for Amy, she's one of nicest girls you could ever meet. Her husband was killed at Anzio. He was an army medic. Killed just about the same day Sarah was admitted to the General. And something else. She is so much like Sarah it's frightening. I mean that in a good way."

"Tom, I'll be leaving Ashworth. The bank has sent me a foreclosure notice and given me until the end of November to pay up the mortgage or clear out."

"What in hell do you mean? You're leaving. They can't do that to you. I won't let them. Sitwell was right. You're a hero. I'll ram that letter down Hinton's throat. I'll raise such hell that . . ."

"No, Tom, I don't want you to. I don't want to fight the bank. I've had enough of fighting. You used to say a house is not a home. Remember. Well, I've only been here a few hours, but I know this house will never feel like home again. Over there a dream kept me alive, but it was, after all, just a dream. I've changed and Ashworth has changed too. I've got some good memories and that's worth a lot to me."

"But where will you go? What will you do? I hear you but I can't believe you mean what you're saying. I'm confused.

Upset. It's Betty, isn't it?"

"No, Tom, it's not Betty. I'll do whatever I can to help her but I don't think she wants me to. But I can't let Cedric hurt her either. As for where to go, Milverton I guess, so I can still visit St. Margaret's. I think I'll go back to school. I can't use my hands anymore so I'll give it a go with my head. Captain Smythe said I was smart. He was probably just being kind but I'm sure going to try. My brain should be in good shape because I haven't used it much. Isn't that what you used tell me?"

"Nonsense. You know I never meant it. What about Amy?"

"I don't know. I don't think either of us is ready for anything like that. War changes things, Tom. That's about it."

"Some homecoming. That's all I can say."

"At least I made it home. I'm one of the lucky ones. Is Marge's diner still open?"

"Yep, and believe it or not, Marge is still there."

"And breakfast is still four bits?"

"Yep, four bits with the works. All day."

"Good. I'm glad at least something hasn't changed. Well let's go then and bring your wallet. I'm the war hero, remember."

Hal glanced around the kitchen. The Mason jars on the window ledge were all in a row, largest to smallest. Mom would have liked that, he thought, as he closed the door behind him.

www.ingramcontent.com/pod-product-compliance
Lightning Source LLC
Chambersburg PA
CBHW030918120626
46554CB00001B/196